THIS GIRL IS DIFFERENT

BY

J. J. JOHNSON

Published by
PEACHTREE PUBLISHERS
1700 Chattahoochee Avenue
Atlanta, Georgia 30318-2112
www.peachtree-online.com

Cover design by Maureen Withee
Book design and composition by Melanie McMahon Ives

Manufactured in February 2011 by Lake Book Manufacturing in Melrose Park, Illinois, in the United States of America
10 9 8 7 6 5 4 3 2 1
First Edition

Library of Congress Cataloging-in-Publication Data

Johnson, J. J., 1973-
This girl is different / written by J. J. Johnson.
p. cm.
Summary: Having always been homeschooled by her counterculture mother, Evie has decided to spend her senior year at the local public high school, an experience that challenges her preconceptions about friendship, boundaries, and power.
ISBN 978-1-56145-578-2/1-56145-578-4
[1. High schools--Fiction. 2. Schools--Fiction. 3. Hippies--Fiction. 4. Individuality--Fiction. 5. Interpersonal relations--Fiction.] I. Title.

PZ7.J63213Th 2011
[Fic]--dc22

For Noah

Life is a daring adventure or nothing.

—Helen Keller, author and activist, 1880–1968

I manage to grab the snake, but not without twisting my foot and falling butt-first into the creek. When I stand, lightning shoots through my ankle.

I take a long, deep yoga breath, an Ujjayi ocean breath, to be calm. Steady. Strong. Hopping on one foot, I hold the wriggling snake and scramble over to a large rock. As I unshoulder my backpack, the snake flicks its tongue at me. It must think I'm crazy.

I can think of worse things. Better crazy than mild. Or timid, or meek, or boring.

From my backpack, I pull out the mason jar I brought for snake containment. "Your temporary quarters." He slithers in, curls up at the bottom. After popping the ventilated lid on, I hold him up for a better look: velvety black, yellow lines running the length of his back.

Garter snake, or ribbon? I sniff the jar. A bit skunky but not overwhelming. Probably ribbon. "Either way, you're a beauty." I set the container down.

Now, to call for help. I flip my cell phone open. It doesn't chime. Of course I forgot to charge it.

Lightning shoots through my ankle again when I shift weight. It's already getting puffy and it's throbbing. Gingerly, I lower my foot into the creek so the cool water can help the swelling.

The snake, nonplussed, watches me. I unzip my backpack and move aside my drawing journal, the tin of colored pencils, the jar of filtered water. Ah, here it is: an emergency kit, packed by Martha. Score one for Martha, and moms everywhere. Hello, blister pack of ibuprofen! I swallow a couple of tablets with a swig of water and paw through the rest of the kit: band-aids and an ace bandage, a whistle, waterproof matches, a mirror. Plus, I packed two homemade oatmeal bars and a jar of peanuts and raisins. At least I won't starve.

Stranded, hurt, but I can handle it.

No freak-outs. No worries. This girl is different.

I wrap the ace bandage around my ankle and dip it back into the water. Crimson maple leaves float by, brown dappling their curling tips. They swirl and laze in the eddy from my foot. I might as well try to slow down too; it will be a while before Martha realizes I'm hurt. After her shift at Walmart, she'll probably stop at the food co-op and the library and who knows what else. Plus, it would take her a long time to hike this far along the creek. So even if she gets home early, *and* she notices my note and doesn't just assume I'm in the barn or doing yoga, I'm stuck here well past sundown. At the earliest.

From the position of the sun, it's not yet noon. Which leaves eight or nine hours to wait, or to come up with a better idea. Just me and my new friend Ribbons.

Hours later, still without an exit strategy, I take a break from drawing in my journal to check my sketches against Ribbons in his container. I ought to let him go, but I like the company. Sighing, I run my fingers over the smooth glass. I should probably try to find him a tasty worm or cricket to eat—

Wait. Voices in the woods.

A twig snaps. The voices get closer. I can pick out a male voice, some words: *school, shop, classes*. Is it two people out there, or three?

"Hey!" I call. "Hello?"

The voices go silent.

"I'm down by the creek!" I regard my throbbing ankle. "Actually, I'm pretty much up the creek!"

The voices return, low and quiet, like they're discussing what to do. Branches move, leaves rustle. A boy about my age, in cutoff cargo shorts and hiking boots, pops out of the trees. I've seen him before, in town—once in the library, a few times at the coffee shop. You can't help but see him. He is that kind of beautiful. A crunchier, leaner version of Kumar from *Harold & Kumar Go to White Castle*. His hair is glossy black, his eyes dark.

Blood rushes into my cheeks.

"Hi," he says. The frays of his shorts brush against his legs when he moves. His leather hiking boots are scuffed and worn into whorls of color, whipped cream melting into milky coffee.

"Hi." I will not sound like a damsel in distress. Although, technically, with a sprained ankle and no cell phone, I kind of am.

But where is the source of the other voice, or voices?

As if on cue, someone else stumbles out from the woods.

Kumar turns to catch the jumble of limbs. Coltish legs steady themselves and unfold to reveal a girl, very pretty. I've seen her around too.

"Hi." I fan a small wave. "I'm Evie." My heart won't stop pounding.

"Hi!" The girl is all eyelashes and toenail polish, in flip-flops and a short sundress. Not the most practical hiking attire, but who am I to judge? After all, I'm barefoot. The girl is petite and thin and gamine, Audrey Hepburn in *Breakfast at Tiffany's*, but with richer, tawny brown skin. Indian maybe, or Latin American?

"What's up?" She pokes her fingers into her short, jet-black hair, like she wants to fluff and spike it.

"I hurt my ankle. It won't take weight, and no one really knows where I am."

Kumar looks around. What's he looking for? Is someone else with them?

Audrey Hepburn asks, "You came out this far alone?" and I realize she is voicing Kumar's thoughts. She says it like it's unimaginable, like, *You just flew back from the moon?*

I shrug. "I live about five miles downstream."

"You live here?" the boy asks. They look at each other.

The girl juts out her hip, sets her hand on it. "Did you, like, just move or something?"

I know what they're thinking. Our town only has one high school, so everyone knows everyone. Well, obviously not *everyone*. I shake my head. "I've lived here two years. I'm a homeschooler."

They look at each other again. They are saying a lot with those looks.

"I'm normal, I swear!" I smile to reassure them. "I'm actually going to school this year. Starting Monday."

Only three days away. I can't wait. I want to see what it's like; Martha is horrified that it will ruin me. It took a protracted battle to convince her to let me enroll. I finally wore her down—a brutal campaign of attrition—with ceaseless appeals for my own empowerment and personal decision-making. Also I convinced her I could be a gonzo journalist and treat high school like ethnographic research.

"I'll be a senior." I lift my foot out of the creek so I can turn all the way around to face Kumar and Audrey.

"That's awesome!" says the girl. She wiggles her thumb at herself and the boy, "Us too."

The boy's eyes go wide; he is staring at my ankle. It looks swollen even with the ace bandage.

"You weren't kidding about your ankle. Nasty sprain." He steps closer and bends down to look at it. "All right if I have a look? I've had some experience with these."

I nod. He kneels in front of me. My heart is thumping. Please tell me he can't hear it. The closer he gets, the harder it hammers. These two are probably together, they're a couple. Isn't that what I'm supposed to assume? I'm not really an expert at this kind of thing.

"Can I unwrap the bandage?"

I swallow hard, and nod again, and hope that my heart can take the strain of him touching me.

Audrey tucks her dress behind her knees and dips into a knees-together, ladylike squat next to Kumar. Her eyes skim my bare feet, slide up to my cutoffs and tank top, stop at my makeup-less face. Why do girls always look me over like this?

My heart sinks. Which makes me feel lame, because my life is not about feeling insecure. But if Audrey is the kind of girl Kumar likes, he would have zero interest in me. Petite I'm not. I'm not fat, I'm just...built. Muscled and solid and tall. As for girly? Put it this way: I'm proud of being a girl, but girly? Not so much. I glance at my bare feet and unpolished toes, the light hairs on my unshaved shins, and I reach back to tighten my long brown ponytail. Whatever. I am what I am.

Besides, if they're together I shouldn't even be thinking these things.

Kumar cups the back of my foot and lifts it. I take a deep breath because it hurts, and because my heart is beating so hard.

Audrey and Kumar confer. Their words seem to float between them, bubbles that glint and pop.

"OHMIGOD!" The girl scrambles backward.

The boy frowns at my ankle. "It's not *that* bad."

The color has drained from her face, leaving it ashy. In terror, she points at the jar. "Snake! Snake!"

"Oh no. I'm sorry! I should have warned you." I hate

that people are afraid of such wonderful creatures. I don't want to be the cause of any snake-hate. "He's just a little ribbon snake. Completely harmless."

She shakes her head, apparently unconvinced. She takes another step back.

"Would it be better if I let it go? Or do you want me to keep it contained?"

"Con...contained."

"Okay. Don't worry. I'll keep it in the jar and—"

The boy rolls his eyes at Audrey. "Don't be such a wuss." He turns to me and asks, "Planning on keeping it?"

"No. I was just doing some—"

"Drawings." He's spotted my journal. "Wow. Can I see?"

"Sure."

He picks it up and thumbs through the pages. "Holy crap. These are amazing."

"Thanks."

"What?" The girl tries to see without moving closer.

"Drawings. The snake and other stuff." He flips my journal shut and hands it to me, then turns to the girl. "Jay, why don't you start back? We'll wait until you get far ahead before we let the snake loose."

"No no no no no no no. I am not liking your plan. Trudging back through the forest alone? I don't think so." She wraps her arms around herself. "There might be more snakes or other various reptiles. Or what if I take a wrong turn and get lost forever?"

The boy groans.

"How about this?" I say. "On the count of three, you run, and I'll let the snake go in the other direction—"

"And I'll carry you out of here," Kumar says.

Oh yeah. My ankle. He's going to carry me, like I need to be rescued? How humiliating!

Plus, can I handle being that close to him? His beauty is pathological. Which pisses me off, really. Me being all swooning and hyperventilating—it's so lame.

But he's already counting: "One, two..."

The girl takes off, and I hurry to let Ribbons the snake go. The boy picks me up, grunting a little with the effort. Yeah, I'm not small.

"I'm not a damsel in distress, you know."

He laughs. "Trust me: the thought did not occur."

You know there are moments such as these when time stands still and all you do is hold your breath and hope it will wait for you.

—Dorothea Lange, photojournalist, 1895–1965

Audrey Hepburn's real name is Jacinda and beauteous Kumar is Rajas.

Rajas. He's carrying me piggyback to his car, which he says is parked on the state forest access road not too far away. When the trail is wide enough, Jacinda walks beside us. She scrunches her nose as she picks her way through the flora. "Tell me if you see any snakes." She laughs. "Actually, don't tell me if you see any snakes. Just tell me to run."

"Got it." I keep an eye out for any slithery movement. My nose is scrunching too—out of frustration at my heart, which continues to jump around because of Rajas. It won't listen to me, even though I'm a strong woman with strong morals. If the dude's taken, he's taken. Stop it, heart. Then again, I can't blame you too much, heart: I *am* straddling the boy's back, my thighs *are* rubbing against his arms. And he's so warm. And he smells so good.

"What brought you two out this way?" I ask Rajas and Jacinda, to distract myself from my heart (and/or pheromones).

Rajas's attempt at a shrug suffers under my weight. "Just looking around."

"Raj dragged me out here."

"Because it's good for you," Rajas tells Jacinda. "Clear your head from all that girly crap you're into."

"Hey," I interrupt. "Girly doesn't necessarily make something crap."

"Yeah." Jacinda smiles. "Girls rule, boys drool."

"Way to take the conversation back to second grade, Jay," Rajas says. "Besides, Eve doesn't seem like the girly type."

Okay...is that good or bad? In his eyes, I mean. Dang! What is wrong with me! Why do I care?

"What about you?" Rajas asks me. "Why were you out here? Alone?"

"Yeah, do you, like, hang out here all the time?"

"I do," I answer. "I feel most at home when I'm outdoors."

They respond simultaneously: Rajas says, "Nice." Jacinda says, "Ew. I cannot relate." She swats at an invisible insect. "Get me inside already. Seriously. I never thought the Blue Biohazard would seem so appealing."

"I must have heard you wrong," growls Rajas, "because that sounded like you are disrespecting my baby."

Did I miss something? Is he really mad? "The blue what?"

"Biohazard," answers Jacinda. "Raj's car. He gets snippy if you don't bow down and worship it."

"You don't need to worship her. Polishing her hubcabs would suffice."

I lean closer to Rajas's ear. I'm fully supportive of naming inanimate objects, but still. "The Blue *Biohazard?*"

"Blue, for obvious reasons. Biohazard, because she averages a stately five miles a gallon." Rajas puffs out his chest in a show of pride.

"And because it, like, leaks fluids everywhere."

"Just my baby's way of sharing the love, Jay."

"Wow." I lean back a little; Rajas shifts his hold to adjust to my weight shift. More skin against skin: it sends a tingle. "Five miles a gallon? I think that might be worse than a Hummer."

Rajas laughs. "You know it. Figured I'd save myself the sixty thousand, and just drive grandpa's car until it falls apart."

We all settle into happy quiet. Around us, nuthatches and chickadees skitter on tree branches. Rajas's boots pad softly on the earth. Jacinda's flip-flops *thwup thwup thwup* against her soles. While I study the shafts of sunlight filtering through the evergreens, Rajas shifts again. Tingle.

"Am I getting too heavy?"

"You're fine." Rajas pops me up to shift my weight a couple of inches higher.

"I must say, this is quite the..." I trail off, trying to think of a word other than *rescue.*

"Quite the non-rescue?" Rajas suggests. "Because you're a non-damsel in non-distress, right?"

I laugh. "Right."

"I always considered myself a non-hero," Rajas says.

"Yeah, non-problem whatso-never," Jacinda says.

"Still. You guys don't even know me," I say. "That could've been a really long wait back there if you hadn't come along."

"Well we love non-rescues, don't we, Raj?"

"Of course." Sweat dews on Rajas's shoulders and chest; our bodies are starting to slip and stick where our skin touches. "We're almost there now."

"Blue Biohazard, here we come!" Jacinda picks up into a jog.

"Fantastic," I say, but really, I wouldn't mind more

walking—miles more—so I could be with Rajas like this for a long, long time.

"Turn here." I point to the gravel road. "My driveway's up the hill."

"Roger that." Rajas turns the car onto the pitted road. The Blue Biohazard is the perfect name for his enormous, leaky, rusty, rickety old boat of a car.

"I shudder to think of the havoc we're wreaking on the environment," I say, "but…this is a great car. Tons of personality." I'm riding in the front, next to Rajas, because of my ankle. I suppose Jacinda usually sits here. God, I wish my heart would stop pounding. But he is so beautiful. And so nice. With a great sense of humor. And he and Jacinda seem to get my jokes, which isn't a small thing, isn't a common thing at all. I haven't had many friends my own age.

"Thanks." Rajas pats the steering wheel. "My sweet, sweet baby. 1976 Buick Skylark."

"I have a feeling you might appreciate my own vehicular transportation."

"Oh yeah?" he asks.

"Mmm-hmm. Martha—that's my mom—and I have a 1961 Volkswagen minibus."

"No way. That is a sweet ride."

"Ugh." Jacinda pops into the space between the front seats. "You two cannot be serious! You are, like, two of a kind with your old piece-of-junk clunkers!"

Two of a kind? If you say so! Sweat prickles my forehead. "That's what we call her. The Clunker."

Jacinda rolls her eyes and groans; Rajas elbows her back to her seat.

"But you have me beat," I tell Rajas, "with all your elite universities." College stickers coat the Biohazard's rear window.

Rajas squints at me like he's trying to tell if I'm serious. "Yeah," he says. "Lends an air of grandeur."

"Very prestigious," I say.

"He's being ironic," Jacinda chimes in. "Because his car is such a heap? And they are such good schools?"

"I think she got that, Jay." Rajas flashes me a devious, gorgeous, lopsided smile that sends my stomach into a spin.

Jacinda makes a face at Rajas before she says to me, "It's the whole Ivy League except Cornell."

"Why not Cornell?"

"I'm waiting"—Rajas lifts his chin in the direction of the backseat—"for Jay to give me that one."

"Because that's where I want to go next year," Jacinda explains.

"Wait, really?" I turn around. The girl is full of surprises. Which you've got to love. But why would Rajas be waiting for Jacinda to go to Cornell before he gets the sticker? They must be together. Why else would he care so much about her plans? "That's where I want to go," I say.

"Get out! That is so cool!"

Rajas looks over at me. "Really? Cornell? You don't seem like—"

"Ivy League material?" I raise my eyebrows. "Why? Because I don't wear shoes and don't shave my legs?"

He looks stricken. "I really didn't mean it like that."

I laugh. "You're right; I'm not their typical profile. But I've been taking online courses and they have this fantastic Urban Planning program with a concentration in Social Justice. You work with architects and planners, plus do antipoverty campaigns and that kind of thing. The point is to learn how to build communities that help people help themselves. A bunch of their students helped Hurricane Katrina survivors rebuild in New Orleans, back when it happened." I take a deep breath. "I'd be into the program whether it was at Morrisville Extension or City College or East Podunk University. But I have to admit, I don't mind that it's Cornell. Ithaca is gorgeous."

This seems to meet Rajas's approval. He smiles. "That should be a bumper sticker."

"It really should." I laugh. He's sharp, this one.

Jacinda says, "It *is* a bumper sticker! I've seen them!"

Rajas says, "It was a joke, Jay."

"Oh."

Rajas looks thoughtful and tips his chin. "Is that why you're going to high school this year? Is it hard to apply if you're—" He jerks the wheel to avoid a pothole. "Do they let in homeschoolers?"

"Colleges love homeschoolers!" Jacinda answers for me. "I read an article about it in the *New York Times*."

Wow. Score one for the girly girl. She's ambitious and well-read. Right on, Jacinda.

"So they say," I agree. I tell Rajas, "High school is a curiosity to me. I only have a year left, so I thought, why not give it a try, see what it's all about? Bells, detention, people getting stuffed in lockers, prom queens, house parties, that kind of thing. *Sixteen Candles, The Breakfast Club, Clueless*. I'm a sucker for movies about high school. Especially the classics."

"Don't get your hopes up," Rajas says. "High school is overrated."

"Don't make her jaded!" Jacinda leans forward. "I think high school is fun. You get to be with your friends, and do all sorts of activities, and some of the teachers are really good..."

Rajas frowns. "And some are sketchy as hell."

"Whatever." Jacinda waves him away and turns to me. "We'll show you the ropes. You'll do awesome and then you'll get into Cornell!"

"I hope so." Cornell is the one thing I don't want to jeopardize.

"That means if you think high school sucks, you can just go back to homeschool." Rajas sounds like he's been following his own train of thought instead of listening to Jacinda. "Nice back-up plan."

"Exactly! Cornell never has to know." I point to a small dirt road on the right. "Here it is. Up near the Christmas-tree farm." I untwist my ponytail and comb my fingers through my hair. "I talked with the head professor in Urban Planning. He seems super smart and super nice. The students I talked to were great too."

"Shut up! You had an *interview?* Already?" Jacinda sounds panicked. "When? I didn't know they had interviews yet."

Gathering my hair back up and snapping the elastic around it, I turn to face Jacinda as best I can without jostling my ankle. The Blue Biohazard's terrible shocks have already given it quite a few jolts. "It wasn't an *interview* interview." I shrug. "Martha and I just went for a visit."

Jacinda's eyebrows knit together in confusion. "Martha? Your mom? What do you mean? You just... showed up?"

I make an apologetic face. "I e-mailed first."

She slumps into the seat. "I didn't...I didn't know you could do that!"

“They’re just people,” I offer. “People love to talk about what they do. You just have to give them the opportunity.”

She’s still frowning.

Okay. Time to change the subject. “So. Why Cornell for you?”

She musters a pretty smile. “Because it’s Cornell. And it’s close enough to come home and do laundry. My mom doesn’t want me too far away.”

“Don’t believe her,” Rajas says. “Jay just wants the sweatshirt. She’s into labels.”

“Shut up!” Jacinda swats the back of his head. “There’s nothing wrong with wanting to go to an Ivy League school.”

“But I’m curious, why *Cornell?*” I ask. “What do *they* have that...” From the look on Jacinda’s face, I’ve lost her. I try another tack. “What are you interested in studying?”

“Oh. Maybe, like, history and economics? My mom is all, ‘Don’t stress yourself, you should follow your dreams,’ or something like that, but I am thinking that I’ll go to law school and get my MBA at the same time.”

“Jay’s already planning to sell out.”

“Am not!”

We bump over another big dip and my ankle throbs. Time for another change of subject. “What about you?” I ask Rajas. “Do you have any plans?”

"Raj is a slacker," Jacinda says. "His plans are to slack."

"Slacker and sellout. You two are quite the combination."

Rajas scratches his head. "Jay thinks anyone who doesn't go straight to college is a slacker."

"I'm not the only one, Raj. Ask your mom."

Is she kidding? I can't tell.

Rajas ignores her. "The shop teacher, Mr. Pascal, hooked me up with a paid carpentry apprenticeship. Sweet deal, because they're hard to come by."

"Sounds fantastic!" I enthuse. "Your parents aren't into that?"

"My dad's cool with it. But my mom thinks I should be a doctor or a software engineer. Same old story. Holy crap, how long is your driveway?"

He seems to be looking for another change of subject, so I oblige. I point at the white dome coming into view. "We're almost there."

"No way! Really?" Jacinda scoots forward in her seat again. "You live in that?"

"I do indeed. Welcome to the Dome Home." Quite an inspiring sight, in my humble opinion. My house looks like a huge luminous igloo, a half sphere rising up from the earth. A soft eggshell covering of polyester and nylon drapes the frame, shaped by beams that converge in triangles. Clear round plastic windows dot the structure. Stretching off the ground on one side of the dome is a gigantic semispherical vinyl window. The entire upper third of our home is another transparent flexible window. Martha and I always dreamed of living in a sustainable home we built ourselves, and now we do. I am so proud of us, and our house.

Rajas parks the Blue Biohazard on a patch of hard dirt near the Dome Home. He gets out and pulls his seat forward for Jacinda while I clamber out my door. I hop over to the hammock and sit back with care. Rajas sprawls out onto the grass nearby.

After handing me my backpack, Jacinda walks around, looking everywhere, taking everything in. Her flip-flops *thwup thwup* against her feet.

"This is a geodesic dome?" Rajas asks.

"Very good." I smile. "You've seen one before?"

"Sort of. A picture of one. In our Environmental Science book." He rolls onto his side and props his head on one hand. "But that one was ugly. Gray steel and asphalt shingles. This"—he nods at my house—"is amazing."

"Thanks." A course in environmental science sounds fascinating, but my school schedule is crammed with requirements for graduation. The guidance counselor left no room for electives. I suppose my whole life has been electives, up until now. I rewrap my hair into a messy bun and tell Rajas, "We ordered the kit from a company in Oregon."

"You built it?" He sounds impressed.

His interest feels as cozy as a warm sleeping bag after a day trek through the mountains. "Sure. The kit comes with all the parts, and a huge book of instructions. It was tricky at first, but once we got the hang of it, it was fantastic." I smile at the Dome Home. "The best part was that, about halfway up, it kind of came alive—it popped up higher on its own. It lifted us with it, on our little scaffolding. We couldn't believe it. We just about fell off from shock. And laughing."

"We?"

"Me, Martha, and Rich. Her brother, my uncle."

"That's it? Just you guys?" Rajas asks.

I nod. "Just us."

"Wow." He lies back down and gazes at the sky. "That's amazing."

"You like to build? I figured that out, see. Because of the whole carpentry apprenticeship."

"Very clever of you." Rajas grimaces; he seems embarrassed. "Yeah. Nothing like your dome, though." He shades his eyes to look at me. "I really just fool around. Have a workshop in my garage. Made a couple of tables and I'm working on a rocking chair."

"Hey, don't sell yourself short. Someone once said 'I'd rather build cathedrals than chairs,' because chairs are so hard to get right." I smile. "I collect random quotes." I tuck some unruly strands behind my ears and reach down to pick up Little Gray Kitty, who's come to say hello. As I smooth down the kitten's ears, I say, "I'd love to see your chair."

Rajas looks startled. Like he's surprised by my interest, or maybe the fact that I just invited myself over. But he smiles. It's dazzling.

Jacinda appears from behind the curved frame of the Dome Home. Right. Jacinda. She and Rajas are together, probably.

We watch her *thwup-thwup* around the vegetable garden to disappear into the barn—a regular barn, wooden and dilapidated, here long before Martha and me. Jacinda pops back out a second later. "Hey! There's a bunch of cats in here! And ohmigod! A cow!"

Rajas shouts to Jacinda, "A cow? In a barn? That is insane."

Jacinda gives him a withering look and disappears again. "And chickens in a hut!"

"The cow is Hannah Bramble," I call out to Jacinda. "She's friendly, but beware the chickens. They're deadly. Like piranhas with feathers."

Jacinda flies past the chicken coop, lifting her knees

high as she runs to us. "Get out! Are you serious?" She turns to make sure there are no chickens in pursuit.

Rajas cracks up. I can't help but join him.

Jacinda collapses on the grass next to Rajas. She pushes him like she's mad but then starts laughing too. "Just what I need! Someone for Raj to gang up on me with."

Rajas carries me inside The Dome. It sets my heart galloping again.

"Thanks. Sit down, guys," I say after Rajas deposits me at the kitchen table. "You must be hungry." Neither of them sits. Instead they wander through my home, looking up through the huge skylight, scrutinizing our mandala-patterned cork floor, pressing their hands onto the luminescent fabric of the walls.

"Holy cow," Jacinda breathes, twirling in slow circles.

"This construction is so smart." Rajas traces his hands over the struts.

I smile and listen to them move around. It's a comforting sound, like a soft wind moving through pine trees. No matter how much I try to distract myself, my eyes return to Rajas.

"You have plumbing." Jacinda sounds pleasantly surprised. She's peeking behind the door to the bathroom. Built of oak planks, the walls and ceiling of the bathroom are the only square, straight, flat walls inside the Dome Home; they support the sleeping loft.

"Mmm-hmm." I hop to the fridge for ice—which I wrap in a dishtowel and tie around my ankle—and the jug of iced tea. "If you need to use the bathroom…this might sound weird, but it's a composting toilet, so the toilet paper goes into—"

"No no, I'm good." Jacinda waves her hands. "I guess I just didn't expect you would have a bathroom in this kind of place."

"Sure. Plumbing, electricity, hot water." I pull a knife out of the block to slice some bread. "The stove and oven use propane from the tank outside. Solar panels do the rest."

"Ohmigod! Raj, come look! Evie has Ganesh!" Jacinda touches the elephantine figure sitting on our ecumenical altar among other sacred objects: more Hindu deities, small Buddhas, ceramic crosses from Mexico, a calligraphic verse from the Qur'an, a Star of David inlaid with mother-of-pearl. Martha and I collect them on our travels. Icons from the world's religions.

Rajas stands next to Jacinda to look at the collection. "No one around here knows who Ganesh is."

"Hazards of living a small town," I say. "Martha and I were psyched there's a food co-op and a Unitarian church. But still, no diversity. Especially with religion."

"So true," Jacinda says. "Here, the biggest choices here are, like, Catholic or Protestant. Or Unitarian."

"But you're Hindu? Both of you?"

"Yeah. Our moms are from Bombay." Rajas picks up a hand-carved Buddha, turns it in his hands. "They drag us to Binghamton University for Diwali and stuff."

"My dad is, like, a Methodist?" Jacinda says. "And Raj's dad is agnostic, so everyone just compromises. Sometimes we go Unitarian."

Why on earth would their entire families compromise with each other? Oh no. Are Jacinda and Rajas engaged or something? Before I can speak, Rajas turns around to face me. "Haven't I seen you there, at the Unitarian Church?" he asks.

"Sometimes." I manage to stay cool, but inside, I'm dying. He's noticed me there before! I take a deep breath. Calm down, girl.

"Just sometimes?" Jacinda asks.

I nod, try to focus on her question. "I think all religions have the same message: Love each other. Respect a Greater Spirit. But I also believe there's a life energy, like a current, going through everyone and everything. You know the Walt Whitman poem 'I Sing the Body Electric'?"

Jacinda's eyes are starting to glaze over. Oops. I guess I was starting to ramble.

"Anyway," I say, trying to sum up. "Martha and I go different places, depending where we are. Or I do yoga or just lie on the grass and meditate. Same idea."

"Sounds like you've lived all over," Rajas says.

"I've traveled all over. But I have a rule that you haven't actually *lived* somewhere unless you're there more than two years. So I've only really lived in Seattle and Montreal. And now here."

Rajas makes a face. "I'd take those other places any day of the week."

"Oh, Raj, don't be a hater." Jacinda flicks her hand at him. "Upstate New York is beautiful, right, Evie?"

"Definitely. What Leatherstocking Country lacks in diversity, it makes up for in natural beauty—"

"Wait!" Jacinda freezes. "Where's your TV?"

You have to appreciate her non sequiturs. "We don't have one." I hop across the kitchen to the other cupboard. "But we're not complete Luddites. Our computer plays DVDs. And we have the...what do you call it?" I snap my fingers like I'm trying to remember. "It's a collection of tubes that information slides through. The Tube-A-Tron? No. The InterWeb?"

"You mean the *internet?*" Jacinda looks concerned about me.

Rajas rolls his eyes. "She's kidding, Jay."

"You are?"

I laugh. "Sorry! You're too easy."

"That's what all the boys say," Rajas mutters. Which seems weird.

"Shut up!" Jacinda says, not mad at all. She turns to

me. "Don't listen to him. I'm saving myself—"

"For her anonymous internet—InterWeb to you, Evie—lover," Rajas finishes for her. Frowning, he adds, "Real smart, Jay."

"Shut up," Jacinda tells Rajas, more serious this time.

What? Are they kidding? I am so lost. Are they not together? She has an InterWeb lover? It makes no sense. But from Jacinda's scowl, now is not the time to ask. Besides, even though they seem comfortable and familiar, I have to remember I just met these guys. It's none of my business.

Jacinda puts her hands on her hips and takes stock of the Dome Home again. "Seriously, this place is pretty cool. But no TV? I cannot relate."

I shrug. "Martha and I usually just talk, read, hang out."

"Or, like, use the InterWeb?"

"Exactly." I smile. Despite her dainty, pretty-girl appearance—which is the polar opposite of what I'm used to—and her way-too-tempting gullibility, she seems solid, like she's got depth and weight. Figuratively, not literally: the girl is teensy. I hop on my good foot to set a jar of honey on the table.

After a quiet moment, Rajas points to the wood-burning stove in the middle of the dome. "You heat with wood. This place is insulated enough? Is there some sort of liner for the winter?"

"Yes." I lean on the table; my ankle is killing me. "The winter liner covers the whole thing, sort of like a huge tarp. Unfortunately it dims the light from all our windows. But there's a vent at the top to keep air moving.

"You've probably figured this out by now." I point to the different areas of our home. "That's Martha's space, behind the curtain. Living room, kitchen, bathroom. I have the loft upstairs."

"No walls. Not much privacy," Rajas observes. He tilts his head to read the spines of the books on our bookshelves, which, along with the curtain, carve out the space between the living room and Martha's room.

"I don't really need much privacy. After sharing a tent with Martha and Rich the whole time we were building this place, my loft is total bliss." I pour iced tea into clean mason jars for drinking and set a plate of sliced bread next to the jars of honey and blueberry jam Martha and I made. "Please, have something to eat." I sit and put the ice, melting into the dishtowel, onto my ankle. *Ah.*

They both seem reluctant to stop looking around, but make their way over and sit. Rajas takes big gulps of his tea.

Jacinda takes a sip from her jar and sets it down, holds up a thick slice of bread. "Is this from that cute bakery up in Sherburne?"

I shake my head while I chew a bite, swallow it. "Fresh from the Dome Home oven."

Her eyes go wide. "You *made* this? Here? Like, rolling out the dough and everything?"

I smile. "Kneading the dough? Yes." Smearing more jam onto my slice, I say, "It's not rocket science, I swear."

Jacinda inspects the bread. "Maybe not. But I don't know how to do it."

"I'm happy to show you sometime."

"How about the jam? You made this too?" Rajas asks.

I nod. "And the honey's from our bees."

"You keep bees. Why am I not surprised?" Rajas smiles his half-smile and bites off another chunk of bread. His dark, dark eyes get round. "Amazing, Eve. Really good."

My cheeks go hot; Rajas calls me Eve, not Evie like everyone else does. It sounds so smoldery on his lips. It makes me feel older. Sort of...sexy. Warm in the tingly bits. *Eve.* Yowza. I hop across the kitchen to plug in my phone.

"You have electricity out here?" Jacinda asks.

Before I can answer, Rajas gripes, "Were you not listening? Did you not notice the solar panels outside?"

Instead of getting snarky, Jacinda smiles and shrugs.

"I must have been distracted by Hannah...what's your cow's name again?"

"Hannah Bramble."

"Right," Jacinda says. "And the piranha chickens."

"Sharks with feathers." Rajas laughs.

"Killer hens." I'm laughing too.

What's it been? Only an hour or two since Rajas and Jacinda and I met. But it's already so...easy. It's amazing: Some people you know for years, but you never get past feeling stilted and awkward. They never understand you. Other people, they walk into your life and *bam.* It's just so right. You feel like you were meant to be part of each others' lives. It's never happened to me with kids my own age. School hasn't even started yet, and already it's happening. Already I know I'll never be the same.

There are only three things that can kill a farmer: lightning, rolling over in a tractor, and old age.

—Bill Bryson, writer, b. 1951

So." I shift the ice on my ankle. "How did you two meet?" Isn't that what I'm supposed to ask, if they're involved? I will be a big girl about it. I refuse to be jealous. This girl is different.

Jacinda and Rajas exchange glances. Rajas lifts his shoulders in an offhand shrug. "Known each other forever." He doesn't say more, like there's nothing more to say.

Jacinda takes a big bite of bread; she swigs some iced tea to wash it down. "Yum, Evie. This is so good." Thank God she's not one of those girls who doesn't eat.

"But how did you meet?"

Jacinda swallows. "If you must know, Raj used to clobber me with blocks—"

"Only when you were being a brat—"

"*And* he used to pee in the bathtub." She sticks her tongue out at him, pleased with herself. Again, I am totally lost. Jacinda must notice my confusion because she says, "Seriously? We've known each other forever, like Raj said. We grew up together."

"So, you've been friends for a long time." How did things get romantic between them? At first I was attempting civilized conversation, but now I'm truly determined to get information.

"Friends?" Rajas laughs. "No."

"We are not *friends*," Jacinda states matter-of-factly. "Our moms are sisters."

"See?" Rajas picks up another piece of bread. "Boring."

"Oh." *Oh!* If their moms are sisters, Rajas and Jacinda are...cousins. Cousins! I smile so big my cheeks hurt. Wow. They seem so close. How cool is that? Family and friends at the same time. Not that I would know; Martha and Rich are the sum total of my relations. "Cousins! That's fantastic!" I enthuse.

"If you say so." Rajas, still eating, sounds noncommittal. But Jacinda stops chewing and narrows her eyes at me, as if she has just figured out why I'm so thrilled with this news. A slow Cheshire Cat grin draws itself across her face.

Quick, change the subject before she says anything.

"So. What's school like? Got any tips or secrets? Am I going to survive?"

It does the trick, because Jacinda's eyes twinkle with excitement. "Don't worry. We'll show you everything you need to know, won't we, Raj? What classes do you have?"

"Let me grab my schedule." I scoot my chair to get up, but Rajas holds out a hand to stop me.

"I'll get it," he says. "You stay put, rest that ankle."

"Thanks." It's a thoughtful gesture, and I try to take it that way, instead of feeling like a damsel in distress again. My ankle is hurting; the ice feels good. "It's on my desk. In the loft."

He looks concerned. "Is it safe to go up there? Should Jacinda go? Is there girl stuff lurking about?"

I laugh. "It's safe. You'll be fine."

He grins his lopsided grin, which makes my stomach flip. He climbs the ladder. "Holy crap."

"What?" Jacinda pops out of her chair to investigate.

I try to see around her. "What's wrong?"

"Nothing. This is just..." Rustling sounds come from the loft.

"Let me see!" Jacinda moves Rajas over to give herself room on the ladder. She climbs, somehow managing to maintain modesty despite her short sundress. The girl's got skills. "Aha!" She grabs the schedule.

"Wasn't talking about the schedule, Jay. Look."

"Holy cow," breathes Jacinda.

I'm already hopping over to the ladder. They must have discovered my scale models—of cities, communities, villages, buildings. I beam; I can't help it. Is there anything better than cool people appreciating something important to you, something that reflects who you are, something you've built yourself? It's so soul-satisfying.

Rajas holds one of the models over the side of the loft, so I can see it. "This is amazing."

"Thanks. Did you see my Eco-Village? It's totally self-sustaining. In theory."

"Ohmigod, you did these?" Jacinda's bare legs disappear over the ladder and I hear her shuffling around.

I smile. "I love to design. It just makes me happy."

"You are seriously gifted. You totally have to go to Cornell."

"Yeah," says Rajas. "Makes sense now."

They are quiet a little longer, looking at my models, before they climb down. Jacinda has my schedule. She looks it over.

"We have Global View and gym together!" Jacinda squeals. "That's so fricking great!"

Rajas grimaces. "So you both have Brookner."

"Shut up," Jacinda practically growls. Before I can ask what they're talking about, Rajas takes my schedule from Jacinda so he can have a look.

"Um...do we have any classes together?" I ask, trying to sound casual.

"Just lunch, if that counts," Rajas says, sitting.

Jacinda studies my reaction. "Oh, it counts all right." She looks at me like I'm very amusing.

The crunch of gravel turns our attention to the driveway. The Clunker shudders to a noisy, clanking stop.

"That would be Martha," I say.

Rajas and Jacinda stand up as my mother bursts into the Dome Home.

"What is that hunk-of-junk gas-guzzler doing—" She stops when she sees Rajas and Jacinda. "Oh. Well, hello there."

"Martha." I give her my dirtiest, tone-it-down look. "This is Rajas and Jacinda. We met down at the creek. The car in the driveway"—I over-enunciate to be sure she gets the point—"belongs to Rajas. Its name is the Blue Biohazard."

In seconds, Martha's face flashes from annoyance to surprise to intrigue—I've never brought two strangers to the Dome Home. She takes my hint and plays it cool. "Good to meet you." She extends her hand. "No offense about the car. I drive a hunk of junk too."

"None taken," Rajas laughs. "Good to meet you." He peeks out the door to get a look at Martha's van.

"Hi, I'm Jacinda." She pumps Martha's hand. Martha looks at me with a Where-did-you-pick-up-this-strange-specimen? look. It's the same look—Did-you-just-get-back-from-the-moon?—Jacinda has been giving me all day. Standing next to each other, they are a study in contrasts: Martha with her big frame and wiry silver hair, a dingy shirt, pants, and practical shoes; Jacinda in her pixie cut and little dress and sparkly flip-flops.

"Jacinda..." Martha's eyebrows twist while she thinks. "That's an unusual name. I swear I've seen it—" She snaps her fingers. "Aha! Are you the babysitter from the flyer?"

Jacinda claps her hands, delighted. "Yes! That's me! Which one did you see?"

"The Horny Singletons Pack." Martha crosses to the kitchen area and opens the refrigerator.

"The...*what* pack?" Jacinda looks bewildered.

"The Help for Single Parents group at the Unitarian Church," I explain. "HSP. Martha says it stands for Horny Singletons Pack."

Martha reappears with a carrot. "Because that's what it is. A wolf pack of unmarried horny horndogs. The fact that they happen to be divorced, and have kids, is somewhat extraneous."

I give Martha a dirty look. "One: it's *not* a Horny Singletons Pack. And two: it's good for you."

"So you say, darling." She chomps a piece off the

carrot, holding the remainder like a cigar, wagging the ferny top. "What's the story here?"

"Rajas and Jacinda helped me out of a pickle. I twisted my ankle."

Martha flies over and kneels to touch my foot. "Is it sprained?"

"I think so."

She drops her carrot—it lands on the table next to my iced tea—and takes a closer look. She moves my ice pack and holds her hands above my ankle. It's a restorative energy thing. She closes her eyes to focus the healing vibrations. I don't even want to look at Rajas and Jacinda; who knows what they'll make of this? Of her? They've been great with me, but Martha's a whole other level of different.

"Nice. A '61 minibus." Rajas is admiring it from the doorway.

Martha opens her eyes and grins at him. "Why, yes indeedy! That's The Clunker. My pride and joy. Are you a connoisseur?"

Rajas nods. "Can I take a look?"

"I'll do you one better." She tosses the keys to him. "Why don't you take her for a spin?"

Rajas looks at her in utter disbelief. "Really?"

"Sure. Take Jacinda in case you stall and need a push start."

Jacinda looks from Rajas, to me, to Martha. "You're, like, just kidding, right?"

"Only one way to find out." Martha shoos them toward the door. "Go on. Live a little. You're only young once, *n'est-ce pas*?"

"All right. Thanks!" Rajas smiles. "Be right back."

"Take your time. If her door falls off, just slide it back on the rails."

Jacinda looks horrified. "Okay..." She sees that Rajas is already outside. "Ta-ta." She *thwup thwups* to catch up with her cousin. Cousin! I let out a contented sigh.

Martha cocks an eyebrow at me. She locks her gaze into mine. Squinting, she sets her palms on my shoulders, and smiles. "Well, well, well, my darling," she says, "looks like lightning's struck."

She's like that, Martha: intense and cryptic and funny. When she was twenty-three and following Phish with her brother Rich, she got pregnant with me by a guy they'd been hanging out with. The family folklore is that, nine months later, Martha went into labor at the start of a show. Her midwife friend had disappeared into the sweaty crowd. So, to deliver me, it was Rich, or no one. He says it was the best—and scariest—trip of his life. And he quit hallucinogens after that.

I know nothing about my dad. "We had some good times," is all Martha will say, "but he wouldn't have been a good father." Rich just rolls his eyes when I ask. The most he's ever told me is, "The worst thing about that dude is he would sell shrooms to anyone. Even if they were clearly going to have themselves a bad, bad trip. Dude had no scruples."

Rich is the only constant man in Martha's life. She says she prefers it that way. The way she talks, it might seem like she doesn't believe in true love. And maybe she has lost faith in the possibilities of finding it for herself. "You and me: we're enough," she'll say, tending the garden or boiling apples for applesauce. "I'm not opposed to the occasional one-night stand, when I get particularly…lonely. If you know what I mean. But you, Evie, will have great love in your life. You will fall deeply and powerfully and fiercely in love. It will be as undeniable as lightning striking deep into your core. And I'm sorry to say, my darling, that with great love can come great pain."

I gape at Martha as she sits down next to me at the kitchen table. *Lightning.* My throat has gone dry. "What did you say?"

"You heard me." She lifts my leg onto her lap, cradling my ankle. "I know lightning when I see it."

I stare out the open door and realize I've been practically holding my breath since Rajas left, waiting for him to get back. Oh man. Martha saying it makes it real. And overwhelming. "I don't feel good." I get up and hop to the bathroom. My stomach is swirling. "I think I'm coming down with something."

"You've got a fever, all right," Martha says, "for Rajas!" Swishing her hips, she begins singing. Some song about fever lasting all through the night.

"It feels more like food poisoning," I tell her.

"Oh, darling." Martha is still moving her hips. "Sometimes lightning takes its toll." She's swirling; I feel like hurling. She wiggles her eyebrows at me and starts singing again, *"You give me fever. Fever!"*

Education, therefore, is a process of living and not a preparation for future living.

—John Dewey, philosopher and educator, 1859–1952

The Clunker bumps hard over our road, swaying and shimmying like the chicken buses we rode to visit Rich when he was in Mexico. Next to me, Martha is practically asleep; her forehead bonks against the window whenever we hit a dip in the road. My ankle is bandaged and sore and it hurts to shift gears, but I'm too excited about school to sit back and let Martha drive.

"You awake?" I ask her.

"Mmm."

"Liar." I smile. "So I'll pick you up around three?"

"Mmm-hmm."

When Jacinda and Rajas left my place on Friday, Rajas offered to drive me to the first day of school.

Why on earth did I say no? Since then he and Jacinda have friended me on Facebook and we've chatted a little. I wish I were in the Blue Biohazard with them now; I wish it so hard it's almost an ache. I want to be where Rajas is. But Martha would have been crestfallen. Riding together, hearing about my day, spending as much time with me as she can—it's her strategy for coping with my decision to attend The Institution of School.

I stifle a yawn and take another sip from my travel mug of yerba maté. I woke up at 5:00 as usual, to shower, eat breakfast, and tend the animals and garden, but mostly I sat; Martha wanted me to baby my ankle. All morning, my heart's been pounding, thoughts in overdrive. I can't stop thinking of Rajas. He and Jacinda stayed for dinner the day of my non-rescue rescue, and they hung out for a long time, talking and laughing and playing Cranium with Martha and me. I attempted to be coherent and add to the conversation every now and then, but mostly I was Zenning out, wondering all sorts of things about Rajas: What does he think of me? Is he as attracted to me as I am to him? Is he involved with someone? After he and Jacinda left, I wrote in my diary, went out and stared at the stars, and sketched a bunch of designs, trying to calm down and fall asleep. Yoga would have helped, but my ankle sprain put the kibosh on that. Point is, every moment since they left I've been thinking about Rajas. I'm dying to see him again.

Further toward town, the road smoothes into pavement, houses begin to cluster. Stores appear, the first of which is Walmart, Martha's place of employ for the last year. She hates it, but without a college degree, she doesn't have a lot of choices. She moves jobs a lot, mostly retail, either quitting when she can't stand one more minute of it, or getting fired for appropriating items for personal use. I can't remember the last time she had health insurance. Which is why she is so supportive of my goal to study planning and design, my dream to get a degree from Cornell. She wants me to follow my bliss, of course, but she loves that it involves a decent profession with potential benefits. Meanwhile, she works for The Man and volunteers at the co-op to put food on the table. I can't wait until it's my turn to take care of her.

"Did you remember your name tag?" I ask.

"Yes, darling."

"And the stickers we made?" Today's guerilla stickering campaign will focus on the dangers of pesticides and food additives and preservatives. She's rotating through the grocery section this week.

Martha leans over to kiss me and cups my cheeks in her hands. "I love you. Don't let that place break your beautiful spirit."

"Martha, please," I assure her despite my nervous stomach, "it's just school."

"Ha. Just like this place is just a store." She yanks the door handle, shaking it until the door rasps open. "Promise me."

"I promise I'll be fine."

"And you'll be true to yourself?"

I give her a look. "I'll pick you up after school."

"Sure you don't want to change your mind? You can hang out—"

"Martha!"

"It was worth a shot."

"See you later." After she's through the doors, I cajole The Clunker back into what little traffic there is and drive past the cemetery, McDonald's, and the tire shop on Broad Street. It's one of the two primary streets in town. Broad runs north-south, Main runs east to west. I pass the Naturalista Food Co-op, Doug's Sandwich Shop, Nano's Pizza, the movie theater. In the center of town, by the county courthouse and a little park, I make a right onto Main Street.

A few blocks up, another right turn, and here I am. Zero hour. School.

All grades, kindergarten through twelfth, share a campus of three buildings on the east side of town. The elementary school is set to the north, surrounded by jungle gyms and playgrounds. To the south is the high school, grades nine through twelve. The middle school, grades seven and eight, is wedged—you guessed it—in the middle.

With sweaty palms slipping on the steering wheel, I turn into the parking lot. I'm more nervous than I thought. I've only been inside the building twice before. Once to interview with the principal, Dr. Folger, who set me to work on The Battery of Tests to determine my placement. Military terminology is truly appropriate; the day of testing left me feeling beat-up and exhausted. The second visit was to meet my guidance counselor, who said I scored well enough to become a senior, as long as I double-up on math and science so I'll meet state requirements for graduation. Starting today, my daily routine will be rather intense: Global View, gym, biology, physics, lunch. With Rajas! Then English, geometry, trigonometry.

The Clunker's brakes squeal as I look around for a parking space. The lot is full, stacked with old Mustangs, battered minivans, pickup trucks, a few shiny new cars. A lot of kids must drive to school, juniors and seniors, I assume. Scanning the throngs, congregated in clusters, I see a couple of vaguely familiar faces, but I don't really know anyone. Deep yoga breath. Jacinda pops into view. And Rajas! A thousand flitty moths take flight in my stomach. The tips of my fingers tingle. *Lightning.*

I park and climb down from The Clunker and limp across the asphalt. My ankle can hold some weight if I go easy.

I am greeted with wide smiles. The most welcome smiles.

"Eve!" Rajas's voice is the best sound I've ever heard.

"Is it everything you expected and more?" Jacinda chirps.

"So far, so good." I give them each a small hug hello. Touching Rajas shoots electricity up and down my spine. He wrestles my backpack from me. Around us, other students are watching. They seem curious, maybe even a little suspicious, but neither Rajas nor Jacinda seems to care.

They walk me into the building and help me find my first class. The halls are like Mexico City in rush-hour traffic, minus the cars. Kids are crammed into every space, zooming around. I had no idea it would be this crowded. "This is Global View and also our homeroom," Jacinda explains.

"Homeroom?" I think I know what that means, but I'm not completely sure.

Jacinda looks surprised. "Homeroom? When the teacher takes attendance and reads announcements?"

"Huh," I say without thinking.

"'Huh,' what?" asks Rajas.

"Nothing. Nothing. I knew they keep records of

whether you show up or not. It's just...I'm not used to that kind of thing." My stomach sinks a little. Education should be exhilarating, not compulsory.

"You'll get used to everything soon," Jacinda assures me.

"That's a scary thought."

The light in here makes everyone look greenish and alien. The classrooms have windows, but fluorescents drone on the ceilings, casting unnatural shadows. The halls have no natural light. Gray tile floors, cinder-block walls, dented metal lockers. It's so sterile and impersonal. I can't think of a less appealing environment. It's like a warehouse. Except worse.

Maybe enrolling in a regular school wasn't such a good idea. But then again, what did I expect?

I take another deep breath and try to focus on the positive: Rajas. Jacinda. Other new friends, new perspectives, a fresh look at things. Speaking of fresh, would it have killed someone to add skylights? Some live plants?

The walls seem lined with eyeballs. And when Rajas leans close to wish me good luck, those eyeballs grow wide. I straighten my shoulders and take yet another deep breath. Hobbling away from Rajas feels like ripping off a band-aid. I check the clock: T-minus three and a half hours until lunch.

Religion is the opium of the people.

—KARL MARX, PHILOSOPHER AND ECONOMIST, 1818–1883

The quote from Marx on the whiteboard in the front of the classroom, and the question below it—*Agree or disagree?*—boosts my spirits immediately. Like I told Rajas the other day, I've been collecting quotes for years. And even better, Martha, Rich, and I have spent many a supper discussing Marx and his theories. I make a tottering beeline to the board and pick up a marker, blue and chemical-fumy, to write my response: *Disagree. TELEVISION is the opium of the people.*

The bell rings, but it doesn't sound like school bells in movies. Rather than a hammer-on-metal bell *brrring,* the "bell" is a prolonged, grating, synthetic beep, a noise so artificial and startling that I almost drop the marker. I hop to a desk near Jacinda, passing a girl who stares at me with her mouth open. Behind Jacinda, a boy is tapping the screen of his phone. Jacinda pats the empty chair next to her. I sit and set my things on the desk.

"Bold move!" Jacinda nods toward the quote, sounding impressed. Something catches her attention; I follow her gaze. Our teacher is coming through the door. He's wearing a button-down shirt tucked into faded jeans. His tie is already loosened. Thick-rimmed glasses frame his eyes. He's good-looking and stylish—in a pushing-forty, post-tragicially hip, old-timey kind of way.

The man clears his throat. "Good morning and welcome back. I'm—"

Static pops from the speaker near the ceiling. It is the only adornment on the cinder-block wall except for two lengths of whiteboard, a television on a rolling cart in the corner, and a big analog clock. Has the teacher not had a chance to decorate, or does he not care?

The teacher frowns, "It sounds as if—"

"Hello students. Teachers," squawks the speaker, "if you'll excuse the interruption, this is Dr. Folger. I'd like to welcome our sophomores, juniors, and seniors back from summer vacation, and extend a warm welcome to our first-year students. I trust you are rested and ready to learn. I'm indeed pleased to announce that, due to your high marks on end-of-grade tests, we are now a

Striving-for-Excellence school. If we repeat a good performance this year, we shall become a Governor's School of Distinction."

No one seems to be listening. Jacinda rolls her eyes, twirling her index finger in a sarcastic whoop-de-doo gesture.

Dr. Folger continues, "I expect this year to be our most successful year to date." Papers rustle like he's moving things around. "I'll turn things over to your capable teachers. My door is always open. Go Purple Tornado!" The speaker sputters and clicks off.

At the front of the class, the teacher half-sits, half-leans on his desk, which is clunky and industrial and looks like it was made in 1950. He uncrosses his arms and smoothes his tie. "Well. As I was saying. I'm Mr. Brookner and this is Global View. There aren't any announcements." He smiles and sweeps his arm toward the speaker. "Well, any *other* announcements, so after I put faces to the names on my list here, we'll jump right in."

Mr. Brookner lifts a folder off of his desk. "Before I call roll, I don't need to remind you that phones need to be silenced and stowed during class." There is a bit of shuffling as phones are put in bags or pockets. Brookner starts taking roll; most kids raise their hands or mumble as he calls their names. I'm semiconscious of gripping the sides of my desk, bracing myself as Mr. Brookner closes in on the first letter of my last name.

"Tera McClernon?"

"Here."

Mr. Brookner checks it off. He pauses and squints at the paper. "Hmm. Is this right?" he murmurs. "Uh—"

I raise my hand to stop him. "I just go by Evie. Please. For obvious reasons."

Mr. Brookner studies me for a moment, then nods. "Understood." He makes a note on his list.

Phew. One roll down, six to go.

When he's finished with the list, Mr. Brookner turns to the board. "Well. I thought we'd start today with..." But he trails off. "Interesting. I see someone has already added a thought." He sounds charmed—and maybe also a little annoyed?

The class titters. Behind me, someone whispers in sibilant *S*'s. I give Jacinda a look, *So I guess it was a rhetorical question?* She sort of shrugs and smiles.

"Class. Settle." Mr. Brookner clears his throat. "Someone has shown some enthusiasm this morning."

Enthusiasm? A response to a question demonstrates enthusiasm? Yikes.

"*Television* is the opium of the people. Hmm. Would the writer care to elaborate?" He levels his gaze at me. The jig is up.

"Um." I shift in my seat. "Sure." I take a breath to

gather my thoughts. "So. Marx was implying that religion is an illusion to make oppressed people feel better without actually confronting the reasons for their oppression. Which there probably is some truth to, in the sense that religions tend to focus on other realms—like heaven or the afterlife—rather than this plane of existence, you know what I mean?"

Mr. Brookner's eyebrows have crept up; they are hovering above the frames of his glasses. "Go on."

His look makes me lose momentum. "Well, uh, with religion, in another sense," I say, "it's something that at least makes you think about your values. And really, at its best"—I'm getting my groove back—"religion prompts you to take action and *do* something to help others. Like the Catholic Workers movement, how they worked for fair labor standards. Or Quakers, who were abolitionists, helping enslaved people follow the Underground Railroad, and who now lobby for peace.

"But television? It's just passive. Worse than passive. Did you know you burn fewer calories watching television than you do sleeping? It's less active than sleep! Plus, it's basically advertisers feeding you a load of crap: that you are defective and not good enough, and that you have to buy stuff to make up for it." Man, I'm on a roll! "Ad campaigns and TV programs dictate your values. It's the opium of our time because it sedates you with bad self-esteem and consumerism while you get type two diabetes from drinking soda and eating potato chips and sitting on your ass."

I look around, pleased with the cohesiveness of my argument. But eyeballs are bugged out. Kids are staring at me. Staring. "Sorry. Sitting on your butts," I amend.

Silence.

"Rear ends?" I try. "Cute little tushies?"

Mr. Brookner chuckles. "I don't think your word choice is the issue." He turns to the rest of the class. "Well. This is quite the jumping-off point. Who has something to add to Evie's assessment?"

Butts, asses, rear ends, cute little tushies shift in seats. A girl in the front row—Marcie, I think?—clears her throat, but no one says anything. It's a thundering silence. Jacinda inspects her fingernails.

"Okay, well then." Mr. Brookner picks up a green marker. "Let's look at the quote in context." He starts adding dates to the board. Around me, students flip their notebooks open and seem to relax, their bodies slouching like deflating tires. This must be what they are more used to: listening. Writing stuff down.

I open my notebook and stare at its blue delineations. My cheeks feel hot and chapped, like I've just been in a windstorm that no one else even felt. Ten minutes into the first day of school and I'm already weirding people out. This must be some kind of record.

Gym class, the other class Jacinda and I share, is next. As I limp along beside her, Jacinda entertains me with a running commentary: "Ohmigod, that was crazy! Ta-ta, Marcie!" She wiggles her polished fingers at the girl from Global View. "Hi, Neil!" she says to a redheaded guy on the other side of the hall. "The way you went toe-to-toe with Brookner! He is so smart, that was incredible. Hi, Peter, hey, Sarah!" Good God, the girl knows *everyone*. "Okay. Having gym second bell is seriously lame. Like I'm going to get all sweaty in the morning? I don't think so. Too bad we don't have Mr. D, he's awesome. Lord knows I get enough of Ms. Gliss." She waggles her fingers to another girl: "Hi, Carrie!"

Her train of thought is interpolated with so many hellos and goodbyes, it's harder to follow than usual. But "bell" must mean both the horrid sound and the class period itself. Noted.

Our gym teacher, Ms. Gliss, is all business. She's tiny and curvy like Jacinda, dressed head to toe in purple and white, which I'm going to go ahead and presume are the school colors. She's wearing one of those sport skort things and she's got expensive-looking sneakers with fluffy pom-poms on the laces. At the bell, she blows her whistle—unnecessary since we're all milling around in a small group—and marches our all-girl class into the locker room (dim light, rusting lockers, musty smell). She tucks her pouffy blonde hair behind her ears and sets her fists on her small hips.

"Gym class is a *real* class and you need it to graduate," Ms. Gliss begins. "So please do not come to me with excuses. Physical fitness is extraordinarily important in this day and age. September is National Childhood Obesity Awareness Month. We have an epidemic on our hands, ladies, and I for one am determined to do my part in combating it." She pauses as if for emphasis. I'm intrigued—until I realize that she's giving obvious, pointed looks to the heavier girls. Which just seems mean and prejudiced. "So gym class will be strenuous and you will take it seriously. I have no time for senioritis, m'kay, ladies? I *will* fail you if you do not participate. Participation means,"—she touches her thumb to each finger as she lists—"changing into appropriate gym clothes each and every day, completing all assignments..." Good gravy, how many rules do you need for gym class?

"Here are your locker assignments—*quiet!*—and I want to remind you girls that I am not as gullible as...certain male gym teachers. Menstrual periods are a fact of life and you will *not* be excused from class during menses." There is giggling.

Ms. Gliss raises her voice. "*I said quiet!* If you need a sanitary pad or tampon, I am happy to provide you one. Just please do not start thinking of my office as a drugstore." She smiles for the first time. It's one of those lovely, beguiling smiles you sense has served its bearer well.

"I encourage all of you to participate in after-school sports. It's not too late to join the JV or intramural soccer or field hockey teams. And, as usual, throughout the semester I will be having sign-ups for regional walk/jog fundraisers: Crop Walk, Race for the Cure, AIDS Walk, et cetera." Finally, the woman says something I can get on board with! "These fundraisers are not required, but I urge you to participate. They are good for your body and your character.

"Now, as many of you know, it's a big year for Cheer Squad." Her smile starts to sparkle. "We have an excellent shot at making state finals. Isn't that right, Jacinda?"

"Yes, Ms. Gliss."

Ms. Gliss nods and continues talking, extolling the virtues of fitness, sports, nutrition, and weight loss to attain a healthy body mass index, until the bell slices into her monologue.

Jacinda and I make our way out of the locker room. "What was that about?" I ask.

"What? Ms. Gliss?"

"Yeah. The Cheer Squad?"

"Oh, she's the coach. Hi, Julie!" She waves at someone. "It's, like, so *Glee*, right?"

"So *Glee*?"

"*Glee*? The TV show? You haven't seen *Glee*? Seriously, I don't know how you survive without a TV." She waves at another girl going by. "Ta-ta, Andrea! Come on, Evie, let's get you—hi again, Stiv!—to your next bell."

Okay, I'm totally lost. But she's too busy social butterflying to explain.

Biology, physics, and at last it's time for lunch. Rajas—*Rajas! Yes!*—and Jacinda guide me into the serving line of the cafeteria. And holy crap. The food? Horrendous. Beyond horrendous. A forensic scientist would be gobsmacked. Hamburger patties on soggy white buns... how would you ever trace this oily gray circle back to a cow? Uck. And the jello. Show me any food in the natural world that shade of neon green. You can't.

The salad bar offers the only food bearing any semblance of...food. Note to self: pack a lunch tomorrow. And forever.

I limp through the cash register line and start to follow Jacinda and Rajas to a table.

"Hold on," I call to them. "It's such a beautiful day, why don't we dine alfresco?"

Rajas grimaces. "Sorry, Eve. Outside's not an option unless you want detention."

Even a total school virgin like me knows detention is something to be avoided, so I follow Jacinda to a cramped table. There are two empty chairs, which seem to have Rajas's and Jacinda's names on them.

"Sit," Rajas tells me. "I'll go find another chair." Too tired to argue, I plop down and Jacinda introduces me around the table. Most of the kids smile. The placement of their cheeks and lips are right, but there is a hollowness, a hesitancy around their teeth. One of the girls—Megan?—looks up from her phone and frowns, her eyes going up and down my body, taking in my Levis, my shabby T-shirt. Her lips purse and she looks back down, resumes tapping her phone's screen. The boys, in general, seem friendlier and less judgmental. The girls need to step up their game.

Jacinda smiles and laughs at someone's joke, someone else's bit of gossip, while I inwardly quiz myself on people's names. Marcie, Stiv, Megan (I'm pretty sure), Matt, Jim. This blur of faces and hair and clothes and food and phones and chatter, it's more than a little overwhelming. When Rajas returns and sets his chair down next to me, I melt with relief, and I touch his elbow with mine to convey my gratitude. He seems to shiver at my touch—or am I just imagining it? Wishful thinking? He smiles. My stomach flips, my heart thumps. Being near him is the heart-rate boosting equivalent of ascending a Mayan pyramid.

"How are classes so far?" Rajas asks, nearly shouting to be heard over the din. Our table seems to be the epicenter of the cafeteria.

"Okay," I shrug. "I'm a bit whiplashed from the newness of it all. But so far, so good."

Across the table, Jacinda peels her orange and leans into our conversation. "Ohmigod, stop being so modest!" Turning to Rajas, she says, "You should have seen her in Global View!"

"Not a big deal," I say, poking at my shredded iceberg lettuce in its Styrofoam (Styrofoam! How has that not been banned yet?) bowl.

"Whatever! You totally went toe-to-toe with Brookner!" She pulls off the last bit of orange peel and picks at the white membrane. "Raj, will you please tell Evie The Way of The Brookner? And more specifically, his quotes?" She sections her orange and offers me a piece. "Raj took Global View last year."

Rajas's eyes widen. "Holy crap! You discussed the quote?"

"Not only discussed," Jacinda squeals, "she wrote her response *on the board*!"

Rajas grins. "Nice." He shakes his head and takes a section of orange. "Be warned that Brookner takes those quotes seriously."

Jacinda nods. "They are, like, his thing."

Rajas says, "It's his intellectual gauntlet. He always starts class with a quote. He'll swear that he wants a discussion, but really he just wants to explain it himself and then jump into his lecture."

"That's not true!" Jacinda comes to Mr. Brookner's defense.

Rajas gives her a dubious look.

"Well," I say, "either way, people must discuss the quotes with him all the time."

Rajas and Jacinda shake their heads, their gazes sticking on me so their eyes roll side to side while they say no. Rajas says, "Not really. Not until today, sounds like."

"Well, that's just weird," I say. "I can't be held responsible for throwing down the gauntlet if I didn't even know that's what I was doing."

"Now you do, though. Know, I mean," says Jacinda. She pops another piece of orange in her mouth and turns to Rajas. "He seemed impressed. And slightly irritated." She spits out a seed into her napkin. Leave it to Jacinda to make seed spitting look polished and ladylike. "I wish it had been me sounding so smart about his quote," she sighs.

Rajas leans toward me—and I almost drop my plastic fork because Oh God he smells so good; today it's cinnamon and coffee beans and oranges. He speaks into my ear, "Jacinda gets wiggy when it comes to Brookner. She's been lusting after him for a year." He says it in a kidding-but-not-really kind of way, and his disapproval is clear.

"Shut up! I can tell what you're saying!" Jacinda scrunches up her face; her eyes dart around our table. People keep looking at us, but it's so loud in here that I don't think anyone can hear our actual conversation. Jacinda leans closer to me and says, "Okay, maybe I have a crush—but you cannot tell anyone."

"Well, he does seem pretty cool. For a teacher." More interesting than any other teachers I've encountered this morning. "Besides, who am I going to tell? You two are the only people I know at this school."

Rajas lowers his voice to say something to Jacinda, and I manage to catch a word or two: *I mean it...careful...sketchy*.

Jacinda pouts. "Those are just rumors and you know it." She reaches into her purse and pulls out her phone.

I take a forkful of salad. They're talking about Brookner—they must be—but I can't catch the exact words. Should I ask? Would that be too nosy? I'm still debating when my phone buzzes in my pocket. I dig it out and flip it open. I don't have to look at the number to know who it is. "I'm fine, Martha."

"Darling! I just wanted to check in. How's it going? It's pretty slow here at the Mart of Wal."

Typical Martha: she calls to check on me but talks about *her* day first. Gazing out the window, I muse, "Maybe it's because it's so nice out."

Rajas catches my attention. He looks horrified, like I'm mutilating puppies, or something equally heinous.

"What?" I ask, but he's looking over me now, behind me. So is Jacinda and everyone else.

"No phones!" A voice from earlier in the day. A small hand appears in front of me. "Hand it over."

I turn to face the owner of the hand. Ms. Gliss.

"I'll be off in a second," I tell her. Speaking into my phone, I say, "Martha? I have to go, but I'll see you when I pick you up, okay?"

Sighing, "I'll be waiting with bated breath, my love."

"Okay. I love you—"

But the cell phone has been yanked out of my hand by Ms. Gliss. Apparently in this case, The Man is A Woman.

It is not desirable to cultivate a respect for the law, so much as for the right.

—Henry David Thoreau, writer and philosopher, 1817–1862

Ms. Gliss confiscates my phone. "The Fourth Amendment protects from illegal search and seizure," I tell her. "So you can't take my phone." Ha! Schooled.

Her forehead wrinkles, but she recovers quickly. "The Fourth Amendment protects you in your own home. You're in *my* house now."

Whoa. The woman seems to know her history. But she can't be right. Even at school, you can't be subjected to search and seizure, can you? Not without a warrant. Anyway, it's moot now. She already has my phone.

"You can pick it up at the main office at the end of the day," she says. The smugness in her voice is almost tangible.

I look around the cafeteria. What's with all the other kids tapping away on their phones? Why isn't she giving them grief?

"I'd say you're not off to a very good start here, young lady." Ms. Gliss writes something on a form, rips off one of a triplicate page, and hands it to me. A yellow carbon copy. "Your parent or guardian will need to sign this."

"You could have just talked to her. That's who I was on the phone with."

Her eyes harden. "You watch your step."

"Are the rules written down somewhere? Because I didn't get the memo about phones." I am now beyond confused.

From the look on her face, Ms. Gliss isn't a big fan of explication. Or levity.

As soon as Ms. Gliss is gone, Jacinda, who has been silent, studying her hands in her lap, starts talking. "I'm so sorry, Evie! Ms. Gliss can be a real stickler. We should have told you that you can't use your phone in school."

I still don't get it. Jacinda follows my gaze to the other kids with phones. "Oh! You can't use your *phone* in school. But you can use the *internet*. During lunch, before and after school, and also if you have a free bell. Which you don't," she remembers.

Internet, okay. Phone calls, not okay. Interesting. "Does the school give out iPhones?"

Jacinda looks at me like I'm crazy. It's the Did-you-just-get-back-from-the-moon? look. "This is a *public* school, Evie."

"Then that's discriminatory."

"How do you mean?" Jacinda asks.

"Smartphones are expensive. The school should either ban them completely or provide them to everyone. Otherwise it's biased, socioeconomically."

"There are computers in the media center," Jacinda offers. "Anyone can use those."

"Are they portable? Small, and up-to-date?"

"No," Jacinda frowns, "they're big old desktops."

"And how many are there?"

"I don't know. Like three or four?"

"For the whole school?" I shake my head. "That's not the same. It's less convenient, *and* there's a limited number."

"You're right," Rajas says. "The policy isn't fair. I've thought about that too."

Jacinda stares at Rajas. "You want to give up your iPhone?"

Rajas ignores the question. "Technically, you're only supposed to use them for academics. But it's not really enforceable."

"Yeah," Jacinda agrees, "they don't, like, check your internet history or anything." She makes a face. "At least, I don't think they do." She looks around the table. "Can the school check your internet history?"

Marcie and Stiv shrug. Matt says, "Mr. Wolman said you can be investigated for anything you do during school hours."

"Really?" Rajas says, like he doubts it.

Stiv says, "Doesn't matter. You can always erase your history and delete your cookies."

Man, I have a lot to learn.

After lunch, I limp my way—figuratively and literally—through English, geometry, and trigonometry. The teachers seem decent, if not super exciting, and I recognize a few faces from the morning. The English teacher, Mr. Wolman, asks us to write down our favorite books on index cards so he can get to know us. When he sees I've filled the entire front and back of my card, he smiles. It's promising.

Megan has English with me, and she's friendlier than she was at lunch. Matt, the guy from Global View and lunch, invites me to sit next to him in trigonometry. All in all, I survive my first day intact.

After the dismissal bell, I limp to the main office to retrieve my contraband. Ms. Franklin, the secretary, seems sweet. "Rough first day, hon?" She tilts a plastic container toward me. "Fudge? It's my specialty."

"Ah. You're speaking my language." I select a piece of fudge; it melts in my mouth. "Mmm. Chocolate heals all wounds. Thank you so much."

"Anytime." She opens a drawer in her desk and hands me my phone. "Maybe you should leave this at home tomorrow."

"Or hide it better."

She smiles. "I'll just pretend I didn't hear that. Take another piece of fudge for the road."

"Love to. Thanks again." I hobble to the parking lot. My backpack is heavy with homework. Such a strange notion.

Halfway to the parking lot, Rajas finds me. He reaches out to take my bag.

"It's okay, I've got it."

"This is not chivalry," he says. "Just while your ankle heals." His hand is still out.

I give it over. We don't talk much, but it's a companionable quiet, comforting while we travel through the hectic lot. What I would give to be alone with him. I sneak a glance at his lips. How amazing would they be to kiss? He's often chatting with girls, but I haven't seen him sticking to any one particular girl besides Jacinda. So maybe he isn't involved? Could he be interested in me? My legs turn to blueberry jam thinking about it.

We get to The Clunker. I climb in and he hands me my bag. "See you tomorrow," he says.

I'm reluctant to leave, but I can't think of anything else to say. "See you."

He waves as I rumble off to pick up Martha.

She is waiting at the side of the building. "Tell me all, my love." She swings herself into the passenger seat. "Have you been completely corrupted yet? My day was just awful. I almost got busted and had to flush our stickers. Which clogged the toilet. How's your ankle?"

"Sore. Better overall, but worse than this morning."

She nods. "It needs rest."

We bump through the streets, then onto gravel roads home, and I listen to her recap her shift. As usual, she complains about overconsumption, the customers who come in every day to buy things they don't need. After a while she loses steam. "Okay, let's have it. How was The Institution of School?"

"The jury's still out. It was mostly okay. And weird. I got detention, you'll be pleased to know."

Martha grunts. "For what?"

"Socioeconomic status." I explain the phone rule.

"Darling. I'd say it speaks volumes about a place when the best punishment they can cook up is to spend more time there. It really brings to mind Freire's theory of banking education—"

I hold up a hand to stop her. "Please do not commence rant. I don't need a diatribe right now."

"Fine. But let me say this." She reaches over and musses with my hair. "If your goal is The Great Social Experiment, then you shouldn't waste time before you start shaking things up."

Right. The investigative reporter, the school shaker-upper. That's what I'd told Martha to get her to let me enroll, but... "What if that's not my main goal right now?"

"What else could possibly—" She chuckles with delight. "Ooh. And how is Rajas?"

I can't help but give her a big, sloppy grin. "Wonderful."

"Lightning."

My stomach does cartwheels. I nod.

"Is he spoken for? Will you have to steal him away from someone?"

"Don't know. His Facebook status doesn't specify."

"So that means he's available?"

I sigh. "It means he didn't answer the question."

She gives me an incredulous look. "It hasn't occurred to you to ask?"

"It seems like an odd question to just vomit out."

"My love, my darling," she clucks, "I raised you to be bold. But, *c'est la vie...*If you don't want to ask Rajas, ask Jacinda."

"Isn't that kind of lame? I feel like it's going behind his back. It's cowardly."

"Darling," Martha says, "information is what girlfriends are for! Anyhoo, that boy's got eyes for you. I can tell these things."

My stomach flips again. "It does seem like it."

"So don't just stand there—"

"Bust a move?" I cajole The Clunker up our driveway.

"No wallflowering. *Viva la revolución* already! And if you must fall in love in the meantime, well..." She tugs my hair. "I suppose that's allowed. Not that you need my permission."

"You got that right." I pull in next to The Dome and The Clunker shudders to a stop.

Hallelujah. Home. I hobble to the porch.

"You know what, my love?" Martha reaches into a tree to pluck an apple, one of the first of the season. "We're both tuckered. You could use some company. I'm going to ditch Horny Singletons tonight."

"Don't even think about it, Martha. You need to hang out with people your own age." I crunch into the apple. "Besides, I have homework." Heaps of homework.

Martha screws up her face. "It's my turn for Share Your Divorce Story night—"

"So make something up! Something torrid and lewd, with lots of drama and intrigue." I wag my fingers at her. "Or better yet," I say, "tell them the truth! 'Truth is stranger than fiction.'"

Martha laughs, "I do what I can."

I'm in the barn with Hannah Bramble's warm company, my ankle propped on the milking stool. I'm writing in my diary, daydreaming about Rajas, when The Clunker rumbles home. Next to me, a pail of milk is cooling, steam twisting in languid circles over the creamy top. The cats have long since finished their milk—I always give them the first bit—and retreated to private corners to tidy their whiskers and paws. Nearby, the chickens cluck softly in their coop. In a few minutes, Martha appears with a glass of wine. She holds it out to offer me a sip. I shake my head and set my journal and pen aside. Martha sits in the straw.

"How was HSP?" I ask.

"Wouldn't you like to know." She motions for me to move closer.

I lean back onto her leg, sigh as she pulls my hair elastic out of my hair. She nods toward my diary. "Planning the revolution?"

"Not yet. I'm making notes for a beautiful, sustainable school. Holistic architecture, natural materials, solar panels. Lots of natural sunlight. My goodness.

Why does the place have to be such a factory? I bet every student there has a vitamin—"

"Vitamin D deficiency," she finishes my sentence. "I have no doubt." She sips her wine. "Well, darling, did you talk to Jacinda? Is Rajas a free man?"

I shake my head. "I feel sort of weird calling or texting her just to ask about Rajas. I'll ask her first thing tomorrow."

"Please do, my love." We settle into quiet, listening to Hannah Bramble swish her tail. Martha strokes my hair, and I feel her divide it into three sections. I love it when Martha plays with my hair. It's the most relaxing thing in the world. It's her way of letting me know she's listening, that she wants to hear more about my life, my thoughts.

"It was weird, school. Problematic."

"*Par exemple*?"

I sigh. "Several. For one thing, there's our gym teacher, Ms. Gliss."

She snorts. "The one from the detention form?"

"That's the one. You wouldn't believe the way she took my phone. Just grabbed it right out of my hand. She acts like because she's a teacher and I'm a student, I have no rights at all and she can do whatever she wants. With impunity."

"Typical," she harrumphs. "You said there were several things?"

"Well, it's not as overt, but she's also obsessed with fitness. I know she's a gym teacher, but the way she looked at the heavier girls? Her lecture about body mass index seemed more about appearance and being thin than it was about being healthy."

Martha keeps braiding. "And this surprises you?"

"I just couldn't believe how blatant she was. I'm surprised she didn't whip out a scale and weigh everyone."

"So do something. Expose her. Write something, publish it somewhere. That's why you're there, isn't it?"

"Yeah." I shrug. "I don't know. There's probably a student newspaper."

Martha tugs my hair to tell me she's unhappy with my blasé attitude.

"I'm just tired, Martha."

"Biding your time."

"Sure." If that's what she wants to call it. Right now I'd just call it exhausted.

"Biding your time until you get it on with Rajas."

I swat her. "Martha! Boundaries, woman! You are my *mother*."

"You know I'm kidding, my love. And as your *mother*, I am required to advise you not to get it on until—"

"I know, I know: wait until I'm good and ready."

“Wait until you're good and ready, and then wait some more just to be sure.” Martha smiles into her wineglass. I close my eyes and lose myself in daydreams about Rajas, picking up right where I left off.

I really don't think life is about the I-could-have-beens. Life is only about the I-tried-to-do. I don't mind the failure but I can't imagine that I'd forgive myself if I didn't try.

—Nikki Giovanni, poet and activist, b. 1943

To: editor@purpletornadonews.org
From: eviepeaceandjustice@gmail.com
Re: for publication in the student newspaper

To the editor,

I am writing about injustice. It is occurring right now, every day, at this school. I've only been here a few weeks and yet it is clear to me there is an appalling lack of civil liberties for students. Not to mention a gross disparity between the rights of faculty and the rights of students, and an unsustainable, inhospitable environment.

First, let's talk about the crazy lack of civil liberties. Example: Why can't students use our phones for actual phone calls? Sure, it would be disruptive in class time but what's the problem with calls during lunch or free periods? It doesn't make sense (and discriminates against students who can't afford smartphones). Also, why can't we have lunch or free time outside? It is a scientific fact that, due to lack of exposure to sunlight, three quarters of teens and adults in the U.S. have a vitamin D deficiency, a problem that can lead to cancer, diabetes, and bone and heart disease.* Let's combat this problem by going outside! And those are just two examples out of the multitude that happen all the time.

As for the disparity between teachers and students, I could go on and on but I'll stick to one example. The bathrooms. Ever been in a faculty bathroom? They are a veritable breath of fresh air compared to our facilities! I mean, just consider the student bathrooms. First there's the reek of cigarette smoke and rancid pee. Then there is never any toilet paper. Never! And even with four stalls, there's only ever one garbage can. Which is next to the exit. Why, a reasonable person might ask, is it positioned thusly? Is it just so when you have your period you get to carry your pad or tampon out of the stall—again, without toilet paper—to throw into the garbage? Well no wonder the toilets are always overflowing from people trying to flush their pads.

Fact: the women's faculty restroom has garbage cans in each stall. It has toilet paper to spare. It has lovely soaps, and its clean sinks actually drain. And guess who can't use said restroom? Students can't. I know this because Ms. Theodore gifted me with five detentions, just for using the faculty toilet.

Um, where was I? Oh yes. The unsustainable, inhospitable environment. If you're paying attention, you've noticed this dovetails nicely with the aforementioned lack of sunlight, and disgusting toilets. Also I'll mention that the cafeteria uses Styrofoam and disposable plastic, which is totally unsustainable. How hard would it be to use regular dishes? In conclusion (See, Mr. Wolman? I can write a persuasive essay!): Perhaps you, my fellow students, have, after spending most of your lives subjected to these injustices, become inured. You have gotten used to these things. Or maybe you are simply apathetic. But that doesn't mean that the way things are is the way things should be! It doesn't mean student inequities are okay. There's a saying: Just because no one complains doesn't mean all parachutes are perfect.

If you're with me, speak up! We can make this place better!

Sincerely,
Evie M., Senior

* You don't have to take my word for this. See Scientific American, March 23, 2009, "Vitamin D Deficiency Soars in the U.S., Study Says," by Jordan Lite.

To: eviepeaceandjustice@gmail.com
From: editor@purpletornadonews.org
Re: Re: for publication in the student newspaper

Hi Evie. Stiv here. We are in the same Global View class. I just want to say thanks for the letter to the editor. It is very well written and funny. Unfortunately, the Purple Tornado News can't publish articles that reference specific teachers. It's a school policy. So if you want to try rewriting your letter without any of the specifics and without naming names, I could read it again. If I think it's okay, and the advisor (he's Mr. Wolman, I didn't show him your letter) approves it, then it can go to print.

Thanks again for writing. See you around,
Stiv Wagner
Editor in Chief, Purple Tornado News

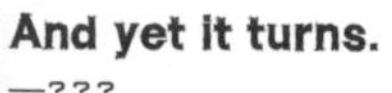

Well well well. Brookner has upped the ante. "Class, settle." He claps his hands. "How about it, Evie? Who said it?"

All eyes are on me. I swallow hard. Word has spread about my daily *tête-à-têtes* with Brookner, my detentions, my letters to the paper. Rajas and Jacinda haven't come right out and said it, but their worry is palpable. Apparently I hopped a train from interesting to exasperating, and now kids are talking about me—not in a good way. In Global View, Marcie and editor-in-chief Stiv are friendly enough, but others are not so generous. Megan, in particular, seems like a bit of a hater. During lunch, in my safety zone wedged between Rajas and Jacinda, people are polite. Yet there's something missing. You hear it in the curt, one-word answers people like Matt and Jim give when I attempt to strike up a conversation. Their eyes say things: *weirdo, misfit, hippie*.

On Facebook, I have been friended...and then unfriended.

Sure, I could quit my rabble-rouser ways. Conform to the norm. Go with the flow. Giving up things like my letters to the editor and this repartee with Brookner would make life easier. And since I have so much fun with Jacinda and Rajas—beautiful, uninvolved (according to Jacinda) Rajas—why not relax, let it roll, just enjoy? Tempting. So tempting. But what would be the point? I came to school to experience something new *and* be true to myself. Get a different perspective without losing my own. Put to use all the stuff that Martha's taught me about standing up to injustice and questioning authority.

Besides, I love discussing the quotes with Brookner. He's an interesting guy, much more so than my other teachers. I like Ms. Crandall and Mr. Wysent, and while I'm not a big fan of Ms. Gliss, and I've had some heated disagreements with Mr. Wolman and Ms. Theodore, the other teachers seem okay. I've gotten to know the detention monitor pretty well; he helps me with my physics homework. But Brookner is far and away my favorite.

I clear my throat but don't say anything yet.

Brookner comes onto his toes, pauses like a pendulum and rocks back onto his heels, adding a rhythm to the uncomfortable quiet. "No, Evie? Hmm. Okay. This quote is from Copernicus." His eyes flit to me. "He's referring to the revolution of the planets—"

The man is goading me. "Mr. Brookner."

He smiles. "Yes, Evie?"

"I'm pretty sure it was Galileo."

A groan emanates from the back of the class. To my right, Matt whispers, "Dude, would you just *let it go!*" It stings.

Brookner tilts his head, "Really, Evie."

I take a deep breath. "Yeah. I'm pretty sure."

"Would you care to elucidate?"

"It's about speaking truth to power."

A glint in Brookner's eyes. "Is it now."

I nod. "It is." Marcie rolls her eyes. At me or Brookner? I can't tell.

Fortitude. "Galileo figured out that the planets circled around the sun, right?" I look around, smile at Stiv and Jacinda and Marcie, to encourage them to get into the discussion. No go. I continue, "The Church said this was heresy because God made the earth, so it must be the center of the universe. During the Inquisition, the Church made Galileo recant his theory. He did, but then he said, 'And yet it turns.' Because he knew you can deny the truth, but that doesn't make it any less true."

Brookner smiles. "Ah. Speak-ing truth to pow-er." He punctuates each of his syllables as if to mark this as an important moment. He locks my gaze in that way of his that there's no getting used to, like he wants to penetrate deep into your soul. It's three-quarters flattering, one-quarter creepy, because sometimes it lingers too long. It reminds me of one of Martha's random friends back in Montreal, who thought he could cure headaches just by pressing his fingers to your head. He figured his belief in himself was so strong, it superseded all others' beliefs. Brookner is like that. In another life, he would have been an evangelical revival preacher, or a transcendentalist acid-tester, a devotee of his own powers, basking in his followers' approval and praise.

Maybe I'm being too hard on him. He is the smartest teacher by far, and I'm a sucker for how he quotes books and music and movies and ties them all in together in surprising ways. Like his wacky theory that world social order can be traced back to the trade of coffee, opium, and chocolate. Not to mention his charisma, which can be mesmerizing. I can see why Jacinda has such a raging crush on him. They are exactly the qualities that make Rajas warn us about him, over and over; he's worried that Brookner will snare us in a lethal trap of attention and charm. And then what? Turn us into vampires?

I meet Brookner's eyes and can't help but smile, feel a tingle of thrill. "You know it. Speaking truth to power."

"Truth." He holds my gaze. "You are a believer, then, Evie?"

Behind me, someone snorts while I consider Brookner's question. "I wouldn't necessarily say that."

"I see. But you believe in one unifying truth?"

"Yes." Love.

He sweeps his arm in a grand gesture and begins to pace. "Then you, Evie, are a believer. But what if your truth is wrong?"

"The truth can't be wrong. That's why it's the truth."

"Doesn't it vary according to your point of view?"

I tighten my ponytail. "Maybe your *view* of the truth varies. But the truth is...untouchable. It doesn't vary. It just *is*."

"Ah. A true believer, indeed."

My cheeks burn. I glance over at Jacinda. Lips pursed, she's staring at Brookner, in thrall. Brookner is, in turn, staring at me.

"Yes, well. Time shall reveal all, hmm?" He opens the textbook. "Now. Moving on. If you will all open to page 110, we can read the words from Galileo himself."

Textbooks knock onto desks, pages flip, the room relaxes. I stare at the drawing of Galileo Galilei on page 111. As I suspected, Brookner knew the source of the quote. He credited Copernicus to get me talking. Tricky man.

Jacinda clicks her pen, poised over her notebook. Thank God she doesn't think of me as a weirdo or smart-ass or know-it-all; she clearly holds a lot of social influence around these parts. If Rajas and Jacinda didn't have my back, I would've already been thrown to the wolves.

At least it's only a few more periods until lunch. And Rajas. Available, not-involved-with-anyone Rajas. Who seems very glad I'm here. Unlike Ms. Gliss, who hasn't given me a break since the dreaded Lunchtime Mobile Phone Incident in September. Since then she's slapped me with two more detentions, both for insubordination.

Insubordination. The perfect foil for abuse of power. A catchall for anything a teacher doesn't like. Such as my ankle taking too long to heal.

"You need to join the class," Ms. Gliss had informed me. "Your fitness is already suffering." She made a point of staring at my stomach. "I have no doubt your ankle has healed by now."

"It's not ready for field hockey, but I'm happy to do gentle yoga." My offer degenerated into a debate about whether students have the liberty (my word) to subvert (her word) their teachers' class plans. *Bam.* Detention.

The next Gliss detention was for not having the right kind of sneakers. I argued that students should not be required to buy sweatshop products. She remained unmoved. I told her there was no way I could ask Martha to pay for overpriced sneakers. Ms. Gliss remained stoic. So then I asked her whether Nike paid her for endorsements. *Wham.* Detention.

And Jacinda had defended her, urging me to bite the bullet and buy the sneakers. I love Jacinda, but I don't think she gets the concept of limited means. Martha and I have everything we want, but that's because we don't want much. There's no getting around the fact our budget is tight.

Another detention had nothing to do with sneakers or faculty bathrooms. I was feeling sorry for the python who lives in our biology classroom, so I took him out of his habitat for a little snuggle before the bell rang. Mr. Wysent was pretty nice about it. He seemed apologetic, but said it was policy to assign detention to anyone who, under any circumstances, opened a school animal habitat. Mr. Wysent alluded to some sort of frogs-in-the-cafeteria-jello fiasco a few years back. So, again with the detention.

Gym with Ms. Gliss, a smelly hay infusion bio lab with Mr. Wysent, then the mind-bending study of physics. It's a long morning.

At the appointed lunchtime rendezvous location,

Rajas is waiting for me; my heart pounds its customary Rajas rhythm. I look around. "Where's Jacinda?" She always waits here in the hallway with Rajas, usually checking her phone for e-mail from her Internet Lover.

"She has a Cheer Squad meeting." He shrugs. "Some crisis or other."

"Oh." I still can't believe Jacinda's a cheerleader—captain, no less. At first, I thought she was kidding. But it does explain her weird dynamic with Ms. Gliss. And all the *Glee* references. "I wonder why didn't she tell me?"

"Maybe she thinks you wouldn't approve."

"Why wouldn't I approve? I'm not *that* judgmental!"

Rajas laughs. "Oh, so you *do* approve?"

"Um...no." He's right. I have a strong anti-cheerleader bias. Well, not strong so much as colossal. From Martha, maybe? Or all those movies about catty girls? Note to self: there's a lot more to Jacinda than some superficial, airhead, mean-girl cheerleader stereotype. Maybe it's time to reexamine said stereotype?

"Brought your lunch?" Rajas asks, bringing me out of my thoughts.

I lift my cloth lunch bag to answer.

"Good." He looks around, all shifty-eyed, and takes hold of my arm. His touch electrifies every nerve ending, scalp to toes. "Come on." Careful of my not-fully-healed ankle, he jogs me away from the cafeteria, past the gym, turning a corner into a hallway I swear I never knew existed.

"Where are we going?"

"Shh," he says. "Be stealth."

We turn another corner and stop in front of a classroom. He pulls a key from his pocket and unlocks the door, peering into the room like he's making sure the coast is clear. He motions me to follow.

In the dark, I bump into him. He fumbles around until a switch clicks and fluorescents flicker on, bringing the huge room—about half the size of the gym, but without its wall of windows—to light. Table saws, circular sanders, miter boxes, work benches.

"The mythical shop class," I marvel. "You have a key to Camelot?"

Rajas cocks his half-grin. "Mr. Pascal just gave me one. Not supposed to let anyone else in here but...I figured you'd like it. Plus, look—" He points to a door I hadn't noticed, on the outside wall. "We can duck outside for fresh air. Which I know you've been jonesing for."

"It's perfect!" I throw my arms around him. "I love it!"

His muscles tense. Oh nooooo. Is he uncomfortable or just surprised?

I shrink back, unhugging, but he stops me.

He leans in. I lean in. And I don't believe it, because it's all happening so fast, but our lips pull into each other and we're kissing, his tongue warm but not as wet as I'd imagined, and our chests pressing together and it smells like sawdust in here and my stomach floats because I'm in free fall. It's not a face-mashing kiss like in the movies. It's the perfect first kiss. Gentle and sweet and slow and sexy all at the same time.

Rajas pulls away. "I swear this wasn't my plan. For bringing you here."

"Fine by me if it was." I smile, but now things feel awkward. "So. Show me around?"

He wipes a thumb across his chin.

"Crap!" I clamp my hands over my face. "Did I drool or something? I'm kind of new at all this."

"Really? You don't say." Laughing, Rajas tries to pry my hands from my cheeks.

I grab his hands. "Maybe I just need more practice."

"Just what I was thinking."

We kiss again. Oh God. If we keep going, I will melt into a puddle on the floor. Deep breath. I pull back just enough to say, "Okay. What are we doing here?"

"Um, hooking up?" His dark eyes twinkle.

"No, I mean what are we doing *here*, in shop class."

"Oh yeah." He laughs. "Well, remember when we met?"

How could I not? One tends to recall being struck by lightning. "What part?"

He nods toward a corner of the room. "I brought my rocker in. I finished it."

So he did have an innocent reason. Damn. Does that make our kiss more exciting—a spontaneous our-attraction-cannot-be-suppressed thing? Or is it lame that I practically jumped him?

Wait. What am I doing? What's with the self-doubt, Suzy Self-conscious? I'm nothing if not thick-skinned and confident. But...the way I feel about Rajas. It makes me soft and exposed, like a raw oyster. My protective shell has been shucked. And then tossed out to sea. And then sucked away with a riptide. I wonder about Rajas: does he feel insecure and vulnerable too? Sometimes I think I catch glimpses of it.

Rajas takes my hand to lead me to his chair.

Oh man. What a chair. It's amazing. It's not fancy, not cheesy or ornate. It's simple, classic, well-made. Clean lines, with bark on the arms and splats, so you can appreciate the wood's origin. It is functional and artistic, totally connected to the natural world.

It is stunning. Wow. He made this.

We're still holding hands. His hands are a little larger than mine, a bit rougher. The calluses on his palm bump my own; his thumb is wrapped in a band-aid. They are strong, capable hands. I sensed all this before—this guy carried me out of the state forest, after all—but seeing his work, it's all coming together: his hands, his subtle mind with a gift for constructing things, for discerning beauty and utility. This is a person who can make something exquisite and real.

And it is a truth, an immutable, unchangeable truth: I am falling in love with Rajas.

I'm a believer.

He reaches out to the rocker, gives it a push to set it in motion.

"Wow. This is fantastic," I say about the chair—and him, and being here. "It's like something you would see at a Blue Mountain art festival. It's beautiful." It *is* beautiful, and not just the chair. The lightning. Subjecting myself to the cheese grater of love. Rajas is worth it. The chair proves it.

"You think?" His smile flashes a glint of vulnerability, like he can't hide the fact that he was nervous to show me and now he's relieved and proud.

"I really do." I study the wood. "Maple?"

His eyebrows rise like he's impressed with my knowledge, but not surprised. He nods.

"I love the style. Not quite Shaker, but close. Strong but delicate." I squeeze his hand before I let it go. I kneel to look along the chair's lines and run my finger along its arm. "You used tung oil instead of stain?"

He nods again.

I stand up and walk around the chair, taking it in. "Most people go through their whole lives without creating anything this beautiful. You should be so proud."

"It's my first chair."

"I guess it's a day for firsts." Ha. I'm funny.

"Guess so." He grins. "Let's eat."

"Sounds great." I realize I'm beyond hungry, I'm ravenous. Maybe it's a metaphor for being alone with Rajas, like my libido is fueling my appetite. Or maybe I'm just really hungry. Give a girl a break—even Freud said sometimes a cigar is just a cigar.

Opening the door to the outside, we pull two stools into the sun. We're in a hidden nook near the breezeway between the high and middle schools. It seems safe from detection. We unwrap our lunches. Being here with Rajas is easy and exciting and awkward and comfortable, all at the same time. How are such simultaneous contradictions possible?

"You have detention today?" he asks.

"Mmm-hmm," I mumble through the first bite of my cheese, mustard, and arugula sandwich.

"What's this one for?"

"This one is for snake liberation."

He laughs. "Only you, Eve."

"What?" I wipe mustard from my lip with a cloth napkin. "The poor thing looked miserable!"

"So you thought you'd take it upon yourself to set it free."

"I didn't snakenap him or anything. I wasn't sneaky about it. I just held him in the sunlight for a few minutes between bells. I still don't see the problem."

"Mr. Wysent's cool. Don't hold it against him. It's just school policy." He laughs. "Too bad you weren't here last year. You should have seen those frogs flying out of the jello." Shaking his head, chuckling, he crunches into an apple. "Guess it's still taking some getting used to, all the rules."

"Not the rules. Well, not *just* the rules. It's the abuse of power and lack of civil liberties I can't get used to."

"It probably feels that way, to you."

"It doesn't to you?"

Eyebrows converging, he says, "Never really thought about it that way. I don't love it, it just...is what it is, you know?" He chews his apple. "But you know what I do hate? All the labels. Rich kid, poor kid, nerd, goody-goody, troublemaker, jock—"

"Popular cheerleader," I offer.

He laughs. "Popular cheerleader."

"Misfit homeschooler."

"Misfit home—" He frowns. "You're not a misfit, Eve. You're just...different." He looks at the sky, thinking. "Plus, you're not a homeschooler anymore. You busted yourself out of that particular label, didn't you?"

Whoa. I guess I did, didn't I? Can I still consider myself a homeschooler if I go to public school? It's such a huge part of my identity, I can't just shed it like a snakeskin. I appreciate reptilian skin-shedding, but I'm not capable of it myself.

"Why can't we all just get along?" Rajas says in a high voice like he's quoting someone. Taking another bite of apple, he continues, "Everyone's so stuck in their labels they can't see past the zits on their own noses. I cannot wait to get out of here. Graduation, and I'm gone. Real world apprenticeship, here I come."

Which seems pretty lame. But he's a smart kid; maybe it's a smart survival skill? Keep your nose low, keep out of the line of fire. Still, "Don't you want to try to make this place better while you're here?"

"Nope." He smiles. "I'm just getting the hell out of Pandora."

"Pandora?"

"From *Avatar?*"

"Oh. TV show?"

"It's a movie! Incredible special effects. You haven't seen it?" He looks shocked and appalled.

I shake my head.

"Okay. That's hard to imagine. Just please tell me you've seen *The Matrix.*"

Again, I shake my head.

"Unacceptable. Not on my watch. We're going to have a DVD night. You've got a lot of catching up to do."

DVD night with Rajas. I get feverish just thinking about it.

"Consider it your cultural education." He pauses, drinks from his water bottle. "Anyway, I know you don't watch TV, but I thought you liked movies. Isn't that why you started here? All the movies about teenagers and high school?"

"Not *all* the movies. Rich introduced me to the classics. *Ferris Bueller's Day Off. Pretty in Pink. Footloose. Dirty Dancing. Grease.*"

"And now you're trying to change everything those movies stand for?"

"I can't help it!" I'm laughing but I'm serious. "It just makes me crazy, all the injustices. Is that such a bad thing?"

"No," he sighs. "No, it's part of what I like about you. You see things in a totally unique way. And you have the guts to actually do something about it. I just wasn't expecting you to be so gung ho."

"I wouldn't say I'm gung ho."

"No? And you've written how many letters to the *Purple Tornado News*?"

"One."

He narrows his eyes at me. Gorgeous eyes.

"One! That I edited and submitted three times," I admit.

He smirks that disarming half-smile. "Stiv still won't print it?"

"I toned it down and took out the names, and then toned it down some more. And then you know what I did? Toned it down some more. And then some more. But he still says he can't run it. It's like hitting my head against a brick wall."

He reaches over and touches my hair. "Don't do that. Your head is beautiful."

Heat floods my cheeks and toasts my ears. I manage to say, "You're sweet." Translation: *you're amazing and smart and hilarious and you* get *me and even your hands are sexy and your carpentry skills are mind-blowing and you just called me beautiful...*

With his bandaged thumb, he pushes my hair back onto my shoulder. My heart thumps. We're quiet awhile. I eat my sandwich. "It's so lame."

He looks at me, confused. "What's so lame?"

"The newspaper," I explain. "It's lame that they won't print any actual news. Stiv needs to grow a pair."

He laughs. "Cut him some slack. He's a good guy. His hands are probably tied by the administration. Or his advisor or whoever."

"Hm. I'm detecting a theme here. Stiv's a good guy. Mr. Wysent's a good guy. Their hands are tied. They're good people, just following the rules. Isn't there a quote about a Nazi soldier saying he was just following orders?"

"Whoa there, cowgirl. Mr. Wysent's not a Nazi. And Stiv—although he does look like he could belong to the Aryan nation, I'll grant you that—he's definitely not a Nazi."

"No," I acquiesce. "They aren't Nazis. I shouldn't have said that. I just—" I just what? "I just expected more. From teachers. And students. I know that people agree with me. They must! Students should be treated with respect and equality. Who's going to argue with that? No one, that's who. So why is it so hard to speak out and change things?" A thought: "Wait. How about student government? Isn't that what it's for?"

"Student government?" Rajas laughs. "Student government is for looking good on college applications."

"Aren't they supposed to be the student leaders? A voice for change?"

He almost rolls his eyes. Like he wants to be supportive of my naiveté...but can't believe my naiveté. "You can try, Eve. But..." He frowns. "Just be careful. They're not used to—"

"People rocking the boat?"

"I just don't want you to get hurt."

"Why would I get hurt?" I ask.

He presses his lips together.

"What? What are not saying?"

"I don't know. I just honestly don't think student government does anything, apart from—" He stops midsentence. "Okay, I have no idea what they do…"

But I lose track of what he's saying, because in my mind, I'm already writing a petition.

Our problems stem from our acceptance of this filthy, rotten system.

—Dorothy Day, radical Catholic activist, 1897–1980

Minutes of Student Council Officers Meeting
Second meeting of fall semester
Present: Megan Atwater (Secretary), Kelly Lupito (President), Tera McClernon (Treasurer), Stiv Wagner (Vice President)
Minutes submitted by Megan Atwater, Student Council Secretary

First order of business: Treasurer's report. Tera says student council has $428. After our upcoming $200 donation to senior class's homecoming preparations (for decorations), we will have $228. Stiv suggested having a fundraiser so we can have money to donate to the other class's upcoming activities. Kelly said funk that, seniors rule. We all laughed. Tera recommended a car wash. Kelly said no way, doodles, it's too cold. Tera recommended a donut sale during lunch. Megan (me)'s brother works at Dunkin so she (I) will ask him if they can donate donuts for the fundraiser. Stiv will get approval from Dr. Folger. We will put this on the agenda for student council general meeting, with a sign-up sheet for volunteers. All in favor of donut fundraiser: 4.

Second order of business: Petition written to student council. Evie M. (she didn't put her whole last name on it?) submitted a "petition" to the student government mailbox (see attachment). She wants us to present it at the next student council meeting. Kelly says funk that, the demands are unrealistic and we're not hippie homeschoolers. Tera wondered about the actual purpose of the petition. Megan (me) doesn't think we (the officers), should take an official stance on political issues. Stiv suggested that we put the petition on a desk at the next student council meeting and if anyone comes up and reads it and wants to sign it, fine. That way we've done what Evie asked but not really. All in favor: 4.

Third order of business: None.

Meeting adjourned.

Attachment: petition from Evie M.

TO STUDENT GOVERNMENT OFFICERS: You guys are the leaders of this school so please discuss at your meeting and distribute for signatures! And then we will present it to Dr. Folger and the administrators!

PETITION TO DR. FOLGER AND THE SCHOOL ADMINISTRATION AND THE SCHOOL BOARD

This is an official petition for a redress of grievances. Students demand the rights granted to us in the U.S. Constitution and Bill of Rights. We should have the same rights in school as we have outside of school. These include, but are not limited to, the following:

- Students should be treated with the same respect and dignity from teachers that teachers receive from students. After all, we're part of this community too!
- Students have a right to a clean environment, especially toilets and restrooms
- Students have the right to use phones to make phone calls during lunch and free periods
- Students have the right to healthful choices in lunch foods
- Students have the right to fresh air and sunlight

We, the undersigned, petition Dr. Folger and the school administration to address these matters in a timely and responsive fashion.

Sincerely,
(Add names here)(Class)
Evie M., Senior

[Attach more signature pages as necessary]

The internet is the first thing that humanity has built that humanity doesn't understand, the largest experiment in anarchy that we have ever had.

—Eric Schmidt, chairman of Google, b. 1955

Today, Brookner doesn't ask for a response to the quote. As soon as the bell rings, he rocks onto his toes and says, "Let's jump right in, get the lecture over with, so we have time for something different today, hmm?"

After a bout of lecturing, he pauses and surveys the room. He claps to refocus attention. "Now. Move your desks aside and arrange your chairs in a circle."

There are groans, like everyone's feeling lazy, but the protests seem superficial, because people rearrange the desks and chairs pretty fast. A shift in routine is welcome, especially on a day like this when it's drizzling and chilly and the sky is a low ceiling of musty concrete. After the chairs are circled, Brookner takes a stack of index cards from his drawer, along with a box of safety pins. "Take one of each. It doesn't matter which card, so just pick one and pass it along, right? Pin your card to your shirt so that everyone can see it. Please."

The cards and pins travel around the circle; by the time they get to Jacinda and me, only a few cards remain. We exchange glances. This is why I love Brookner. He piques your curiosity.

My card says, *Artist, 55, three kids.* I poke my safety pin through and fasten it onto my sweatshirt.

Jacinda pins *Gay prostitute, 32, no kids* through a buttonhole in her top. "So it doesn't leave a mark," she says.

Brookner says, "Everyone got one? Good. Take a look around. Peruse your cohorts."

The class has become a montage of cards listing varying occupations, ages, family statuses:

Doctor, 62, three grandchildren

College student, 19

Student, 8

Housewife, 42, two kids

Movie star, 35, three adopted kids

Lawyer, 50, two grown kids

Firefighter, 30, one kid, divorced

Factory worker, 45, one kid

Burglar, 47, no kids

Cashier, 35, five kids, divorced

Writer, 90, lots of grandkids

Teacher, 39, two kids

Bartender, 22, no kids

Drug dealer, 25, one kid

Carpenter, 60, ten grandchildren

Janitor, 42, two kids

Priest, 35, no kids

Computer programmer, 33, one kid

Brookner clears his throat. "Class. Settle. Here's the deal: You are in the middle of the Pacific Ocean. Your cruise ship has sunk, the water is full of bloodthirsty sharks, and your lifeboat has sprung a leak. If you don't throw someone off within five minutes, you will capsize and everyone will die."

There's a flood of smiles. Everyone gets engaged, studying each other's cards and posturing so others can read theirs. Brookner's plan—which, I assume, was to change venue enough to involve everyone in some actual dialogue—seems to be working. Clever move. Why did it take him this long to come up with it?

"Okay. Time starts..." Brookner makes a show of pressing a button on his wristwatch. "Now!"

After a moment of quiet, Jacinda clears her throat and lifts her hand skyward. It's the first time she's raised her hand without Brookner calling on her. "You should throw me off," she announces.

"Not so fast," Brookner interrupts, adding, "Sorry, Jacinda." She blushes—she does this every time

Brookner says her name. He continues, "I forgot two important rules. One: no one can volunteer himself or herself for sacrifice. Two: all decisions must be unanimous." He presses the button on his watch again. "Five minutes. Go."

Across the circle, Stiv clears his throat. "I vote for Jacinda, the gay prostitute." Rajas keeps telling me Stiv's a decent guy, and he's nice enough, but he's got some work to do to convince me of his *cojones*. "She doesn't have any kids, so no one will miss her," he shrugs. "Plus she might be spreading AIDS."

"And she's a fag," Matt says.

Shocked, I look at Brookner. He is frowning but doesn't say anything.

Jacinda says, "Shut up! That's a hate word. Besides, just because I'm gay doesn't mean I have AIDS." Go, Jacinda!

"No, not because you're gay," Stiv says. "Because you're a prostitute."

Heads nod around the circle. Marcie says, "We'd um...we'd probably be saving lives in the long run by sacrificing her."

"Okay," says Stiv. "Let's vote. All in favor?"

Hands rise in unison, flowers reaching toward the sun. Stiv, Marcie, Matt, Jacinda, everyone's except mine. Stiv looks at me. "What's the problem?"

I make an apologetic face. "It's not right to base a

decision on someone's occupation. Or sexual orientation. Or whether they have kids, or if they have AIDS."

Stiv frowns and crosses his arms like he's thinking.

I lean forward. "Okay. Just for the sake of argument: What if Jacinda became a prostitute because her mother has cancer? What if being a hooker is the only way she can pay for her mom's expensive medicine? Maybe she uses condoms every time and gets HIV tests every month. How can we possibly know people's motivation for what they do?"

"That's true," Jacinda agrees. "You don't know."

Encouraged, I press on: "And why is it relevant that she's gay? No one else's card specifies their sexual orientation."

Jacinda chimes in, "Totally. Do we just, like, assume that straight is the norm?"

I beam at her.

Stiv says, "You guys have a point, but if we don't choose someone, we all die. Most of the rest of us have kids, or are like—"

"I'm a fireman, dude," says Matt. "You can't kill a hero."

I squint, thinking. "What if we—"

"We don't have much time," Stiv reminds us. "We should vote. All in favor?" Hands, including Jacinda's, reach skyward. Everyone's except mine.

Groans.

"Time!" calls Mr. Brookner. "Well. You're all shark bait."

"Thanks a lot," says Marcie.

Jacinda bumps me on the shoulder. "Whatever!" She raises her voice so everyone can hear. "Personally, I appreciate not being thrown to the sharks."

But she voted for herself! I was the lone voice of dissent. Obviously this was just a pretend lifeboat—but the lesson feels real. And harsh. People talk a good game, yet when it comes down to it…who can you trust? How do you know for sure? You think you've got friends but suddenly it's Mutiny on the Brookner Bounty.

"Class, settle. Interesting." Brookner rocks forward, claps his hands and swings back. "You are the only class to all die."

"Thanks to Evie," someone mumbles—Matt, I think, but I'm not sure.

"Yes, thanks to Evie." Brookner squeezes his way around the circle. He stops in back of me and presses his hands onto my shoulders. The bell buzzes. Like Pavlov's dogs, everyone pops into motion, trained to move to the next class at the synthetic beep. "Chairs back where they were!" Brookner calls. "Don't forget: Tomorrow is global event day and your report is due. Print or internet, just be certain to cite the source. It *will* be graded!"

I move my chair and gather my things, but Brookner

holds a finger up. "Evie. If you'll stay behind."

Jacinda's eyes go wide. "I'll catch up with you later," she says, adding in a whisper, "tell me *everything*."

As the class files out, Brookner closes in on me and hovers a little too close. Is it on purpose? Or does he have a warped sense of personal space? Was he raised in a cage full of battery hens, or is it some strange assertion of power? Either way, I refuse to budge an inch.

"I wonder," he whispers, leaning even closer and lowering his voice like a conspirator, "did you have something else in mind just then?" His breath smells like coffee and sour milk.

I do not move. "What do you mean?"

"Surely you didn't just want everyone to die."

"Of course not."

"Mmm-hmm. I thought so. You had something in mind."

"I didn't get time to explain it."

"Please, enlighten me."

I cross my arms. "Okay. Clearly you wanted us to base our decisions on what's listed on the cards. That's not rocket science."

He smiles. "Go on."

"But there's a lot more to a person than age, occupation, whether they have kids. And who are we to judge anyway?"

"Condemning people to death is better than placing value judgments?"

"No. There's a better way—better ways. I can think of at least two."

Brookner leans close enough that I can smell the soap on his skin. He's way, way too close; it's immensely distracting. I give in and pull back a little.

"Well?" he prompts.

"Um, right. One, go by age, starting with the oldest. They've lived more, so they should give the younger people a fighting chance. Or two, draw straws. Make it completely random. Otherwise you're placing your values onto other people. You have to go by age or nothing at all."

"Interesting."

"Everyone gets a chance that way. It's called fairness?" I'm goading him now. "You may have heard of it?"

"Sounds more like anarchy."

I snort without meaning to. "No, it doesn't. But even so, what's so bad about anarchy? There are worse things. Fascism, for one. Authoritarianism."

Brookner chuckles. He leans on the corner of a desk. "Hmm. Well, you can go now. You're not in trouble."

"Why on earth would I be in trouble?"

He smirks. In the space of a millisecond, his eyes flick down to my shoes, travel up my Levis, skim over my dark gray hoodie, jump to my eyes. He looks intrigued, as if he thinks of me as a challenge. A puzzle he can solve. It's both flattering and unsettling.

"I should go." I pick up my books.

Brookner steps toward me, compressing the air between us again. Is this a power thing? Is he *that* concerned I'll forget who's in charge? Why is he so invested in making me uncomfortable? He sighs and turns, reaching for a notepad. "You'll be late for your next class. Let me write you a pass."

There it is: another assertion of power.

I do not say thank you, because I refuse to let him feel superior.

As he hands me the pass, his fingers graze my palm. I can feel the heat from his fingertips. They linger a little too long.

Lunch in the shop room with Rajas. Oh, how it can take my mind off everything. Ms. Gliss giving me more crap about my ankle, and then ranting to the class about body mass? Gone. Mr. Wysent's confusing assignment about Punnett squares? No longer an issue. Power dynamic weirdness with Brookner? It all just floats away like wisps of cloud in the wind. Now it's just me and Rajas: kissing, eating, talking. So far we've managed to keep our shop room trysts a secret.

Jacinda doesn't miss us during lunch, because she started scheduling regular lunchtime practices for Cheer Squad. God only knows when they eat. Jacinda is committed to qualifying for state cheerleading finals at the expense of almost anything else. I have to hand it to her, she excels at what she does. Her squad respects her leadership and, in the little bits of their practices I've seen, it does seem like it takes skill. Especially their dance routines. If I tried to do them, I'd look like a charging bull moose. With rabies. On meth.

After lunch, down the hall from shop class, Rajas and I start to peel apart. But near the gym, a sustained screeching stops us cold. What *is* that? I look at Rajas, he shrugs at my unspoken question. We step into the gym to investigate.

From inside a crowd of cheerleaders, Jacinda spots us. Her eyes go wide and she holds up her hand to tell me and Rajas to stop where we are. We do—and stay to listen. It's difficult to understand the shrill shrieks. When the yelling finally starts making sense, my stomach tightens. The words are awful.

"I have *had* it with this squad!" Ms. Gliss screeches. "Look at yourselves! It's like you don't even care!" She appears to start crying. "I've never seen such muffin tops! You're bulging out of your uniforms! No wonder you keep dropping your lifts!"

I start toward her.

"Wait, Eve." Rajas catches my arm and whispers, "What are you doing?"

"I don't know yet. Something!"

Ms. Gliss hiccups. "Fitness doesn't just mean exercise, ladies! It means *limiting* your *calories* for heaven's sake!"

Jacinda catches my attention. Eyebrows knit, lips pursed into a concerned O, she shakes her head. She doesn't want me to intervene.

Rajas is shaking his head too. "This is Jay's territory. Let her handle it."

We stand, horrified, as Ms. Gliss wipes her running mascara and continues, "Get yourselves together, ladies! Your appearance is inexcusable. Inexcusable! Especially you," she wags a finger at Marcie. "Don't think I haven't noticed those five pounds! Or is it ten?"

Ms. Gliss walks toward her office, her white sneakers squeaking on the floor. She turns around. "And do not make me out to be the bad guy here, ladies." She sniffs. "I don't mean to sound harsh. But the truth can be painful. I'm telling you this for your own good. You've got a pep rally and homecoming soon. If I don't say something now, the whole school will be talking later, and that would be much worse." She whips open the door to the locker room and disappears into her office.

Girls start whispering. Jacinda hugs Marcie, who is crying. The Cheer Squad converges en masse. Their eyes seem to plead with Jacinda, their captain, to *do* something. Across the gym, a cluster of boys is loitering by the door to their locker room. Marcie's was a very public humiliation.

"Ohmigod, Marcie, you are not fat." Still holding on to her, Jacinda walks Marcie toward the door where Rajas and I are standing. The other girls follow. Jacinda pulls her shoulders back and straightens up to address the group. "I think that we just need to practice our lifts more. Work up our strength and balance, right, squad?" Jacinda smiles gratefully at her cousin as he holds the door for them.

"But—but Ms. Gliss—" Marcie tries to say; it comes out as a sob.

"Ms. Gliss bullshit," Jacinda spits. Wow. I've never heard her swear. Judging from Rajas's shocked look, she must not do it often. "She can be mean when she's stressed. But, still! That was out of line! Don't listen to her, Marcie."

I touch Marcie's shoulder. "Jacinda's right. She can't do this to you. We won't let her."

Rajas brushes my hand with his, like he doesn't want to interrupt. "See you later," he whispers.

I nod.

Marcie watches Rajas go and wipes her eyes. "Ms. Gliss is right, I am so fat."

"Bullshit!" Jacinda lets out a big breath. "Here's what you're going to do. Go to Ms. Cleary and fake a migraine so she'll send you home. Take the rest of the day off. That is, like, captain's orders. And don't you dare start starving yourself!"

Marcie dabs her nose with her sleeve. "Okay."

Jacinda turns to the rest of the group. "Everyone else? Let's take a break from after-school practice today, but we'll definitely meet tomorrow as usual. Just put this behind you, have a healthy dinner, and come back better than ever. We are strong, we are a team. We are the fricking Tornados Cheer Squad!"

Murmuring agreement, the group disperses toward lockers and classrooms. I hang back with Jacinda, walking slowly, turning the corner into a more crowded hall.

"You okay?" I ask.

"That fricking witch!" she explodes. "God! She's always been high-strung. But lately she's getting worse. I mean, you saw that! That was out of control, right?" Jacinda bumps into someone, a first-year student I think, but doesn't apologize or break her cadence. "She's always been totally overboard about 'fitness'"—Jacinda makes quotation marks in the air—"which we all know what that means! Like it's some sort of secret code? Please. It means be skinny or else. I mean, it's a lot of pressure, you know? But she's never, ever singled someone out like that before. Saying those things to Marcie? Isn't that, like, illegal or something?"

"It's definitely harassment."

"We should tell Dr. Folger." Jacinda picks at her nail polish while we walk. For once she isn't greeting by name every person we pass. "Principals can fire teachers, right?"

"You're asking me?" But she's too upset to see the irony. I say, "From the very little I know of school bureaucracy, I doubt a principal can fire a teacher. Not easily, anyway."

"We have to do *some*thing."

Wait. The quote about the internet on Brookner's board. Our conversation after his lifeboat game. Forget trying to change things through the student newspaper...or student government...but what about...

Jacinda looks at me, bewilderment screwing up her forehead. "Why are you smiling like that?"

"Because. I have an idea."

11

I want to live in a society where people are intoxicated with the joy of making things.

—William Coperthwaite, educator and builder

After school, Jacinda comes home with me. We stop at Walmart for Martha on the way. When we get home, Jacinda and I set up camp in my loft with the computer and a notebook.

Martha bangs around the kitchen as she starts cooking supper. "Why don't I skip my thing tonight?" she calls up to us.

"The co-op?" I lean down over the ladder. "You should go."

"Not the co-op. It's a Horny Singletons thing."

"Again? Didn't you just go?"

"Oh, it's nothing," she says a little too breezily. "A couple of the Singletons are getting together for coffee. It's extracurricular." She waves her hand. "But I think I'll skip it. I'll just hang out, keep you two company." She twists the top off a jar of fresh milk and takes a swig. I don't have to look to know that next to me, Jacinda is wrinkling her nose.

"Martha!" I scold. "One, pour yourself a glass, you heathen. And two, you should go. Have a life."

"I have a life—"

"Have a life with grown-upicals."

Now it's Martha's turn to crinkle her nose. "Yes, *Mother.*" She brings the back of her hand to her forehead. "Your authority is too strong for the feeble likes of me. I suppose I'll just disappear and go do the chores."

I laugh. "Poor Cinderellie, mayhaps the mice and bluebirds will help you."

Martha squints and shakes a finger at me. "You owe me an evening of weeding, darling. That ankle's all better and you know it." Martha breaks into a chorus of Bob Dylan's "Maggie's Farm" as she puts the milk back, turns the stove to simmer, grabs the garden basket, and clomps out the door.

I open the computer and type in some notes as we brainstorm ideas. Jacinda taps her fingers against my Eco-Village model, wiggling her foot as she thinks.

"It's like, I'm shocked on the one hand? But then again I'm totally not surprised on the other." She lies back to stare out the huge skylight. "Ms. Gliss has always had a thing against Marcie. And it is hard to hide a few pounds under our uniforms and spanky pants."

"What-y pants?" I ask as I move Eco-Village to a safer location.

"Spanky pants. The granny panties we wear over our real undies?" She shakes her head. "It's, like, you get more sexism when you're on Cheer Squad. Like Ms. Gliss and Marcie today, obviously." She shivers, as if she's remembering Marcie's sobs. And Ms. Gliss's rant. "I mean, in what other sport do they pick on you about your weight?"

"Gymnastics?" I answer. "Wrestling? Figure skating? Boxing? Swimming?"

"Okay, true. But that's not what I mean. With Cheer Squad, it's not just about what you weigh, it's about how you look. People ogle you, and they think you're stupid or superficial or backbitey, just because you're a cheerleader. Like you're straight out of *Bring it On* or something."

"So why do you do it if it's so much trouble?"

"Why do you go hiking if it's so dangerous?" she snaps.

"Good point." I backpedal. "I'm sorry. I didn't mean to offend you. You must really like it."

"I used to love it. Now it's just a lot of stress. But the dance routines still make me happy." She chips at her nail polish. "Then again, I think it's complicated, you know? Because it's good being in Cheer Squad. We can get away with more than other kids. Like how many detentions have you gotten? I cannot relate. I never get in trouble, even when I should."

"That's the trick, though." I pull my ponytail elastic out and twirl my hair into a loose bun. "Oppressors—people in power—do that on purpose so you lose your motivation for change. They're especially careful with natural leaders. They put you in charge of something to give you a stake in the system. That way, you buy into the status quo instead of leading a revolution."

Jacinda hugs her knees. "Like being captain of Cheer Squad instead of fighting sexism?"

"Maybe."

Her bottom lip starts to quiver. "You think it's stupid. Cheer Squad. Like I'm some tool of The Man."

"No, Jacinda. I don't."

"Don't lie."

I take a breath. "Okay, truth? At first I thought it was"—what word won't sound too harsh?—"um, different...than what I'm used to. But that's *my* problem. You're a fantastic person. You're smart and capable and a great friend. If anyone should be Cheer Squad captain, it should be you. You shatter the stereotype, but all stealth and sneaky-like."

"Ohmigod, you really think that?"

"I really do. You can be the cheerleader revolutionary."

She sinks into my bed, a lumpy futon mattress. "I'm so relieved. I was afraid you thought it was silly or something."

"No." I prop my head on my hand. "Look, it's most

definitely not my kind of thing. You couldn't pay me to put on one of those little skirts. It wouldn't cover half of one butt cheek."

"Oh, come on now, you know you want to rock some spanky pants," Jacinda laughs.

"How do you know I don't have them on right now? Maybe Rajas can't get enough of my spanky pants."

Jacinda slaps her hands over her ears. "Ew! Shut up! I do not want to hear about my cousin's sex life." Her eyes go wide. She sits up. "Wait! *Is* there a sex life?"

"I thought you didn't want to hear!"

"I need details. I'll just pretend he's not related to me."

I pick at the tapestry on my bed. "It's not a sex life. It's a kissing life. So far."

"That's so cute! Raj and Evie sittin' in a tree, K-I-S-S-I-N…" She trails off. "What's wrong?"

I pull my hair around so I can hide behind it. I don't want to know, but I have to know: "Is Rajas…has Rajas…?"

"Is he experienced?"

I pretend to examine my hair.

Jacinda sighs. "He's not a virgin, let's put it that way."

My stomach churns. I keep quiet.

"Ugh! I can't believe I know all the girls my cousin's been with! It's not like we talk about it. But I *am* friends with, like, everyone." Apparently I'm not hiding my devastation—*all the girls he's been with!*—because when she peeks through my hair to see the look on my face, Jacinda waves her hand. "But whatever! Pish-posh. I mean you're not worried about it, are you?"

With zero conviction, I shake my head.

"You're a virgin?"

I nod. "Are you?"

She scrunches up her face. "Sort of yes, sort of no. I've, like, hooked up with Stiv—"

"What! Global View Stiv? Newspaper Stiv? You didn't tell me that!"

"It's so not a big deal. We hooked up a couple of times last year and again over the summer."

"Does Rajas know?"

Her mouth curls into a pretty frown. "I think that he kind of knows. He, like, maintains denial about my sex life." She sighs. "Or lack thereof."

I comb my fingers through my hair. "What do you mean 'lack thereof'? Surely you, of all people, could have anyone you want."

She gives me a reserved smile. She looks sad.

Realization dawns: "Oh. Right. Who you want is your InterWeb Lover."

She shrugs. "I'm kind of waiting for him."

"Who is he, Jacinda? Just spill it."

Nothing.

"Does he live around here?" I ask. "Is he worthy of you?"

She stares through the skylight, her foot wiggling so hard it shakes the bed. "Let's, like, change the subject."

"You never want to talk about it. What's with all the secrecy?"

She doesn't respond. She's so open about most things that it's jarring when she does keep something hidden. Maybe she just needs more time?

Jacinda rolls on her side and smiles. "Anyway. Raj? He, like, really likes you. I mean he *really* likes you. I've never seen him so into anyone. He talks about you *all* the time." She sighs dramatically. "Honestly, it gets a little boring."

My cheeks get hot; birds fly around inside my body. I am freaking out with happiness.

She grins. "He's my cousin and all, so I'm biased? But he's the best. He's so cool. You know how some people need attention at all costs? He's the opposite of that. He's so comfortable with who he is. He has no need to, like, broadcast his status."

"On Facebook?" I'm kind of joking and kind of not.

"Right." She laughs again.

"Like his relationship status?" Which hasn't changed despite our hanging out together.

"Exactly. I would fall over if he ever put 'In a relationship.'"

"Why? He doesn't like labels?" I'm suddenly craving Jacinda's perspective on this.

"I guess. He's never been boyfriend-girlfriend with anyone. Like nothing serious."

"So he's not serious with me? But I thought you just said he really likes me? I'm confused."

"I'm confused too!" Another laugh, but with less mirth. "Maybe he wants to keep you all to himself?" Wrinkling her forehead, she adds, "And seriously, don't worry. Just because he's done it before doesn't mean he expects it from you."

Even though I'm still not comprehending all of this, I dissolve into lake of relief. I hadn't realized I was so stressed about sex, about my total inexperience. "Are you really sure?"

"I think that you should talk to him if you're worried about it. But yes, I'm sure."

We are quiet awhile. "He does love my spanky pants though," I say.

She whacks me with a pillow. "Ew! Do I want the details of my cousin's—*ew!* I don't think so. Come on. Let's get back to work."

Over the course of the evening, I manage to shift my focus off Rajas. Jacinda and I brainstorm: We decide on a name for ourselves, for our plan. We create a blog so people can add comments.

Martha leaves for her HSP coffee thing and still we are working.

We fine-tune our manifesto, a team effort between

Jacinda and me, with a little help from the much-underlined book, *Feminist Theory: From Margin to Center*, by bell hooks.

We read, we talk, we bounce ideas off each other. We take turns typing, and we are laughing and thinking and raging and finishing each other's sentences all night. Jacinda calls her parents and we have the dinner Martha set out. I spoon out extra helpings onto Jacinda's plate. "*Mangia*. Eat."

Much later, Jacinda yawns and stretches like a cat. "What time is it?"

"12:45."

"Does Martha always stay out this late?"

Seeing Jacinda stretch makes me need to stretch. I rotate my ankle to strengthen it. "Sometimes. She finally seems to be making some friends." I twist to crack my back. "Okay. Break for lemonade, and then post it on the InterWeb?"

Her eyes go wide and she grins. "Are we really going to do this?"

"Yes, we're really going to do this."

"Holy cow. This is so going to rock!"

"I'll call Rajas. You really think he'll risk it?"

"For us? For you? Totally!"

"Lightning strike. Like a scarlet letter!" I'm practically jumping up and down. If my ankle wasn't still sore, I *would* be jumping up and down.

"Okay, but you've got to, like, speak his language. Tell him it's a prank; he'll like that better than a scarlet letter."

"Let's call him now so he has time to start working on the lightning."

She can't stop giggling.

I stand on the futon, stooping a little so I don't bump the ceiling window. "InterWeb manifesto! We shall take the fight for justice into our own hands!"

She stands too, and we wrap our arms around each other's shoulders.

"Blogs and glue and lightning forever!" she shouts.

We jump around, me on one foot, chanting "PLUTOs! PLUTOs! PLUTOs!" like a couple of little kids until we are out of breath. Then we climb down to the kitchen and pour lemonade into two clean mason jars. We hold them up high and clink them. "A toast," I say, "to friendship."

"To trust," she says.

"To keeping each other out of trouble!"

"Yes!" she agrees. "All for one and one for all!"

We can hardly drink for laughing. At last, a way to shake things up! I can't wait to see the reaction at school tomorrow.

12

When a woman tells the truth she is creating the possibility for more truth around her.

—Adrienne Rich, poet and feminist, b. 1929

Hell yes! The PLUTOs plan has the desired effect and then some. Word spreads even before the homeroom warning bell rings. The place is abuzz; neurons are zipping across synapses like the whole school snorted Ritalin. Conversations fly, phones ping, questions reverberate through the halls and bounce into Brookner's classroom.

—Did you see it?

—What's it supposed to mean?

—The web page says it's a mark against someone being a racist or whatever.

—That's deep.

In Global View, Marcie swoops in on me before I have a chance to sit down. "Was it you?" she whispers.

Next to me, Jacinda shoots a look: part freaking

out—*Ohmigod! Don't say anything! This is so cool*—and part annoyed—*Why isn't Marcie asking ME if I posted it?*

"I don't know what you're talking about," I tell Marcie.

"Uh-huh." She looks suspicious. "Well, I'm kind of scared that Ms. Gliss will think it's me!"

"She won't," says Jacinda. "The whole Cheer Squad was there when she yelled at you. Anyone who heard her could have done this. Plus, the boy's soccer team was on the other side of the gym."

Marcie groans.

"Not that they would have heard anything! They were too far away." Jacinda touches Marcie's arm. "Don't worry, okay?"

"Seriously?" Marcie says.

"Seriously."

Jacinda and I catch eyes. *Never tell, never be divided, never be moved*: the oath the three of us—Jacinda and me and Rajas—swore to each other in the middle of the night. All for one and one for all. Our actions have to be anonymous and we have to stick together. Because if Mr. Pascal finds out Rajas used his shop room key to help us, he'd revoke next year's apprenticeship. And who knows what would happen to Jacinda? No more Cheer Squad captain? Her first-through-twentieth detentions?

The bell sounds, jarring all of our jumpy nerves.

Brookner rushes in, uncharacteristically late, with a laptop tucked under his arm. As he clears his throat to speak, static pops from the PA speaker.

"Teachers, if you'll excuse the interruption." It's Dr. Folger. "I'll be brief. Students, good morning. I would like to remind you that vandalism and defacement of school property is a crime. Indeed, it is not just a school infraction but punishable by law as well. I'd also like to remind you that we have a zero tolerance policy for bullying, whether the target is a teacher or student. This goes for online bullying as well. Violators of this policy *will* be identified and summarily suspended, with recommendation for expulsion. People's good names are not to be trifled with. That is all. Good day." The loudspeaker emits a series of clicks and goes silent.

Well. That answers my question about what would happen if we get caught. Poor Jacinda and Rajas. Thank God I've got a safety plan. I can always go back to homeschool.

"Yes, well." Brookner opens the laptop and prods a button. He rocks onto his toes. "I trust that word has traveled?"

Most of the class nods. A couple of students stare at their desks, like they are reluctant to admit ignorance. Marcie is so antsy and agitated she looks like she's about to combust.

Brookner taps some keys on the computer. "To

recap, for those of you who may not know: It seems that a lightning bolt, made of cardboard or perhaps a thin veneer of wood, has been affixed to the gymnasium doors, as well as to the door of Ms. Gliss's office. The lightning bolt suggests a website to look up for further elucidation. The lightning bolts have been glued quite robustly and are not coming off, despite the Herculean efforts of the janitorial staff."

Good God, I hope my cheeks aren't as red as they feel. Is Jacinda holding herself together? I don't dare look.

"Yes, hmm." Brookner presses his fingers onto his desk and leans toward the laptop, scanning. As he reads, his eyebrows rise until they are levitating over his glasses. "Interesting, to say the least." He turns from the computer screen to stare directly at me. "Most interesting, indeed." A flash of something passes over his face before he looks away. Amusement? Approbation? "Since it is current events day, why not start with this particular current event? Anyone interested in what the website says?" Without waiting for an answer, he finds the cable from the classroom TV and connects it to the laptop.

Our blog pops onto the TV. Brookner steps back to survey the screen. He rocks onto his toes, crosses his arms. "Thoughts? Hmm?"

The class is quiet, taking in the words on the screen.

It is a manifesto, *our* manifesto, mine and Jacinda's, with a pinch of Founding Fathers, a dash of Martha, and a sprinkling of bell hooks. This publicity is even better than expected—broadcasted threats of expulsion, Brookner donating classroom time to our cause. Are other teachers doing the same? My heart thumps with pride, basking in our words writ large on the TV screen.

We, the **P**eople's **L**ightning to **U**ndermine **T**rue **O**ppression (**PLUTOs**) hold these truths to be self-evident:

1. ALL people should be Free to Be You and Me! It ain't just a song, people!

Everyone—EVERYONE—deserves RESPECT, all the time.

This includes kids and adults, students and teachers.

2. When disrespect and inequality is built into a system, it becomes oppression. Some examples:

A. Students who can't buy smartphones are expected to do without the internet privileges afforded to wealthier students.

B. Teachers are given better bathrooms than students.

C. Teachers show disrespect toward students by raising their voices and assigning detention whenever they want for ***insubordination***. Can you imagine students yelling at teachers? We would get suspended!

These are just a few examples. Therefore, be it resolved, that our school is an oppressive system, and many of its members are complicit in enacting various forms of oppression.

3. Types of systemic oppression include, but are not limited to, the following: racism, sexism, elitism, ageism, authoritarianism, sizeism, homophobia, and religious intolerance. **ALL** of them occur in our school.

4. Any attempt to oppress any person or group is unacceptable.

5. Everyone makes mistakes. However, when someone does something super egregious, or when the accumulated number of someone's ***mistakes*** indicate **HABITS** of oppression, we **WILL** take action to hold that person **ACCOUNTABLE**. Lightning will strike!

6. People struck with lightning will be listed on this site by initials, along with their infractions against humanity.

7. The founders of **PLUTOs** will remain anonymous. So don't ask!

Join our cause, anytime, anywhere,
by uniting against oppression!
Post comments on this page!
Free speech for all!
Speak up! Start the revolution!

COMMENTS

First lightning strike: Ms. G. for blatant sexism and sizeism and disrespect of students by yelling at students for their weight and size. She thinks it's appropriate to humiliate and shame students, but guess what? You can't hide from justice! Ha!

A staccato *rap rap rap* shakes the classroom door, snapping my attention away from the genius that is the PLUTOs blog.

Brookner opens the door, and there stands Dr. Folger. Jacinda gasps and the color drains from her face; she looks terrified.

"Mr. Brookner. Students. Excuse the interruption." Dr. Folger bows slightly. "A word?" He motions Brookner forward and whispers something. Brookner nods, listening, his hands clasped behind his back.

When the two men separate, Brookner swivels around to regard me with what seems like a mix of interest and pity. "Evie. Dr. Folger would like a word with you."

Jacinda doesn't move; she is frozen, staring straight ahead. I take a deep breath.

"Bring your things," Dr. Folger says.

I guess this means I might be out of class a while. Which does not seem good.

Another deep yoga breath. I pick up my stuff and stand tall.

My heart is pounding, pounding, inching its way into my throat.

If particular care and attention is not paid to the ladies, we are determined to foment a rebellion, and will not hold ourselves bound by any laws in which we have no voice or representation.

—Abigail Adams, abolitionist, 1744–1818

Dr. Folger settles into a swivel chair behind his big wooden desk. Plaques and degrees coat his office walls. A huge herd of Slinkies populates the horizontal surfaces of his bookshelves, desk, filing cabinet. I set down my bag and move one of the two empty chairs toward the door, so that we are on a diagonal. I don't like being maneuvered into talking over a wide expanse of desk. It's a proclamation of authority. Dr. Folger raises his eyebrows at my move, but he doesn't object. A thin manila folder floats in the middle of his desk. What's in it? Results of my Battery of Tests? Grade reports? The inscrutable white copies of those triplicate detention forms?

"Thank you for meeting with me," he says, as if I had a choice in the matter, "Ms. Morningdew."

"I prefer Evie."

He tilts his head: an inquiry.

"Martha—my mom," I explain, "went a little crazy naming me. She didn't just make up my first and middle names, she made up the last name too."

He smiles. "Fair enough. But you may have to remind me. Evie." He picks up a rainbow-colored plastic Slinky and ripples it. "I've been meaning to officially welcome you to our school."

"Thanks," I say, "for the welcome. But isn't this really about something else?"

He smiles, not an unfriendly smile. "Indeed. Yes, it is."

Time for another deep breath.

"I've asked you to meet with me to discuss certain...events."

"The lightning? The PLUTOs website?"

He looks surprised. I bet he's accustomed to students trying to sidestep him instead of confronting him head-on. He sets down the Slinky and opens the folder. "It looks like you've had some trouble with Ms. Gliss and Ms. Theodore and Mr. Wysent."

"I've served my time." I'm about to say something about the bathrooms or the socioeconomic bias of the phone policy when I remember we talked about it on the PLUTOs blog. So I keep quiet.

He scans the folder. "Yes. But you've had some other trouble."

"Can I see that?" I hold my hand out.

He jerks the folder back as though he's astonished—simply astonished!—that I would ask.

"It's about me, right?"

"Indeed it is."

"So why can't I see it?"

He clears his throat. "I'm happy to tell you what is in here," he says, tapping the file, "but I can't let you read it. I have to protect my teachers' confidentiality."

My eyes bug out. "Your *teachers'* confidentiality? *They* can write in my file? *They* can see it?"

He strums a different Slinky, this one small and metal. "They can add a note or two if they so desire."

"Uh-huh. Okay. Right." I undo my hair elastic, snap it around my wrist like a bracelet. "Can I add a note too, then? Since it is my file?"

Dr. Folger smiles and chuckles. "Ms. Morningdew—"

"Evie."

"Evie. It's unorthodox. But…yes, I would include a note from you. What will you write?"

"I'm not sure yet."

"Ah." He returns to my file and is quiet for a moment, reading. "I see you've expressed interest in attending college."

"Yes. Cornell. They have a program for Urban

Planning with a concentration in Social Justice."

"So they do." Smiling, he points to a frame on the wall.

I glance at the framed diploma and jump up for a closer look. *Cornell University confers...James Charles Folger, Baccalaureate of Science in Urban and Regional Studies.* My hands fly to my mouth. "You're kidding! I don't believe it!"

Dr. Folger chuckles.

"That's the same department!" I study the diploma, visualizing having one of my own, with my name on it, and then I look at the one next to it. "And you got your doctorate from Harvard. Not too shabby."

"The Ed school at Harvard. A bit more down-to-earth than the rest of the place. All of the excellence, less of the hubris."

"Wow." I shake my head as I sit. "Did you like Cornell?"

"No."

"No?"

He grins. "I didn't like it—I loved it." He swivels in his chair. "It was a wonderful program, phenomenal teachers. I learned so much there, both from classes and the practicums. And I made lifelong friends."

"Wow. You could write me a letter of recommendation!" It's a thought and suggestion and question—until I remember why I'm here. That he pulled me out of class, ostensibly for a big-time infraction.

He looks at his hands. His suit jacket pulls a bit at its shoulder seams. "I would love to, Ms. Morn—Evie. If," he raises a finger, "if I were certain I could do so in good conscience."

My heart sinks. Wait for it…

"Now. You and I both know that this…lightning strike…is a rather alarming development. I must take it quite seriously." He clears his throat. "And it coincides with your appearance at this school, as well as your interest in, shall we say, social justice activism."

So. There might be a copy of my petition to the student council in that folder. Possibly even my letter to the editor? Both of which went over like lead balloons. What else lurks in those pages? "Correlation does not imply causation," I say.

"Indeed not," he concedes. "And yet, where there's smoke there's often fire."

I pull the elastic off my wrist and wrap my hair into a long ponytail. How much should I say? Dr. Folger seems cool, but what if he's playing Good Cop, only to become Bad Cop two minutes from now? After all, he is the principal. He is The Man. I take another deep breath before asking, "Just for the sake of argument, it isn't a crime for a student to create a blog, is it? I mean, free speech is protected by the First Amendment. I assume that public school students can exercise their constitutional rights. Although I could be wrong. Freedom of the press seems pretty subjective around here."

"How did you know the website is a blog?"

"Mr. Brookner just showed it to us." Thank God! That was a close one.

"Did he, now?" He picks up the rainbow Slinky again. "As it happens, you are correct. Keeping a blog is not a crime. However, as it pertains to school systems, First Amendment rights must be tempered by the best interest of the institution."

"Yeah, I'm starting to figure that out. So let me get this straight: You can and would, in good conscience, deny individual students their rights? As in, the greatest good for the greatest number? You're that much of a utilitarian?"

"Not strictly, no." He smiles, very slightly, like he is impressed with our discussion. "However, the fact is, Evie, that bullying is a crime. We have specific rules about online bullying, internet bullying." He sets up the Slinky to watch it flip. "And libel is a crime—the crime of defaming someone in print. We are talking about a teacher's good name."

"Are you sure her name is good?" I ask carefully. "I mean, hypothetically, what if the website was telling the truth? What if she did say horrendously awful things to a student?"

"I have an obligation to protect my students, of course. So without divulging anything, I can tell you that Dr. Jones—the superintendent—and I shall investigate the claims."

I nod. Our eyes meet. He clears his throat. It's a standoff. I wouldn't be surprised if tumbleweeds rolled across the floor between us.

Clearing his throat, he says, "Without sounding too nefarious, I will be keeping an eye on you, Evie." He dips his head like our conversation is finished. "Ms. Franklin will write you a pass. Thank you for your time."

"Right. Okay." I pick up my books.

I'm opening his office door when he says, "Evie."

I turn around. "Dr. Folger."

"I want to make sure you realize something."

"What's that?"

He taps his fingers on my file. "This is your first time attending a traditional school. And it is your senior year."

I smile. "So far you're not telling me anything I don't already know."

He returns the smile. "What you may not know is that your record will follow your application to Cornell."

"Right, right. The dreaded *Permanent Record*."

"Indeed."

"Thank you for the warning." I turn back to the door.

I can't wait to rehash this with Jacinda and Rajas. She would have told him by now and they'll both be dying to hear.

"It will follow you even if you decide to…cease coming to school."

What? My brain falls to my stomach, and they both drop to the floor. Holy freaking crap. "You mean—"

"If you drop out of school, Cornell shall still have access to your record. A record that will detail all the events concurrent with your time here."

I head back to the chair and sit.

"You may go."

No. School and PLUTOs just changed from interesting novelty to a really, really bad idea. Now my dreams for the future are at stake.

"I just wanted to be clear about that."

He's managed to silence me. I nod.

"I will also need to call your parents about this," he says. "I generally follow up conversations like these with parents. Over the years I have learned it pays to keep them in the loop, as it were. To avoid surprises further down the line."

I can't help but snort.

"Is something funny?"

"I'm sorry. Go ahead…call her. But be prepared."

He looks perplexed. "She's very strict? You'd rather I

didn't contact her at this time?"

"Martha's as anti-strict as they come. Go for it. But you might want to brush up on your educational philosophy. She'll probably throw Dewey at you."

"Ah. 'Education, therefore, is a process of living and not a preparation for future living.'"

Despite the turmoil Dr. Folger has spun my entire future into, I eke out a smile. "One of my favorite quotes."

He bows a little, a nice gesture that seems meant to convey respect. "I will look forward to talking with her."

We leave his office for the main office. Ms. Franklin, who was not here when we came in, looks up. She sets a can of Diet Coke down next to a needlepoint tissue box holder. "Hi, hon."

"You two have met," Dr. Folger says.

"Yes." She smiles. "Evie, right?"

I nod.

"Shall I write a pass?"

Dr. Folger says, "If you would."

Ms. Franklin pulls a blue notepad out of a drawer and begins writing.

"Thank you for your time, Ms. M—" He shakes his head. "I'm sorry. Evie. Do stay out of trouble. So I can write you that recommendation for Cornell."

Cornell. In case I'd forgotten.

A Permanent Record that is truly permanent.

All along, Martha has said this was a bad idea, and now I have to agree. Another fine mess I've gotten myself into.

Stare. It's the way to educate your eyes. Stare. Pry, listen, eavesdrop. Die knowing something. You are not here long.

—Walker Evans, photographer, 1903–1975

14

Well darling, it ain't a revolution if nothing's at stake," Martha tells me when we get home from school and work. She wiggles her eyebrows. "And not for nothing, I planted a seed in Dr. Folger's ear."

"That's quite an image. A seed sprouting in earwax." I frown. "He called already?"

Martha hands me a mason jar of lemonade and clinks hers to mine. "I talked to him during my allotted twenty minutes of freedom. Congratulations, darling. You've made it to the top of The Man's priority list."

"Thanks."

"Why so blue?"

"Cornell." I sip some lemonade and try to pull myself together. "So. What's this seed you planted?"

"Hell, I thought you'd never ask!" She turns a kitchen chair around to straddle it, crossing her arms over the backrest. "He told me the situation, of course, being very careful not to actually accuse you of anything. But he gave me an overview of PLUTOs and the lightning, which I already *knew*—"

"You didn't tell him it was us, did you!"

Martha gives me her most insulted look. "I would sell my own flesh and blood and her friends down the river? How can you even—"

I put up my hands. "Okay, okay! Abort rant, please. The seed?"

"Right. So he told me what happened." She twirls her hand to show she's skipping to the good part. "And, because I am a grown-up, he listened to me." She sniffs. "I think." She tilts her head. "Yes, he listened. Seems like a decent guy. How the hell he ended up as principal of a—"

"Martha. Keeping you on point is like herding cats."

"What? Am I rambling?"

"The seed!"

"Right. The seed." She takes a swig of lemonade. "He told me what happened. I told him that, when all is said and done, sunlight is the best disinfectant." She flips her hand to say, *Ta-da!*

I wait for more. "That's it?"

"Of course, that's not it! Well, yes, that's it." She sets down her lemonade and sighs dramatically. "The trick is to make it seem like his idea, *n'est-ce pas*?"

"Make *what* seem like—"

"That sunlight is the best...that free speech is the best thing, in the long run."

"I don't think he would agree. In fact, I'm pretty sure he wouldn't."

"Listen. The point of your revolution is empowerment, is it not? If students feel empowered, they speak up. Nothing scares The Man more. But," she adds, holding up a finger, "if The Man can feel like he has some control, some influence over people, even if they are bucking the system, well, then..." She trails off and smiles, very satisfied with herself.

"I'm still not following."

Martha rolls her eyes. "Just you wait, my darling. I planted that seed. And if things get crazy—*when* things get crazy—he's going to come back to it and think it's his own idea."

At this point I'm completely lost. "*What* is his own idea?"

"*Sunlight*, darling. Free speech." She shakes her head. "I'm a tad disappointed you didn't think of it yourself."

"News flash, Martha? I *did* think of it—the free speech part—if that's what you're talking about. The whole point of the blog is to encourage students to write comments and air grievances."

"Ah, but the trick is in the *strategery*, darling. Make Dr. Folger think it's his own idea." She stands. "Anyway. When are you gonna see that gorgeous boy Rajas again?"

Good question. I am dying to be alone with Rajas somewhere other than shop room Shangri-la. But the rest of it? The stuff about strategy and Dr. Folger? That's about as clear as mud.

On Friday night, Rajas and I have a date. Martha has some HSP get-together and Jacinda is babysitting, so it's just me and Rajas, with nothing tugging us in separate directions. We're meeting Jacinda downtown at 11:00 after her baby-sitting gig; she's sleeping over *chez* Dome.

Rajas has parked the Blue Biohazard by a little-used playground on the edge of town, just past McDonald's and the cemetery.

The stars are barely visible, dimmed by the light of the moon. I can feel the air turning my cheeks apple red, crisp and rosy. Rajas has spread a picnic blanket onto the hood of the Biohazard. We've been lying here, kissing, for hours...or minutes...or weeks. I've lost track of everything except his tongue, his lips, his hands, his breath, his eyes.

I'm evanescing into him.

Until something buzzes in my pocket. My phone vibrates, then rings.

"Ignore it," Rajas mumbles through a kiss.

"Planning to." I stash my phone under the blanket. Whoever it is can wait. This is the most…the ultimate—I don't have the words to describe it, the tautness of my nerves, the tingling in every inch of skin. Rajas's hand finds its way under my sweatshirt. My cotton tank wrinkles as he moves his palm up my ribcage. His thumb is so close to my breast I think I might stop breathing at any moment.

We roll over on the blanket, squishing the baguette that Rajas bought for our picnic. We kiss more, and more, and the moon is nearly full, bursting with light like my breasts surely will when he touches them. His fingertips could start fires.

"Hang on a second." I take a breath of courage and sit up to pull my sweatshirt over my head. Rajas's look of surprise and delight makes me feel strong. "Don't tell me you've never seen a girl do this before," I tease.

"Not like that." He smiles. "I usually do it."

My heart drops like it's tied to a bucket of rocks. I tug my sweatshirt back over my head and pull it down. "Really."

"Hey. I didn't mean it like that." He leans in, but there's a hint of frustration. At my displeasure? Or because my sweatshirt's back on?

"Listen, I'm here with you. That's what matters." Rajas raises his eyebrows, like that statement should clarify everything.

"I know I shouldn't care, but I have to ask. Have there been a lot?"

"A lot of what?"

"A lot of girls."

He's looking amused. He doesn't want to make this easy.

"You know what I mean! A lot of girlfriend-y type people."

"Hundreds," he says. "Thousands." He runs a finger down the bridge of my nose. "Does that make you feel better?"

"No."

"Then how about if I said I've never had a girlfriend?"

"No, because I know that's not true."

"But it is. I don't believe in the whole boyfriend-girlfriend thing."

"Because you hate labels."

"Yes. Boyfriend, girlfriend, it's demeaning. A girl is a complete person in her own right. She shouldn't be identified by her relationship to me. Plus, it just complicates things."

Okay, I'm with him on the girl power thing. But why would a label complicate a relationship? I don't love the word "girlfriend" either, but in this case it would be so nice. It would clarify a whole lot; I would know where I stand with him. Actually it would be downright lovely. "Right. Okay. Well." I'm trying to pick my heart up from the ground. It must be around here somewhere. "I just thought—"

"Eve. I really like you. I want to be with you. Why put a name on it?"

Swallowing the lump in my throat, I manage a weak "Sure." Breathe. "Sure. I get it. I'm anti-label. I'm an anti-label kind of gal. Anti-sweatshop too. And pesticides. And definitely labels. Labels, bad. Unless they say organic or fair trade or sweatshop-free..." I can't stop talking. I sound like an idiot. Why can't I stop? "Or, you know, phthalate-free, or—"

He touches my cheek and kisses me. "You okay?"

I nod instead of talking. God forbid I should blather on about sustainable, fair trade, shade grown, organic, bird-friendly coffee standards.

Rajas smiles his amazing half-smile. His gaze goes foggy. "Eve. We can do, or not do, whatever you want. We can just hang out and look at the stars if you like."

Damn it. I'm acting insecure and jealous. Which I hate. I refuse to be that girl. This girl is different. This girl is true to herself. What do *I* want? I want *this.* I sit up straight and meet Rajas's molten eyes and peel my sweatshirt off again. I smile at Rajas and smooth my hair, which is staticky from the sweatshirt's repeat trips. Rajas reaches, slowly, toward my breast. And action! I'm back in the moment in an instant. Bubbling, tingling, evaporating.

My phone rings again. Rajas swears under his breath. Without looking, I reach under the blanket to silence the ringer.

His hands are on the move. My body rises to meet him.

The phone vibrates wildly.

"Gah!" Rajas moans in frustration. "Turn it off!"

"Already done." Flipping open the phone to power it off, I frown at the display. "Why would Jacinda be calling? Over and over? And wait, there's three texts telling me to call, it's an emergency."

"Probably because I told her *not* to bother us." Rajas rubs his face. The phone starts buzzing again. "No! Don't—"

"Hello?" I answer, shrugging an apology to Rajas.

"Evie? Ohmigod! I need help!" Jacinda's voice is a squeak attack. She sounds like a dolphin.

"What's wrong? Jacinda, calm down. Come down an octave. Only whales can understand you."

After listening to her panicked explanation, I say, "Okay. We'll be right—"

"No!" Rajas grabs my phone. Is he playing? His tone is intense. "Jay. Don't be ridiculous. We're busy." He jabs a button and chucks my phone into the open window of the Biohazard. "Now. Where were we?" He pulls me to him.

"Rajas. I want to stay, believe me." I have to get the words out before I melt into thick hot liquid again. "But Jacinda needs me."

"I need you."

"And you," I tell him, grabbing my sweatshirt, "can have me. After I help Jacinda. The snake got loose."

"Not yet," he teases, "but if you're ready for it—"

"Wow. That is lame, my friend." I laugh through my sweatshirt as I pull it back on. "I'm not making an innuendo about your..." I wrinkle my nose. *Penis* sounds so clinical and ridiculous, yet the other options aren't any better: *wiener, cock, dick, package?* They sound either preschool or prostitute; there's no middle ground. I change approaches. "The kid Jacinda's baby-sitting has a snake. It got loose—again, not a double entendre—but she can't get ahold of the parents and she's freaking out."

Rajas breathes a heavy, mournful sigh. "Fine. Let's go."

At the address she gave us, Jacinda is waiting on the front porch, clutching her cell phone, hopping from foot to foot. She jumps at every noise, as if, out of nowhere, a snake might fling itself onto her, poison dripping from enormous, glistening fangs.

"Watch out, Jay." Rajas shuts the Biohazard's door and takes the porch steps two at a time. "Snakes move like lightning." He fakes a karate chop for emphasis.

Jacinda makes a sour face at Rajas and brings me into a tight hug. "Ohmigod, thank you so much for coming! Um, okay. You two can just go in. I'll stay in the Biohazard and keep trying to call Brook—"

Rajas freezes. "Keep trying to call *who*?"

Jacinda covers her mouth, eyes wide.

"This"—Rajas points—"is Brookner's house." He sounds pissed.

Why? I look from Rajas to Jacinda.

Rajas glares at her. "Isn't it?"

"Okay. I know you think he's sketchy and all, but just listen. His regular baby-sitter canceled and so he called me to see if I could fill in. Should I just leave him in the lurch? Just because my overprotective, paranoid cousin heard some rumors?" She crosses her arms. "I don't think so. That is, like, totally unprofessional. It's against the baby-sitting code of ethics."

"He has your number?"

"Everyone has my number. I've been hanging babysitting flyers all over town."

Rajas shakes his head. "I'm not snooping through Sketchy Brookner's house for some snake on the lam."

I turn to him, surprised he's being so stubborn. What's up with that? These two always have each other's backs. They are the poster children for close family relationships. "Why are you being so harsh?" I ask. "You can't abandon your cousin."

His expression is full of meaning. "Eve. There are other things I'd much, *much* rather be doing right now. And," he says to Jacinda, "Brookner isn't just sketchy. He's bad news, Jay. You know what Nishi said." Nishi is Rajas's sister, Jacinda's cousin. But what does she have to do with any of this?

Rajas's frown deepens. "And why isn't Brookner answering his phone? What about his wife? Doesn't she have her own phone?"

Jacinda crosses her arms. "It's just him. He's divorced."

Rajas snorts. "Figures. She probably left him because he's a letch."

"Whatever, Raj. Thanks a lot." Jacinda sounds annoyed and looks apprehensive—probably about a snake ambush. She looks at me. "Okay. Booker's in his room. You just go all the way through—"

"Wait." I stop her. "Did you say *Booker*? The kid's name is Booker?"

She nods.

Rajas finishes my thought: "Booker Brookner. He named his kid Booker Brookner. Now I *know* the guy's an asshole."

I sigh, and repeat the line I've had to say a thousand times. "It's a parent's prerogative to name a child what they want."

"You don't really think that," Rajas says.

"No. I don't." But for now I'll table my feelings about terrible names for children. "Where does Booker think the snake is?"

Jacinda smiles like she's relieved that I'm back to business. She pushes her fingers through her hair, making it spiky. "Booker's room is in the back of the house on the first floor. Off the kitchen?" She shivers. "He's looking for it in there."

I nod to Jacinda and throw a scowl—only half teasing—toward Rajas. "Sure you won't help?"

"Sure as—"

"All right," I cut him off. "I'll be back." I open the front door and step into Brookner's living room.

It is not at all what I would have thought. You'd think neat, adult, literary: rooms lined with mahogany bookshelves. Maybe some iconic pieces of modern furniture sitting atop a faux-zebra rug, as indicated by his trendy eyeglasses and decent sense of style. But this place is more *Animal House* than *Dwell.* A stained, naked futon slouches on an unfinished pine frame; stacked pizza boxes serve as end tables. One of those awful halogen torchiere lamps spotlights cobwebs and ceiling cracks. The staircase is covered in laundry. There is not one book in sight. Not even a magazine.

"Hello?" I call. No answer. I keep going, into the kitchen. It is bright, functional, less filthy than the other rooms. Maybe Jacinda tidied up earlier? "Hello?"

"In here!" A child's voice, overrun with panic. "He usually goes under my bed, but this time I can't—" A muffled crash. "Nope, crud! He's not anywhere!"

Booker's room is stuffed with toys, clothes, a bunk bed, books, boxes, junk. Butt sticking up, he is kneeling to look under the bed. "He likes it where it's dark." Booker crawls around to face me. "I can't find him." His cheeks are mottled from crying. He looks about eight or nine, but I'm bad at judging little kids' ages.

"Don't worry. We'll find your snake," I say.

"What if he gets lost or hurt or something?"

"We'll find him. What's his name?"

"Javier." Booker starts plowing through toys and clothes on the floor. "He's a Colombian red tail boa."

"Oh, I bet he's a real beauty." I inspect the empty snake habitat in Booker's room. "It's cool that you're more concerned about his well-being than you are freaked out."

He stops digging through clothes to give me a withering look. "Why would I be freaked out? I'm not a *girl* or anything."

Wowzer. Hello, incipient sexist. "Perhaps it's escaped your attention that I am a girl? And I'm here to help you?" I smile to soften the words. "Just consider it your first lesson in feminism." Surveying the room, I point to the radiator. "At least you have steam heat, so there aren't air ducts for him to get into. That's good news."

Booker just blinks, his little chin trembling. We start searching.

An hour later, the downstairs sufficiently ransacked, Booker and I head upstairs. He is trying hard not to cry. "What if he starves? What if he gets in the street and someone runs him over?" He rubs his eyes.

I pick my way through the piles of clothes on the stairs. "We'll look up here and then we'll...do you have a basement?"

He nods, sniffing.

"And an attic?"

He nods again.

This would be simpler if they lived in a yurt. "Javier will want warm before cool," I say. "So we'll check the attic next if we don't find him up here."

"Okay." His eyebrows are completely bunched together. "You do Dad's room, I'll do the library."

"No no no. Back it up there, buddy." I am not stepping foot in Brookner's bedroom. It's way too personal.

He shrugs. "Okay. Library's that one."

The library. Ah. Now this is what I expected. Heck yes. The big desk, the antique wooden desk chair, the laptop perched on a pile of papers, it's all here. An open dictionary, a baby monitor, a phone. Hanging above the desk, there's an old sign that says *Loafer's Paradise.* The oak floorboards groan when I move; the floor is straining under the weight of the books.

The books. They encase the perimeter of the room. Dragging my fingers along their spines, it looks like Brookner has organized them into fiction and nonfiction, sorted by category. And then alphabetically by author. Big candles are interspersed with his books. It's a shrine to literature. I inspect the shelves for my own canon, my favorites, the books I return to over and over: for comfort, or inspiration, or to know that someone out there feels the same things I do, knows the words, has written them down. Soul medicine.

Brookner has my canon. Every title. *My Ántonia,* by Willa Cather. *Ahab's Wife,* Sena Jeter Naslund. *The Poisonwood Bible,* by Barbara Kingsolver. *Be More Chill,* Ned Vizzini. All the *Little House* books. *His Dark Materials*, the trilogy by Philip Pullman. Even Daniel Pinkwater's *Alan Mendelsohn, the Boy from Mars* is here. And he has nonfiction essentials: *A Pattern*

Language, by Christopher Alexander, et al., *Pedagogy of the Oppressed,* by Paulo Freire. *Feminist Theory, from Margin to Center* by bell hooks. Howard Zinn's *A People's History of the United States. Incidents in the Life of a Slave Girl,* Harriet Ann Jacobs. *Endurance: Shackleton's Incredible Voyage,* by Alfred Lansing.

Okay. He's got a ton of books. Why should I be so surprised that my favorites are all here? It's not like he pressed his fingers to my temples, read my aura, and cataloged it by color, according to the books I love.

But then again it *is* like that, somehow. That is the paradox of the Brookner—the way he can be alluring one minute, slightly shady and standing too close the next.

Just as I start to tip out the hardcover of *Ahab's Wife*, I freeze. There's a scraping sound from behind the bookcase. Yes. It's reptile scales slithering over wood.

Quietly, I slip the book back and tiptoe to the end of the bookcase. Javier is sliding himself behind it. Only his sinewy midsection and brick-red tail are in view.

Another sound, voices exploding. From where? No one is in here! Oh—the baby monitor. Its indicator lights glow brighter as the voices get louder.

It's Jacinda and Brookner.

I make for the monitor. I have a bad feeling that whatever they're about to say is none of my business. But behind me, Javier is on the move. Crap. "Come here, you,"

I whisper, trying to project good vibes. "I won't hurt you." Just before he disappears, I grab the very tip of his tail. I pull slowly, slowly, hand over hand. He's heavy and strong, but he doesn't put up a fight. "It's okay, Javier. It's okay, boy." When I can, I lift him, holding his head with one hand, supporting his body with the other. He rotates to get a good look at me and flicks his tongue.

"Hi, sweetie. How do I smell?" I stroke him. He is lovely. "Booker! I found—" I start to say, but my attention snaps to the baby monitor. I heard my name. Is it still none of my business if they're talking about me? No, I'm sure it's nothing. Jacinda's probably telling him about Operation Snake Search and Rescue.

I shift Javier and look for the power switch on the monitor. It shouldn't be that difficult to turn this thing off—

Another name spoken: *Rajas.*

Sliding his head into my hair, Javier wraps himself around me like I'm an old friend. Where the hell is the stupid off switch?

"You brought them *here*?" Brookner's voice. Annoyed.

"I needed Evie!" Jacinda. Pleading. "If you answered your phone like you promised, would it have been a problem? I don't think so." Jacinda sounds uncharacteristically irritated—and very, very, strangely, on way-too-familiar terms with Brookner.

A pause. "The point of all this was to have a good reason for me to call you and see you outside of school—"

"A deadly viper was not part of our plan!"

Oh man. Jacinda, what are you doing? You and Brookner have a *plan*? Why are you seeing him outside of school?

My stomach roils. I'm terrified that I know what she's doing—and I do not want to know. Tell me I'm wrong. Brookner's habit of standing too close, of grazing his fingers across my palm as he hands over a hall pass. It's all falling into place.

But he's such a cool teacher. He actually seems to want to teach his students something interesting.

A little *too* interesting.

Rajas is right. He is so right to be worried.

I don't want to hear another word. Grabbing the monitor wire, I yank the plug out of the wall. "BOOKER! I FOUND YOUR SNAKE!" I scream, willing to risk setting Javier on edge as long as the entire house can hear. Anything to interrupt Jacinda and Brookner. "DID YOU HEAR ME? I'VE GOT JAVIER!"

Javier squeezes me, coiling tighter, but he's the least of my worries. I trust him a lot more than I trust the snake that's downstairs scheming with my friend.

Booker comes tearing out of Brookner's bedroom,

almost collapsing with relief. "Thank you thank you thank you! Evie, you are the *best*!"

I run my hand down Javier, coaxing him to unwrap himself.

Booker takes Javier as I continue to uncoil him from around my chest and arm. He gushes a stream of words and love: "Javier where were you I was so worried about you come here boy don't you ever do that again!"

Down in the kitchen, Brookner and Jacinda are waiting for us. The air is tense. Jacinda's arms are crossed close to her chest and her foot is tapping. Brookner is leaning against the counter. Oblivious, Booker disappears into his room, still whispering sweet nothings to Javier.

I blow out a breath and muster a smile. "So. We meet again."

Brookner adjusts his glasses. "Good evening, Evie. Nice to see you." He tips his head toward Jacinda without looking at her. "Jacinda tells me that the great Javier liberated himself again, hmm?" He rocks onto his heels. "Thanks for...ah...thanks for your help. Apparently my baby-sitter is quite frightened of snakes."

Lips pursed, Jacinda's movements seem prim and skittish. "Evie knows I'm fricking terrified of snakes. So she, like, rescued me."

I look from my friend to our teacher. They don't

seem to realize they are repeating each other, recapping events I was here for.

On the counter behind Brookner, near the doorway to Booker's room, the other baby monitor sits there... monitoring. Booker isn't a baby, but this house is big, old, creaky; I bet Brookner uses it at night, when he's up in the library and Booker's in bed. Listening out for bad dreams. Will Brookner notice that the one upstairs is unplugged? Maybe he'll assume that I snagged the wire while searching for Javier. The last thing I want is for Brookner to know I unplugged it because I overheard him and Jacinda.

"No problem at all," I say. "But you might want to put something heavier on the lid of Javier's habitat."

Brookner claps once. "Well! That is a fantastic idea. We will do that." He points at me as though I'm a genius. "We will definitely do that."

Awkward, heavy silence.

"So, Jacinda. We should get going, right?"

"Um. Yeah. Let's go." Sounding subdued, overwhelmed, she turns to Brookner. "Okay. Ta-ta. I'm sleeping over at Evie's tonight." Brookner lifts an eyebrow like he already knew this. Jacinda pulls her purse over her shoulder and walks out.

"Um, Jacinda?" I say.

She spins to look at me.

"Don't you want to say goodbye? To Booker?"

"Ohmigod. Booker."

Back in his room, Booker is stacking paperback books onto the lid of Javier's habitat.

"I'd use hardcovers. They're heavier," I tell him. Jacinda is silent. "Well, we're going now," I say. "See you later."

"Thanks again, Evie!" Booker places a Harry Potter hardcover on top of the pile. "Javier is so happy to be home. Aren't you, Javier? Yes, you are."

Taking hold of Jacinda's hand, I lead her out of the house and down the front steps.

Rajas slides off the hood of the Biohazard. "Crisis averted?" He draws me into a kiss.

"Not quite," I whisper.

With those incredible dark eyes, he squints, like he's trying to glean information from my face.

"I'll fill you in later."

Next to us, Jacinda is staring into the middle distance. She might as well be in another dimension.

"Can you take us home?" I ask Rajas.

"Already?" He makes a face. "Fine. But you owe me an uninterrupted evening." He turns to wag a finger at his cousin. "You got that, Jay?"

"Hmm?" She looks up. "Sorry. I guess I was, like, spacing out."

"Toxic effects of Brookner. Come on, let's get the hell out of—"

"Pandora?" I say.

He smiles. "You got it."

Jacinda looks back at Brookner's house. Her forehead is creased, her feathery lashes hide her eyes. I open the door of the Biohazard and motion for her to get in.

We have a whole lot to talk about when we get home.

Nearly all men can stand adversity, but if you want to test a man's character, give him power.

—Abraham Lincoln, American president, 1809–1865

It's a tense ride to The Dome Home. Rajas's eyes glint with annoyance at Jacinda for interrupting our date. Jacinda stares out the window. I don't bother attempting to generate conversation; my mind is racing, replaying what I heard. Brookner said something like *so we could be together outside of school* and *the point of this plan*... They had a plan. A plan! My stomach is still in knots. Jacinda, what are you mixed up in?

Rajas maneuvers the Biohazard up my driveway. At The Dome, we lean together to kiss goodnight. Because Jacinda's here, we keep it short, but our arms find their way around each other. I ache for more time alone with Rajas. But I need to talk to Jacinda.

We wave goodbye, and as the Biohazard's taillights disappear down the driveway, a long sigh floats out of me, carried off by a crisp autumn breeze. I turn. The Clunker is here; Martha's home early. Too bad. I'd hoped to talk to Jacinda alone, stat.

"Darlings! Hello!" Martha ushers us inside, careful not to spill her glass of wine. She pulls Jacinda into a hug, then me, and takes a drink. "I had quite an evening. Members of the Horny Singletons titillated with drama and intrigue."

"You're home early." I try to hide my disappointment.

She laughs, swirling the wine in her glass. "It ended rather abruptly. Ah, *c'est la vie.*" Martha takes another sip. "How was your night, my love?"

"Good."

She lifts an eyebrow. "Good? Or *gooooood*?"

Jacinda slumps into a kitchen chair. "Evie helped me out."

Puzzled by the non sequitur, Martha looks from Jacinda to me.

I shrug and sit down too. My ankle's still a little sore. "It was a long night."

"I'm all ears, darlings!" She tops off her glass, holding the wine bottle upside down and shaking out the last drips.

Jacinda seems abjectly miserable.

"I think Jacinda and I need to talk," I tell Martha.

"Agreed! Go right ahead."

I hesitate. "Alone."

Martha deflates. "Oh. Okay." She takes a drink of wine, swishes it around her mouth. "Well. Tell me later."

I tell Jacinda, "Let's go outside."

She crinkles her nose, but shrugs. "Okay."

I lead us to the barn and am soothed by the earthy, familiar smells of cow and chicken and straw. I flip the light on; golden dust motes float around the bulb. I lay out an old blanket for Jacinda to sit on. She does, and tucks her short skirt under her folded legs.

I pat Hannah Bramble's warm side. "Hey, sweet girl. How was your day?" With a swish of her tail, she shifts her weight to accommodate me. "Oh, Hannah. It's not milking time." Cats and kittens appear from all corners of the barn to mewl a chorus. "Everyone thinks I'm here to milk," I explain to Jacinda.

Jacinda smiles, almost a grimace. She reaches for a kitten but it squirms away. Jacinda frowns. Even her pout is dainty.

"Don't take it personally," I tell her. "After he gets some milk he'll let you hold him."

I rest my forehead on the warm, soft depression between Hannah Bramble's belly and her flank. If I don't milk her a little, there'll be a feline mutiny. I grab the cats' bowl and start to milk. As the first squirts hit the bowl, I look over at Jacinda. "Hey, you want to try?"

"Try what?" She pulls the ends of the blanket around her to ward off the chill.

"Milking."

She looks at me like I'm crazy. "Ohmigod. No thanks!"

"I'll have you milking yet. You wait and see. A few more weeks."

She gives me a wan, pathetic smile.

Finished for now, I wipe my hands on my jeans and set the bowl in the middle of what is now a cat maelstrom. The mewing quiets as kittens and cats clamber for drinks. When the last of the milk is gone, Jacinda plucks a kitten from the group. It settles into her lap to lick cream from its paws and whiskers.

"That's Ferocious Tiger."

"For the stripes?"

"Mmm-hmm."

She presses the pads of his paws and inspects his claws. She touches their points, lets them retract. She runs her hand down his back. Ferocious Tiger purrs and pushes his cheek into Jacinda's hand.

I know how Ferocious Tiger feels. It's how I feel about Rajas's touch: I rush to meet it, press myself into him.

Oh man, please do not tell me that's how Jacinda feels about Brookner.

And please, please do not tell me that's how Brookner feels about Jacinda! I'm all for following your heart, but not if your heart is a nasty old wolf trying to seduce an innocent puppy.

"So. That was kind of weird, at Brookner's," I say. Sitting on the milking stool, higher than Jacinda, feels too cross-examiny. I plop down on the straw.

Jacinda keeps her eyes on the kitten in her lap. "Yeah. I am really not liking snakes right now. Not liking snakes at all."

I readjust my ponytail. "You and Brookner seemed very...comfortable together."

Her head snaps up so fast that Ferocious Tiger mewls. "What do you mean?"

"I mean"—I select my words with care—"he seems quite...familiar with you. And you with him."

She smiles down at Ferocious Tiger. Her cheeks darken. "You think so?" She asks it the same way I talk about Rajas. This is not good.

"Uh-huh." I undo my ponytail and twist it into a bun.

She doesn't look up. "Like what, for instance?"

Oh no. The girl wants to bask in the details. I need to change the course of this conversation. "Don't get mad—but when I was upstairs looking for Javier, I overheard something."

Her eyes get wide. "What do you mean?"

"The baby monitor was on in his office."

All color leaves her face.

"The transmitter part is in the kitchen, next to Booker's door," I continue.

Her hand is poised, motionless, over Ferocious Tiger.

"I didn't mean to eavesdrop. But it was on while I was catching Javier."

"What did you hear?" On the blanket, her foot starts wiggling. She sets her hand on the kitten but forgets to stroke him.

"It kind of sounded like something is going on."

"What's that supposed to mean?"

She's not making this easy. Fine. I'll just put it out there: "Is Brookner crossing the line with you? Are you two—" What are the right words? "Uh, involved? Romantically?"

Her face becomes ashen. "I don't think that's, like, any of your business."

"I don't mean to be nosy. But I'm concerned. You can talk to me."

She pats Ferocious Tiger's head. She seems deep in thought. She opens her mouth to speak, but closes it again.

I wait.

"Ohmigod, I'm so fricking tired," she finally says, stretching and yawning for emphasis.

Okay, she needs more time. Press gently, ask the questions, wait. Let the person come to you, let it be their own idea.

"Come on." I offer my hand. "Let's get some sleep. You can bring Ferocious Tiger in, if you want."

"Martha won't mind?"

"We usually don't because of fleas and ticks in summer. But you may have noticed we're not real sticklers for rules around here. Besides, it's cooling off, so it'll be fine. He seems to really like you."

In the morning we pull on sweatshirts and thick socks and jam our feet into rubber chore boots. Jacinda follows me to the henhouse. She tips her mug to her lips—real coffee instead of yerba maté to ease her introduction to hippie farm life. "Do you always get up this early?" she asks, cupping her mug for warmth. "It's fricking freezing."

"Hannah Bramble and the piranha chickens wait for no one. We usually take turns, but Martha had to do it the whole time my ankle was hurting, so I owe her." I open the door of the chicken coop and shift the hens to gather eggs.

"Ew! Those eggs are all covered with dirt."

It's not dirt, it's chicken poop, but I'll keep that tidbit of information to myself for now.

"We're going to eat those?" she asks.

I laugh. "Where do you think eggs come from, exactly?"

"The grocery store, exactly?" She shivers.

"The barn will be warmer. Go on in. I'll be there in a sec."

"Okay."

She's already settled on the blanket when I come in. I scootch up the milking stool, wash Hannah Bramble's teats, grab the cats' bowl. Kittens and cats come tumbling out from the nether reaches of the barn.

"Ferocious Tiger!" Jacinda squeals. "There you are!" He disappeared at some point last night. Martha must have let him out.

We are quiet. Jacinda drinks her coffee, the cats mewl until I give them their bowl of steamy cream.

Breathing in Hannah Bramble's warm, honest scent, I plunk down a clean milk pail and milk her in earnest.

After an interval of quiet, Jacinda's foot starts wiggling. "Can you keep a secret?"

I laugh without breaking my milking rhythm. "Maybe you should have asked me that *before* we started PLUTOs." Hannah Bramble's tail swishes. "You better hope I can, or you're not getting in to Cornell."

She gives a wry smile. "I think you mean that *you* won't be getting in. Blackmail works both ways." She sighs, changing the subject. "Okay. You know how you eavesdropped on me and Brookner last night?"

"Overheard. Eavesdropping implies intent."

"Whatever." She reaches for Ferocious Tiger, lifts

him onto her lap. "So, yeah. Brookner and I have been, like, talking. On the internet."

"You've been talking on the internet, as in e-mailing about assignments? Or talking on the internet, as in—" Oh no. I flash back to her checking e-mail on her phone, saving herself for...*Please* no. "Is Brookner your InterWeb Lover?"

"Shut up!" She sounds almost pleased. "He's not my *lover*. But, yeah, he's, like, the one I've been sort of...seeing...online."

"Jacinda. That is *so* not okay." Hannah Bramble lows a complaint about my tone. Deep yoga breath. Rein it in. Managing to sound a bit calmer, I say, "It's not okay, you know that, right?" I pat Hannah Bramble to let her know we're done milking. "He's a cool teacher. But he's our *teacher*."

"It's not like that! He knows I'm young—"

I can't hold back my snort. I regret it right away.

"I am really not appreciating your judgmentalness right now." Ferocious Tiger jumps off her lap and prances out of the barn.

"I'm sorry. I am. But—"

"We don't *do* anything." She picks at the blanket. "Even though I want to. Last week at his place I told him I'm ready to—"

"Last week! You've been getting together with him? In person?" I can't believe this.

She sighs like I'm slow. "Just once. Before last night's baby-sitting, I mean."

"Why didn't you tell me? Wait. Does Rajas know?"

She levels a stare. Right. Of course he doesn't know. He would burst into flames.

"You have to stop. It's not okay. He's our teacher, for crying out loud."

"It's platonic!" She hits the blanket, releasing straw dust into the chilly air. "He says we have to wait until I graduate before we can do anything."

I stare at Hannah Bramble without really seeing her. "Jacinda. Any way you look at it, this crosses the line. There are boundaries."

Jacinda pops up from the blanket. "He told me this would happen! That in the end you'd be just the same as everyone else. I stuck up for you!"

"You talk about *me*?"

"No! Just that he said you might not be as cool as you appear." She blows out a big breath. "I don't know, Evie. This, like, sucks. I expected more from you."

Her disappointment confuses my heart.

Agitated, her body is quivering. "You're the one who's into questioning authority. 'Fight the power' and all? But you're judging us because he's older. That's, like, ageism. I thought you were supposed to be different."

Damn. A punch to the gut. This girl *is* different. Am I being hasty and judgmental? Or has Brookner already anticipated my disapproval and done some masterful manipulation? "Jacinda, don't you see? He wants to turn us against each other. Divide and conquer."

She looks frantic, like an animal that's been spooked.

I calm my voice again. "For a teacher to be with his student is an abuse of power. Do any of your other friends know about this?"

"No!" Jacinda uncrosses her arms, recrosses them. She starts to pace, so distraught that she doesn't seem to mind tromping through dirty straw. "It's *not* abusing power! Abusing power is like Ms. Gliss telling Marcie that she is fat. *That* is an abuse of power. John would never do something like that."

"John?" First names now? I swallow to tamp down my emotions. "Jacinda, it is not okay." Maybe repetition will get through to her. "This is as bad as Ms. Gliss, in a different way." Something else is nagging at me, something about how Rajas warns us about Brookner, how Rajas is always alluding to rumors and *what Nishi said*, how he calls Brookner sketchy. "Hold on. Has Brookner done this before, with other girls?"

It's like pushing a button. Jacinda's eyes go wild. She yells, "You don't know anything about any of this! You're a virgin! You just started school!" She whips out her phone.

"What are you doing?"

She turns her back.

I can tell she's tapping the screen. She brings the phone to her ear and shakes her head. No answer? She taps the screen again, holds it to her ear. "Hi," she says in an unconvincing perky voice. "I'm sorry to bother you so early, but can you do me, like, a huge favor? I need a ride? Can you get your mom's car?" She pauses. "Okay. Thanks anyway." Pause. "No, I'm fine. It's fine. I'll see you tomorrow."

"Who are you talking to?" I ask.

She ignores me. More tapping; she's calling someone else. "It's me. I need you to come pick me up." Pause. "No, I'm still at Evie's. How soon can you get here?"

It's Rajas. It has to be. Who else knows where I live? She must have tried other friends first...but how would they have found their way here? The Dome Home is not a main feature on Google maps.

She's listening to her phone, nodding. "Okay. And also? I am so sure that Evie's going to try to tell you some things? You shouldn't believe her. Seriously, it's bullshit." She glares at me, distant and cold. "Let's just put it this way: Evie's not as cool as we thought she was."

The attempt to combine wisdom and power has only rarely been successful and then only for a short while.

—Albert Einstein, physicist and Nobel Prize winner, 1879–1955

16

Monday's drive to school feels especially long. Martha is sulking in the passenger seat, taking it as a personal affront that I'm withholding information. After Jacinda left in her huff, Martha demanded details. I said we had a disagreement about a guy she's seeing—someone at school who is not good for her. Which is the truth, as far as it goes. But Martha can tell it isn't the *whole* truth. It's the first time in history that she hasn't been privy to every last drop of information about my life. I hate holding back, but I can't tell her. Not until I have more time to think, talk to Rajas, talk to Jacinda. I have to figure out what to do, because if Martha found out it was a teacher, she'd tar and feather Brookner, whether I wanted her to or not.

A man abusing his authority with one of her daughter's friends? Good luck, Brookner. You'd need it.

Jacinda and I haven't talked since she left my house. She won't answer my calls or respond to my texts. She made Rajas take her home before I could even kiss him hello or goodbye. Later, when I called him, Rajas was brusque and aloof: "I should go. I have to help my mom seal the driveway."

Seal the driveway? I sat on my hands for twenty minutes and then finally texted him. *R U OK?*

Late that afternoon, he responded. *WNTT. Mon lunch.*

WNTT? I didn't know that one. My mind flipped through the possibilities until it came to me: *We need to talk.* My stomach fell to my feet.

I wrote, *Y?*

There was no response. An entire weekend of total radio silence.

Now it's time for school. As I bump The Clunker onto the paved road, I ask Martha to check my phone for the millionth time.

"Anything?" I ask.

"No. Sorry, darling." She reaches for my hair. "Everything will be okay. Be strong." Martha strokes my hair until we get to Walmart. She's got a bag of peace symbols we made, to paste onto the toy guns. It's her turn to stock the toy section. She kisses me on the cheek. "Call if you need me." She wrestles with the door handle. "But don't let The Man catch you with your phone."

I arrive at school in a daze. It's hard to move with my insides tied in knots, but I cruise the halls looking for Rajas before first bell.

He's nowhere to be seen.

I take my seat in Global View. Jacinda stops talking to Marcie when I walk into the room. She sits, arms crossed, foot waggling. Brookner's not here yet.

"Hi, Jacinda." Can she tell I'm freaking out? About our fight? About her silence? About Rajas? About her freaking *love affair* with the teacher who is about to walk in? "Um. How was the rest of your weekend?"

Jacinda won't look at me.

I try again. "Did you do anything fun?"

She hugs her arms tighter across her chest. "No."

Well, at least she said *something*. More of this silence would be unbearable. "Do you know—is Rajas mad?"

"How would I know?"

"He didn't call or text much, and I was so worried when you didn't call back, either. Hey, do you want to get together after school? I have an extra hour until I pick up Martha."

She keeps her eyes on the doorway, as if she's dying to see Brookner. "No. I've got Cheer Squad." She sits bolt upright and her cheeks go red; Brookner's here.

She whispers, so faint I almost can't hear, "And don't you *dare* say anything about the quote." She nods toward the board, the words about power and wisdom.

But Jacinda used to love that I respond to quotes. Now I'm supposed to keep quiet?

Brookner flicks his gaze at Jacinda but his expression doesn't change. He stands in front of the board, rocks on his heels, claps his hands, rocks back. Blech. I've been so preoccupied with Jacinda and Rajas, I hadn't thought about how it would be to see Brookner again. I don't want to look at him. I'm overflowing with disgust. What kind of teacher thinks it's okay to have a relationship with a student? Revolting.

"Class, settle," Brookner says. "Good morning. Today's quote is from Einstein, about power, hmm? Comments? Reactions?"

Of course no one responds.

Brookner adjusts his glasses. "Evie? How about it?"

He seems vile to me now, like he has an affliction. His lack of boundaries is a pus oozing from his pores.

"Evie?" he repeats.

Jacinda's whispered warning echoes in my brain. My throat stings as I hear myself say, "No."

"You don't wish to respond?" Brookner seems genuinely surprised.

I stare at my desk. My stomach is wringing itself—

and I realize that I am furious. Yes, Jacinda is my friend. But she's not my keeper. I don't take orders from anyone. Why should I feel sheepish about speaking up now? That's not who I am. Or who I want to be. This girl is different.

"Well. I guess we'll get started. If you will all turn to page—"

I raise my hand. "Actually, I do have something to say."

Jacinda takes a sharp breath. Her foot stops wiggling.

"I agree with Einstein," I say, steeling myself against Jacinda. Will she go ballistic? "Wisdom and power rarely go together. If at all."

Brookner smiles. "Yes, well. Wisdom is a fairly rare commodity, isn't it?"

I hold his stare without blinking. "That's beside the point."

"How so?"

"The point of the quote is that wisdom only really matters when someone has power over someone else. A doctor and a patient, for example. It wouldn't matter much if a *patient* was wise. She—or he—doesn't have the power in the situation." I straighten my shoulders. "What's not okay is when the person with power does not have wisdom."

Jacinda's foot is wiggling again, hard—like a rattlesnake shaking its warning. Tense, coiled, ready to strike. Brookner, on the other hand, seems relaxed. He smoothes his tie and waits.

"A doctor," I continue, biting my tongue to keep from adding *or a teacher*, "should be wise. Should observe boundaries. Or he should relinquish his power. One or the other. Power without wisdom is the definition of arrogance."

"Well put. Thank you, Evie."

Does he not see the irony? Or is this fun for him?

I peek at Jacinda. Her expression is a cascade of animosity.

The class period sloshes by. As soon as the bell drones, I turn to Jacinda. "Please just listen. I—"

"Do *not* talk to me. Ohmigod, I cannot even believe that you—" She lowers her voice to a contemptuous whisper. "It's like you wanted to tell the whole class!"

"Jacinda, no! That's not—"

"Do not talk to me."

Bad. This is bad. I search for Rajas between classes. He is in none of his usual places. Is he avoiding me or what? By lunch, my nerves and stomach are completely frazzled. I'm at the shop room door, scared out of my mind. What if it's locked? Are the clandestine make-out lunches history? Head dreading, heart hoping, I try the knob. It turns, the door opens. I breathe deep relief. Rajas is waiting for me.

But something's wrong. Instead of greeting me with a long kiss, he is standing stock-still. His face is serious, fixed.

My heart flops into my neck.

What has Jacinda said to him? Is he giving me the silent treatment too? Or worse—worst of all—is he ending things? Damn it. Do we qualify for break-up status if we were never labeled in the first place? My heart, flopping around like a dying fish, seems to think so.

I've lost my best girlfriend. And now I'm going to lose the boy I'm in love with. Both in one day.

How can things have gone from status quo, to sprained ankle and ecstatic heart, to total train wreck, in such a short time?

I open my mouth to talk—to say *what,* exactly?—but Rajas beats me to it.

"I'm done with this." His voice is steeped in hate. "It has to end."

14

Well-behaved women seldom make history.

—Laurel Thatcher Ulrich, historian, b. 1938

My hands go to my stomach like I've been punched. He's ending it. What did Jacinda *say* to make him hate me so much?

Or have his feelings for me just...changed? Disappeared? As if they weren't even that strong in the first place?

I don't know which is worse.

I can't speak.

Rajas's hands fly up. "Eve?" He takes my elbows.

"Stop," I say through gritted teeth. If he wants to end it, fine. I'll survive. But to be so cold and cruel—*it has to end*—then flip a switch and act concerned? No. It's humiliating. I wrench free of him. "So. That's it." I swipe at my tears and set my jaw.

His forehead rumples in confusion. "What's wrong? I thought you'd agree."

"Agree? Why on earth would I agree?"

"Because Brookner's sketch. It's nasty."

"Because Brookner? What…?" I shake my head, trying to think.

"Yes, Brookner and Jay," he says. "It has to end."

"Wait." Hope! Joy! My heart races. "We're not breaking up?"

His eyes widen. "Eve. Why would I do that? Not that I like the term *breaking up*. It's such a label…" His complexion goes blotchy. "Why? Do you want to?"

"No!"

"Well, good." He gives me his lopsided smile. "Holy crap. You freaked me out for a second."

"I freaked *you* out? You freaked *me* out. What was with the cold shoulder all weekend?"

"There was no cold shoulder. My shoulders are very warm."

I give him a look that says *answer the question.*

He says, "I had to seal the driveway, like I told you. And we had family stuff all weekend. Jacinda was there, so I couldn't really talk."

"You couldn't find one minute to call me?"

"You're right. I should have called," he says. "I'm sorry."

"I was worried."

"Allow me to reassure you."

"With your warm shoulders?"

"Exactly." He wraps his arms around me. We kiss. I make it intense, backing him up against a workbench and pressing hard. It feels so good...so necessary. The world dissolves away.

We are still kissing when the bell rings.

"Damn, Eve," he says, his voice hoarse, "I wish we weren't in school right now."

"No kidding." We kiss again. I can't get enough of him.

"Eve. We have to go."

With great reluctance, we pull ourselves apart and step into the hallway.

"Like I was saying." Rajas speaks only loud enough for me to hear, walking right next to him. "This thing with Jacinda and Brookner is nasty. Has to end."

"I couldn't agree more. But how?"

I meet Rajas in the parking lot after school. We duck into the back of The Clunker and evaporate into each other, kissing.

After a while, I pry myself away from him. "Martha's shift ends soon."

Rajas touches my cheek, his eyelids heavy. "We have a little more time."

"I know," I mutter between kisses, "but we need to talk about Jacinda."

"Do we really?" His hands find their way under my shirt. He glides his fingertips along my ribs.

"How did you find out about her and Brookner?" I persist. "She didn't tell you, did she?"

He sighs. "No. When I picked her up from your place, she said you were being mean."

I start to sink, thinking about Jacinda's anger, but Rajas buoys me. His touch keeps me floating.

"Seemed weird." He shrugs. "Can't see you being catty."

"Meow." I claw his arm.

Smiling, he runs his thumb over my waist. Can he feel my stomach somersault? "She's been acting weird for a while. Then, on Friday—"

"At Brookner's?" His touch is so mesmerizing it's a strain to concentrate.

"Yeah. Jay seemed so out of it. I knew something was up. So I finally managed to drag it out of her yesterday. I told you he was a slimeball." He makes an angry noise in the back of his throat. "Did she come right out and tell you? How did you find out?"

"I overheard her and Brookner when I was looking for the snake."

He grimaces; his fingers stop moving for an excruciating moment. "There are rumors. That he's hooked up with his students before."

"Wait, does this have to do with Nishi? You said

something to Jacinda about 'remember what Nishi said'?"

He rolls onto his back, the moment officially ruined by our miserable conversation. "Yeah. Nishi told us Brookner hit on her friend."

"Nishi's the older one, right?" He has two sisters, both at Boston University.

He nods.

"You could call her." I sit up. "She could check with her friend and find out what really happened."

"But even if it isn't true—"

"There's still Jacinda."

"Yeah." He rubs his nose. "It's like a bad '80s song. 'Hot for Teacher.'"

"We could confront Brookner," I say. "Tell him we know what's up."

"I don't see what good that would do. It wouldn't stop him. And he'd tell Jay we talked to him. She'd probably stop talking to us."

"She's already not talking to me."

Rajas looks surprised. "Really?"

"As of Global View today."

He reaches for my hand, like he senses how painful her silence is for me. "I knew she was mad. But that sucks."

My throat gets dry and lumpy. "Brookner's quote was about power today."

"What else is new?"

"She didn't want me to say anything. But I got stubborn, so I did say something."

"No! You? You got stubborn and spoke out?" He smiles. "That never happens."

"I know, I know. But you wouldn't believe how upset Jacinda got. She told me not to talk to her."

Rajas blows out a big breath. "That's what I'm saying. She's not herself. She's being unreasonable, and weird."

"Love can do that." I lie down and nestle onto his shoulder. "It can make you insecure and irrational and...afraid. It makes you crazy."

"Love? Makes you crazy?"

My heart thumps. I hold my breath.

He shifts. "Are you talking about Jay? Or...us?"

Deep yoga breath, courage. "Both."

He is silent and perfectly still for an agonizing moment. Then he wraps his arms around me. "Love, huh?" He nuzzles my neck. "I can deal with that label. For this, me and you. But not Hot for Teacher."

Even though my heart is leaping, dancing—*love! He loves me!*—I manage to adopt a serious tone. "Right. Love is a no-no for teachers and students. Love is a yes-yes for boyfriends and—"

Rajas groans.

"Oh, my goodness." I make my eyes wide to emphasize how very understanding I am. "What was I thinking?

We are not boyfriend and girlfriend! We are...um..." I frown, serious now. "What are we?"

"We're this." He kisses me. We lose ourselves again.

In the distance, a phone rings.

No, not in the distance. Right here in my bag.

I sit up. "Oh no! I forgot Martha!" I find my phone, flip it open. "I'll be there in two seconds!" I snap it shut to curtail her rant. "I have to go. Crap. When are we going to figure out what to do about—"

"Brookner." He scowls.

Clambering over to the driver's seat, I tell him, "I'll drive you over to the Biohazard."

"Okay." Rajas climbs into the passenger seat. "So Jay's really that into him?"

"She is really that into him." I crank the key in The Clunker's ignition.

"How would you know how into someone you are without even kissing them?" His mouth drops open and he looks horrified. "Holy crap! Has he kissed her? I'll clock that joker!"

"No no no!" I wave my hands for emphasis. "No. According to Jacinda, Brookner says they have to wait until graduation."

Rajas's eyes bug out. "*Brookner says*? Graduation! And then what?" The boy is going to explode.

"Calm down! Breathe."

His breath comes out as a growl. "She did *not* tell me any of that."

"So I gathered." Finally, The Clunker's engine chuffs, sputters, starts. I roll the forty feet to Rajas's parking space, thinking. "What if we tell Dr. Folger?"

He shakes his head. "I don't think I could betray Jay like that. Not to mention, it'd be our word against Brookner's and Jay's, and they'd deny it."

"You're right. And it would alienate her more. Push her further away."

"Yeah." He rubs his face.

Still trying to think, I stop next to the Biohazard. "Wait—I have it!" I slap the dashboard. "Lightning!"

He looks puzzled, and then gives a slow grin. "Oh, nice! That's perfect."

My mind races. "But she'd know it was us."

"Wouldn't matter," Rajas says, "because then the whole thing would be out in the open. And we don't even need to name Jay, or mention her at all."

"Right. Right. It will shame Brookner into stopping."

"If he has any ounce of decency."

"Which is definitely not a foregone conclusion."

He runs his thumb along the dashboard as he thinks. "Jay could rat us out—"

"To Dr. Folger?" I finish his thought. "But how would she explain she knew it was us? She'd have to admit her role in PLUTOs and the lightning against Ms. Gliss. Dr. Folger would drag a confession out of her."

"But she has the right to remain silent," he counters.

"I bet she's not allowed to plead the Fifth. I mean, if First Amendment protections—free speech, freedom of the press—don't apply in school, why would Fifth?"

Rajas lifts an eyebrow at my mini-tirade.

"Don't look at me like that. You're the one who brought up the Bill of Rights."

"The what? The swill of bites? Sounds vaguely familiar. Where have I heard that before?"

"You, my friend, would be in grave danger of flunking homeschool."

"Oh, the shame!" He laughs. "Don't worry. I know my AmHist."

"AmHist? That sounds like cough medicine."

He ignores me. "First Amendment is religion and speech and press. Second is arms. Third was anachronistic and therefore my brain does not care. Fourth, search and seizure. Fifth is 'You have the right to remain silent'." He looks very pleased with himself. "Do I get an A, teacher?"

"I don't believe in grades. They're just a form of labels."

"Doh!" He laughs.

I kiss him.

"Uh-oh. Another teacher-student relationship." He's

joking, but when his words sink in, we pull away. A scowl dampens his sepia features. We're back to Jacinda and Brookner.

"She'll be incredibly furious at us if we strike Brookner," I say. "Spitting mad. Hopping mad."

"She's already spitting and hopping," Rajas says.

"True." Just thinking about her silent treatment twists my insides. "But if we strike Brookner, she won't speak to me for *years.*"

"She'll come around. Jay never holds a grudge for long. We'll give it a few days before we do the lightning. Maybe next week." He reaches out, takes my hand. "She'll be talking to you by then. You'll probably already be sick of all the yammering. Trust me." He smiles his gorgeous crooked grin. "Besides, what's the worst that could happen?"

"Uh, Cornell?"

"Yeah. Okay. That would be bad," he concedes. "But I meant with Jay. She can't not talk to you more than she already is."

"Right. Right." I hug my stomach. "Then why do I feel like horking?"

"Look, even if everything else goes to crap...you have me. We're in this together. All for one and one for all."

"Hmm. Sounds vaguely familiar," I say.

18

Publicity is justly commended as a remedy for social and industrial diseases. Sunlight is said to be the best of disinfectants; electric light the most efficient policeman.

—Louis Brandeis, American Supreme Court Justice, 1856–1941

I sigh and run my hand along the cinder blocks as I make my way to first bell. Global View has become my own personal Ninth Circle of Hell. I can't stand the sight of Brookner—I shudder to think of him letching after Jacinda or any other girls. I keep having images of him as a nasty, youth-sucking, power-hungry lamprey. Worse still is Jacinda's ongoing silent treatment. How can wordlessness be so damned loud? Despite Rajas's constant assurance that she'll forgive me, right now she won't even look at me. The last few days have been torture. In the movies, everyone hates high school, and I'm starting to comprehend why. It has nothing to do with pedagogy or educational philosophy. It's the humans.

Like Sartre said in *No Exit*, "Hell is other people."

Perfect quote for Brookner's whiteboard.

Crap. I'm getting more jaded by the minute. Martha would blame The Institution of School. And I must admit, I'd like nothing better than to be homeschooling right now, designing a community, pulling weeds, cloud watching, mucking out the barn, doing an on-line assignment, sketching wildlife. Actually, no: I'd like nothing better than to be with Rajas right now. Alone. Butterflies flutter in my stomach; my cheeks heat up just thinking about it.

First things first: Global View. Jacinda and Brookner.

But wait a minute. Everyone's milling around the classroom door, students frothing in a small hubbub. Getting closer, I catch snippets of conversation:

—What's this one for?

—Whoever it was...

—I heard something was going on...

Oh my God. Brookner's door is emblazoned with a huge bolt of lightning. The PLUTOs website is written in drippy red paint, caking now, like dried blood.

Rajas and I were going to strike *next* week! To give Jacinda time to cool down and come to her senses.

So who did this?

In uncanny unison, the crowd turns. And once again, it's a wall of eyes.

"Class. Settle." Brookner's here; he parts the crowd. Kids step back like no one wants to stand too close to him. Brookner unlocks the classroom, acting casual. "Please. After you." He sweeps his arm magnanimously. He's clutching a laptop.

Everyone takes their seats. The board is blank—no quote, which could mean that Brookner isn't as calm as he seems. Did he see the lightning strike and turn tail? Fleeing to...where? The men's room? The teacher's lounge?

Jacinda's not here. I say hi to Marcie; we've gotten friendlier since the lightning strike against Ms. Gliss.

Whispers wheeze around the room while Brookner sets the computer on his desk. He wheels the TV cart out of its corner. No way. He's going to display the PLUTOs site? How is that a good idea? Can he seriously be more interested in *what* is written about him than he is worried that *anything* is written about him in the first place?

Well, good. I want to know what it says.

"Sorry, I, uh..." Brookner says, poking a button on the laptop, "...don't have a quote up yet. It's been quite an eventful morning, as you can see." He smiles and looks up, fidgeting with his tie. Marcie titters, catches my eyes, and swings to look away. Brookner rocks onto his heels. "Hmm. Well." He grabs a marker and twists the cap off, begins to write a quote on the board about sunlight being a good disinfectant. Sounds familiar. It's the seed Martha planted in Dr. Folger's ear. Maybe Dr.

Folger passed that little gem on to Brookner.

Around me, students are exchanging wide-eyed glances. Marcie and Matt and Stiv keep looking at me like maybe I know something about this. When the bell rings, Brookner jerks, messing up the *S* at the end of *Brandeis*. The mistake betrays his nervousness; clearly he's not as composed as he wants us to think. He erases the mistake before snapping the cap onto his marker. Looking straight at me, he opens his mouth to speak. And then closes it again when Jacinda rushes past him, her head down. All eyes follow her—she's never late—as she sets her books on her desk and smoothes her short skirt to sit down.

I whip out my notebook and scribble a note to Jacinda: *It wasn't who you think it was!* I stare at the paper, cross out the words, start over. I wish I could just write *This wasn't me and Rajas! Do you know who did it?* but I can't write our names, lest the note fall into enemy hands. I settle on *We need to talk, please!* and tear it quietly from the wire spiral. As soon as Brookner turns his back, I pass it to Jacinda.

She lets it drop to the floor. In slow motion, she turns to lock me in a baleful stare.

Brookner connects the computer to the television. "I chose today's quote because..." His voice trails off. "Well. 'Sunlight is the best disinfectant.'" He shifts his weight and leans against his desk. "Brandeis is saying that things are best put out there in the open, hmm? Rumors, accusations, the best thing is simply to air them." He's looking a little pale. "Just put it out there, and don't let it fester. Light will shine. The notion of transparency, making things transparent." Pulling his glasses off and inspecting them, he uses his tie to clean the lenses. It's as though he's trying to distract himself so he can keep from coming unglued. "Yes, well. Why not just go straight to the website? Anyone remember the blog address?"

Silence.

"No one?" He crosses his arms. "Evie? How about it?"

I shake my head while my stomach mops the floor.

"No?" He sounds disappointed. "Well. Fortunately, we have a reference." He opens the door, startling Mr. Heck, the janitor, who is wielding a spackle knife. He has managed to remove half of the lightning bolt. Brookner picks up two of the larger scraped-off pieces and studies them. "Cardboard this time, I see."

Brookner closes the door unceremoniously in Mr. Heck's face and returns to the laptop. He types in the address from the scraps. The PLUTOs blog appears on the TV. "For those of you without smartphones." He reads, "'We, the People's Lightning to Undermine True Oppression (PLUTOs) hold these truths to be self-evident…' Yes, yes." He scrolls down the screen. "Ah. Here we are.

"'First lightning strike: Ms. G. for blatant sexism…' Yes yes.

"'Second, the PLUTOs put a strike on Brookner's door. Because he crosses the line with his female students.'"

Brookner sits down fast. "Most interesting. Interesting. Yes, well." It's as close to speechless as I've ever seen him. He smoothes his tie again, readjusts his glasses. He looks at me. "Much different tone to this entry."

I nod: a slight movement that doesn't divulge the tsunami of relief rushing through me. Thank God! Brookner, at least, realizes it wasn't me this time. Now I just have to convince Jacinda. I slide my foot out to retrieve the neglected note; I've got to try again. Just before my toe gets there, Jacinda snatches it. Without unfolding the note, she puts it on her desk and lays her hands over it. Turning to regard me with a look of icy hate, she raises her hand.

"Jacinda?" Brookner sounds agitated. Standing, unsteady, he rocks onto his heels. "You…you would like to address the class?" He sounds like what he wants to say is, *Please, for the love of all things good and holy, keep quiet!*

She nods.

"Okay. Well. Enlighten us."

She drums her fingers, her polished nails pounding

her perturbation. "I think that the quote is about trust." There goes her foot again, shaking, shaking.

"Trust?" He frowns. "How so?"

"Because you might think that sunlight is best for things, but it's not. Because you basically can't *trust* people. People spread *lies*. And those people should know"—her fingers stop drumming—"that other people have sunlight of their *own*."

"Yes. Well." Brookner blinks at Jacinda's baffling contribution, but the way he looks from her to me, he can tell something's rotten in the state of Friendmark. "Anyone else?"

Without enthusiasm, I raise my hand. "The quote means that *anyone* can bring things to light and say whatever they want. You might never even know who."

"Yes, that would be the point, wouldn't it?" Brookner asks with an impish smirk.

For a moment I return his smile, forgetting myself, glad to glimpse the intriguing Brookner, the guy who likes coloring outside the lines. Except—no. Having an affair with a student? That's coloring way too far outside the lines. It's another coloring book altogether.

Not that Martha ever gave me coloring books. My childhood was all kraft paper murals and sloppy paints.

Brookner gets serious again. "The problem is that once people speak up, you have no control over it."

"Exactly," I say. Palms up, I ask, "But what can you do? That's the price of democracy. And free speech. Anyone can say anything." I feel like kicking Jacinda's chair and screaming, *Do you get it, girl?*

"Well. Anything except libel, which means defamation in print." Brookner freezes, eyes hazy. "Most interesting," he mutters to himself. He goes back into motion, yanking the laptop cable out of the TV. "Shall we change the subject? Global View. How about it?" He goes to the board, selects a marker, and starts writing.

I take a deep yoga breath. Sure, this seems like a disaster. Someone has hijacked PLUTOs and the lightning, taken things into their own hands. Jacinda thinks it's me. But...breathe. Calm down. Think. I didn't do anything wrong. It's not the end of the world. Rajas is on my side. We'll get everything sorted out.

Still, I have to wonder if this whole Institution of School experiment is really worth it. I didn't meet Rajas and Jacinda at school; I met them in a creek in the state forest. If I'd stayed a homeschooler, Rajas and I could have fallen in love anyway. And Jacinda and I could be friends. If only I hadn't had a class with her and Brookner, if only I hadn't spoken up, if only we hadn't started PLUTOs. If only Cornell wasn't on the line.

But that's a lot of if-onlys, and a lot of lightning has struck between each of them.

I take another deep breath.

A note lands on my desk. From Jacinda. Please tell me she knows Rajas and I didn't do it!

It's the piece of paper I passed to her earlier. She scribbled on it without opening it. My heart sinks while I read her curly handwriting: *Be careful what you wish for—free speech, democracy. YOU are NOT immune.*

What is that supposed to mean? I start to scribble a response, but a rapid-fire knocking stops me. Someone's at the classroom door.

It swings open. It is Dr. Folger, standing next to Mr. Heck.

Brookner's face goes slack with dread; he can't hide it this time.

Dr. Folger says, "Excuse the interruption, Mr. Brookner. Students." He whispers something to Brookner. Listening, Brookner nods. The corners of his mouth turn down; he looks as though he's received a temporary reprieve but knows he's still got a lot to answer for.

"Evie. Would you please go with Dr. Folger?"

As I stand, visions of my future whirl in my mind, blurred images being sucked down a drain. This school is a gigantic toilet, flushing away my chance at Cornell.

There's a very optimistic premise that I have, which is, if you give people tools, their natural ability, their curiosity, will develop it in ways that will surprise you very much beyond what you might have expected.

—Bill Gates, founder of Microsoft, b. 1955

19

Somehow, Martha is here. She rushes out of Dr. Folger's office, where she has been tampering with his collection of Slinkies, setting them up to descend from shelf to filing cabinet to desk to chair. She gathers me into a hug. "Darling."

"How'd you get here?"

"Taxi." She smiles at Ms. Franklin. "Thanks again for the tea, Melinda."

Mrs. Franklin sets down her can of Diet Coke. "You're quite welcome."

Martha relegates me to her left arm so she can shake a finger at Ms. Franklin. "Not for nothing, I'll give you some advice. You've got to quit the juice. Those artificial sweeteners will kill you."

Ms. Franklin looks at her soda can. "I'll take that into consideration."

"Corporations profiting by poisoning. Poison profits," Martha sucks her teeth and seems about to commence rant—I smell a new sticker campaign for Walmart—but Dr. Folger is all business.

Walking past Martha, he gestures to the chairs in his office. "Please, come in."

He slides the nameplate on his door to the center of its track. "Ms. Mornin—" He shakes his head and says, "Evie. And Mrs.—" Frowning, he corrects himself again, "Martha. Take a seat."

We sit. The diploma from Cornell seems three times the size it was the other day. It looms over the entire room. Martha holds my hand.

Dr. Folger tips one of the Slinkies that Martha set up. We watch it walk from one surface to the next until it droops onto his chair. He picks it up and sits. "Evie. This time. Was it you?" No preamble. *This time, was it you?* like he assumes it was me the last time and he's not sure about today.

Martha doesn't wait for me to answer. "Darling. Did...Mr. Brookner...did he do anything to you?"

"No." I shake my head. "It wasn't me."

"Wasn't you he did it to, darling?"

Dr. Folger says, "Or wasn't you who—"

"He didn't do anything to me and I didn't do the lightning."

Martha considers this and pats my hand. "Even if you did do, my love, there's no harm in speaking out." A pointed look over the desk. "Is there, Dr. Folger?"

He grimaces. "Let us unpack that statement, if you will, Martha. And Evie." He clears his throat. "Is there harm in speaking out? Yes, and no. I value freedom of expression. However, I also believe that such freedom comes with responsibility. They are two sides of the same coin, shall we say. We can't go around publishing wild allegations." He ripples the Slinky. "I have a school to run. Students to look after. Teachers' good names to protect."

Martha squirms in her chair. Ten to one she's thinking his language of protection is both cause and effect of the hierarchy of The Institution of School.

Dr. Folger sets the Slinky on his desk blotter. "I happen to like you, Evie. It's clear you possess a keen mind, a strong moral foundation. Perhaps your spontaneity and judgmental streak could use some modulating, but that will come with time and experience, I suspect. The point is, the law is the law. Libel is illegal. Smearing somebody's good name when—"

"It isn't libel if the allegations are true." Martha is working very hard to keep her voice under control, keep her arms from whirling.

Dr. Folger says, "If there is evidence to conclude

guilt, then you are correct: the act is not libelous. Please be assured that I will investigate these allegations. Indeed I take them very seriously. I've already called Dr. Jones, the superintendent of schools. However, in the meantime—"

"Right, right. I get it," I interrupt. "You have to do...whatever it is you have to do."

Dr. Folger inclines his head, waiting for me to say more. Martha stares at me, shocked, I'm sure, at my apparent acquiescence.

"But it wasn't me." *Please,* I add silently, *don't ruin my chances for Cornell!* "I didn't make the accusation about Brookner. Did you notice the posting sounds entirely different?"

"Indeed?" He leans forward. "And how would you know that?"

Martha barricades me with her arm. "Don't answer that, my love!"

I nudge her back. "Martha, please." To Dr. Folger I say, "I know what it says because Brook—Mr. Brookner—showed it to us in class."

Dr. Folger's eyes go wide. "He *showed* the class?"

Martha looks equally surprised. "Why would—"

"He said sunlight is the best disinfectant."

"Did he now." Dr. Folger leans back, steepling his hands in front of him. "Most interesting. Justice Brandeis and the concept of transparency." He looks pointedly at Martha. "Interesting."

Martha shifts. "Huh. That's been coming up a lot lately." She shakes her head like she's refocusing. "Transparency is a concept employed by the most successful factions of the radical and not so radical—"

"Martha," I snap.

"Right." She pulls a pretend zipper across her lips. "Your turn, darling."

I turn to Dr. Folger. "That's how I know that this post is so different from the first one." I've got to be careful. "Whoever posted them, it seems to be different people."

Dr. Folger picks up the rainbow-colored Slinky. He moves it back and forth, as if he's weighing his thoughts. "As it happens, I did note the difference in tone. Of course that's small comfort to Mandy Gliss and John Brookner."

"John Brookner." Martha suddenly seems a thousand miles away. What's going on? I give her a look but she doesn't notice.

Dr. Folger also casts an inquisitive glance to Martha before he continues, "Quite inventive, isn't it, to have created a blog format so that anyone can join the..." He tilts the Slinky. "...discussion, shall we say?"

"Revolution," Martha corrects, still a little distant. She mutters, "The revolution will not be televised."

"No, but apparently it will be blogged." Dr. Folger smiles.

Martha smiles. "Apparently so." It seems like she's come back into the conversation, and, despite herself, is warming up to Dr. Folger. Good. Maybe she'll dial back the fanaticism.

"I just don't want this to get out of hand," I say. "If it's not okay to post lightning accusing teachers unless there's evidence, then it's not okay to accuse students of posting the lightning unless there's evidence. Right?"

"Darn tootin'!" Martha says.

"Indeed, it isn't. However, as you know: where there's smoke there's often—"

"A bong!" Martha quips. She snorts a laugh.

I could throttle her!

"What." Martha shrugs off the look I'm giving. She waves at the diplomas. "Dr. Folger went to school." Not having attended university herself, Martha conflates cannabis with college campuses.

Dr. Folger frowns, but with a glint in his eye. "Yes, well. What I meant is that I will be watching you, Evie. I am quite concerned about these developments."

I keep quiet and pray Martha will too.

Dr. Folger jiggles the rainbow Slinky. "I'm told that you've become quite close with Rajas Messer and Jacinda Harrod."

My stomach churns. I squeeze Martha's hand to keep her quiet. "They didn't..." I don't finish. How can I assert their innocence without incriminating myself?

"Please, Evie. You need not comment. Just be aware that I will be keeping tabs on them as well. Dr. Folger puts down the Slinky. "Meanwhile, it would behoove us all if the PLUTOs blog went off-line."

"Evie wouldn't know anything about that." Martha is indignant.

Dr. Folger regards her a moment, then speaks. "Be that as it may, it would simplify things immeasurably."

Crap. I'm stymied for a response, yet again. Should I plead the Fifth? Should I make a stand for the First Amendment? Should I break down in tears and beg for mercy? Should I scream that Rajas and Jacinda are innocent? I twist my hair. I want to do the right thing. I just have no clue what that is right now.

The Cornell diploma is growing so immense that it would crush all of us if it fell off Dr. Folger's office wall.

In the end, I remain silent, let Dr. Folger excuse us, hand The Clunker keys to Martha, and let her take me home.

This life of separateness may be compared to a dream, a phantasm, a bubble, a shadow, a drop of dew, a flash of lightning.

—The Buddha (Prince Siddhartha Gautama), founder of Buddhism, 563–483 BC

My heart flies when the Blue Biohazard thunders up my driveway. It's the sound I've been waiting for since I beat a hasty retreat from school this morning. Rajas texted during lunch to ask if he could come over after he helped his mom with something. Time has crawled. I need his support, his ear, his ideas for what to do. His lips, for distraction. And I have a question for him.

I come up from boat pose and bow a quick *Namaste* to the trees and clouds, then jog from my favorite grassy knoll to the driveway. Unlike the rest of me, my ankle feels fine. The Biohazard stops and I grab Rajas's hand to lead him to the barn.

"Where's Martha?"

"She went back to work, and I made her promise to

do her volunteer shift at the co-op after that."

"So it's just us?"

"And the cats and piranha chickens and Hannah Bramble."

"Let's go inside," he says.

"First I have a question: it wasn't you, was it? You didn't post the lightning on Brookner's door?"

"We agreed to wait a few days," he says.

Relief! "Oh, thank God. I didn't think you did it, but I just had to ask, you know?" I take his hand. "Come on, I want to show you something." I lead him up the ladder to the hayloft in the second floor of the barn. There's a swing up here, tied to the rafters, with such an amazing parabola you feel like you're flying.

When he sees it, his face lights up. "You put this here?"

"It was here when we moved in."

We swing. And then we kiss. As usual, his touch makes me lose all track of time. Kissing my neck, Rajas says, "Never thought I'd have a roll in the hay, not literally."

"Pretty great, isn't it? Except for the pokey bits." I laugh at the unintended innuendo. Wrapped in blankets to cushion ourselves from the sharp points of straw, I'm down to my tank top and underwear. He's in his boxers. As much as I want to feel his skin on mine—*all* of his skin on *all* of mine—I'm holding back.

Complete nakedness would be too tempting, and I promised myself—not to mention Martha—I'd wait for sex until I was absolutely, without question, completely ready in heart, body, and soul. I refuse to succumb to hormones and horniness. My decision will be rational and intentional. This girl is different.

And this girl is burning in all the right places.

Rajas runs his hand under my tank top again, circles my nipple with his thumb. My stomach does cartwheels. I could die happy, right now. Except for the menacing alternate reality hanging over me: the one where I'm in a big boiling cauldron of trouble, where I might not get into Cornell, where Jacinda's giving me the silent treatment.

I roll onto my back and heave a sigh.

"Worrying?"

I nod.

"Thought so." He tugs my hair, coaxing me to rest my cheek on the hollow below his collarbone. Listening to the comfort of his heartbeat, I watch his belly rise and fall. A thin patch of hair insulates his chest. Not Neanderthal hairy, not pre-pubescent bald, it's just the right amount. I set my palm on his stomach. He seems content, sated. Is it because of the physical stuff we've been doing? Or just from being together? I wonder: would a label set my mind at ease?

We have the love label now. And I do love me some

love. So why am I still itchy? Besides the straw pricking me through the blanket, ha ha. I sigh. The difference is publicity. Being public. When you're officially boyfriend-girlfriend, it's a known thing. You've proclaimed it to the world. That's why you change your Facebook status to "In a relationship."

"Which part bothers you the most?" Rajas asks.

I'm about to say *The part about not going public with our relationship*, until I realize he's asking about school and PLUTOs and Jacinda. So instead, I shrug, my bare shoulder sliding against him. It reminds me of the day we met, how our skin touched while he carried me to the Biohazard, how he non-rescued me and took me home. He and I both know I'm not that damsel in distress. I'm equal and strong. But I'm also learning that it's nice being held.

"The Jacinda silent treatment is ridiculously unpleasant," I say. "And the second meeting with Dr. Folger wasn't a picnic, either." I sigh again, not sure whether I should tell Rajas that Dr. Folger mentioned him and Jacinda. Maybe later. "Martha says it's my first major lesson in social justice activism."

"Meaning?"

"She called it Social Justice 101." I draw the numbers on his chest. "Learning what happens when the revolution you've started turns around and bites you in the butt."

"The butt?" He gives mine a squeeze. "Got an awful nice one of those."

We kiss some more. And touch. Until the clattering of Hannah Bramble in her stall brings us back to the earth, the barn, the chores that need doing.

"I need to milk Hannah Bramble."

"I need more cowbell." He rolls on top of me. "But you probably have no idea what I'm talking about, do you?"

"You're saying you've got a fever. And the only prescription. Is more cowbell."

He laughs. "Eve, you are full of surprises."

"Explore the studio space!" I shout. Ah, YouTube, the great social equalizer.

We laugh and kiss. Our laughter fades and still we kiss: harder, pressing into each other, intense.

Rajas reaches down to slide off my undies. "Can we?" His breath is hot in my ear.

"I don't know." I pull back to look at him, trying to center myself. Yoga breath. "Not yet. Can we just keep fooling around until I'm definitely, one hundred percent ready?"

His face falls for a half a second—or did just I imagine it?—before he smiles. "Yeah. Of course."

But the mood is killed. I tug my underwear up. "I really need to milk Hannah." This time he doesn't argue. We dress in silence.

Downstairs, the kittens and cats mewl until I give them their milk. I set down the cats' bowl and settle into a rhythm with Hannah Bramble.

Rajas sits down and chews on a blade of straw. "That's quite a grip you got there, cowgirl."

"You would know."

He laughs, dispersing the tension from upstairs.

Hannah shifts, and her tail swats me like it does a thousand times, twice a day, every day. As the pail fills with milk, I breathe in the scents of cream and hay and cow. Comfort smells. Habit smells. Home. Everyone on earth should have a place where they feel this peaceful. A world of farming collectives. Designs fly into my mind. Small houses surrounding shared fields and barns: public core, private edges. Wind turbines on a hill, solar panels...

"Eve? Cowgirl? You there?"

"Sorry. Just Zenning out."

"Designing?"

"Mmm-hmm."

"Nice." He scratches his nose. "You okay? With everything that's going on?"

"Yes. No." Thinking. "I just wish I knew who did it."

"Today's lightning?" The straw in his mouth bobs as he speaks. "Does it make a difference?"

"Hell yes." I stand up, stretch. Hannah Bramble leans toward me; I stroke her velvet nose to thank her.

I cover the milk bucket so the cats won't drink it or fall in. Taking out my hair elastic, I let my hair tumble down, and finger through the straw-head scarecrow snarls. "How's Jacinda doing?"

"Terrible. Never seen her like this. All this stuff with you, and now the lightning with Brookner, and cheerleading crap."

"Well, at least Ms. Gliss has laid off the overt Cheer Squad fat attacks. According to Marcie."

He nods. "Yeah. She's being investigated, I guess. Jay says a guy from the school board is hanging around, so Ms. Gliss has to watch her step. So she's always in a crappy mood."

"Jacinda or Ms. Gliss?"

"Both. There's some stupid pep rally coming up that they're all freaking out about."

We are quiet awhile. I stretch more, ending up on one foot, in tree pose, to strengthen my ankle. A thought: "What if it was Jacinda?"

"What was Jacinda?"

"Who put up the lightning and posted on PLUTOs." I start to wobble so I change sides. "Maybe Brookner called things off with her? She could have done it for revenge."

"No. She's more into him than ever." He winces. "I can tell."

“Hm. Maybe some other girl Brookner tried to hit on? I’ve got this weird feeling Marcie posted it.”

“He’s messing with Marcie too?” Rajas looks like he wants to hit something.

“Calm down! I have no idea. Maybe it’s crazy, but since she was the impetus for the first lightning strike, it would be kind of poetic.” I divide my hair to braid while I think. “It has to be someone who has access to the school.”

“Could have come in as soon as the school was unlocked this morning.”

“No. The paint was almost dry. It must have been done last night, by someone with a key.”

Rajas selects a new piece of straw, peels it, and places it between his teeth.

A thought hits me. “Oh, man! It was a teacher!”

He gives me a look of incredulity.

“Just hear me out. Teachers have keys. What if a teacher found out about Brookner and Jacinda, and wanted to say something, but anonymously?”

“Let a student take the fall?”

I snort. “Let *me* take the fall.”

His forehead wrinkles. He seems pained to think about me getting in trouble. “Maybe they didn’t think you’d be singled out.”

“Maybe they thought wrong.”

His eyes flash, shining like onyx. "Not like you didn't bring it on yourself!"

"What?" I step back, startled by this attack. "What are you saying?"

Rajas tosses the piece of straw down. "Just saying, Eve. You make things difficult."

"Oh, okay. So I deserve this? To ruin Cornell and lose a friend, just for speaking out and taking a stand for what's right?"

"Why do you have to be such a magnet for controversy? Why do you have to look at things so differently than everyone else?"

I stare at him. "Funny. I was under the impression you *liked* that about me."

Rajas's face softens. "I do." He scrunches his nose. "Yeah, I do."

"Wow. Is it that hard to convince yourself?"

"No." He gets quiet. "Just that...you're tough to figure out. Not like all the other girls."

God. *All the other girls.* Why not just stab me in the heart? *All* the others. How many have there been? But Rajas is still talking, so I take a deep breath—lungs snagging on my heart—and try to listen.

"...and that's cool about you. But why do you have to fight so hard? Why does every single thing have to be a struggle or a revolution? Maybe you could take it down a notch—"

“Right. I see. I should make things easier for you. Maybe do what you do: hide out in the shop room?”

Scarlet blotches spread onto his cheeks. “Holy crap, Eve. Don’t act like such a—”

“Wait a second.” My body goes cold. Realization seeps through me, gradual and unwelcome. Something about his mood, the way he’s gone from defense to attack. “You never answered my question. Did you post the lightning? You said, ‘We agreed to wait,’ but you didn’t say it wasn’t you.”

He stares at me a long moment, then looks down at his hands.

“Tell me I’m wrong.”

He doesn’t look up.

My words get quieter but drip with anger. “Tell me it wasn’t you.”

Nothing.

“You went behind my back! We agreed to wait. And…you let Dr. Folger think I did it.”

His shoulders sink. “Eve, if I’d have known that would happen…that he would single you out—”

“Well it’s not rocket science!” I draw back, attempt a deep breath. It’s like a python is squeezing my chest. “What about Jacinda? Did you bother to tell her who really posted the lightning?”

He heaves a sad sigh. “She assumes you did.”

“So tell her! Tell her the truth!”

"Eve. I can't. She'd never speak to me again. She's furious as it is."

"News flash, Rajas! She's not speaking to *me* at all!"

"I can't risk it. She needs someone."

"Why the hell didn't you wait like we planned?"

"Because she's getting worse. She told me she's in love with him. I just *had* to do something."

"Are you freaking kidding me? You just *had* to do something? You just *had* to stab me in the back? You just *had* to leave me hanging out to dry?" Hot tears from a brutal betrayal.

He puts his head in his hands. "Look. If Jay knew...if she ever told anyone that I used my shop key—" He shudders. "I could lose my apprenticeship."

"Your apprenticeship! What about Cornell?" I swipe at my tears. "What about us? I thought you were...I thought *we* were—"

"We *are*, Eve. We are." He wades through the straw to take my hands. His cheeks are wet; he's crying too. "I love you."

My heart contorts as I wring my hands free.

"I love you, Eve."

"Sucks for you."

"I love you."

"Bullshit! You don't love me. If you loved me, you wouldn't sell me out like this." Fueled by pain and anger, my brain is starting to work again, starting to recover the capacity for reason and logic. "If you loved me? You'd tell Jacinda the truth. You would accept responsibility for your actions, and take what she gives you." I feel my feet under me again. "And you'd take responsibility for us instead of shirking labels."

"Shirting labels? That doesn't even make sense!"

"*Shirking* labels. Pick up a damn book once in a while and learn some freaking words! Words like responsibility. Ever heard of it?"

He shakes his head. "I can't. I can't tell Jacinda, it would push her away so hard. She needs me right now. I'm worried." He reaches for me again, and again I pull away. Looking at the straw, he mumbles, "And I can't jeopardize my apprenticeship."

"Oh really." I go from cold to frozen.

"Eve. I didn't mean for this to happen." He rubs his face. "I should've seen that Jay would blame you. And Dr. Folger would too." He's weeping. "I'm sorry! I'm so sorry."

I pull air into my lungs. "I won't let you treat me like this."

"I'm sorry," he breathes.

"That's not good enough! You can't have it both ways."

"Have what both ways?"

My ears buzz with foreboding at what I need to say, but I say it anyway: "Either you stand up for me and tell

Jacinda the truth—that you did it, you alone. Or it's over between us."

"Don't give me an ultimatum! Jay's my cousin."

"You should have thought of that last night when you were sneaking around behind my back. It's a simple choice, Rajas: Take responsibility for what you did and face the consequences. Do what's right. Don't let me take the fall. Or it's over."

"Jay's family. It's not an option to walk away from her." He glares at me. "And you're a hypocrite to talk about taking responsibility! You're the one who made PLUTOs and the lightning anonymous!"

"So you've already made your decision."

His eyes go flinty. "No. You're the one making the decision."

"It's amazing, really, your ability to dodge blame. Or own up to anything at all."

"You should take a look in the mirror," he says.

I point to the barn door. "Leave. Now."

He tilts his head, looking angry and regretful. And he leaves.

I slide the door shut, hard, behind him. It ricochets off the doorjamb and lurches back open.

The Biohazard's brake lights glow eerie red in the dusk. The car rumbles down the driveway, scraping dirt and gravel.

I disintegrate into the straw and try to breathe. I look at my fingers. They are numb and tingling, as if I've been electrocuted. Ha, the body electric. How appropriate. Lightning has struck how many times now? And here I am, back where I started: hurt and stranded, alone.

21

It is more difficult, and calls for higher energies of soul, to live a martyr than to die one.

—Horace Mann, U.S. educator, 1796–1859

I now understand why they take attendance at The Institution of School: if it wasn't mandatory, who would come day after day after day? Not me. Especially after a break-up. Not that I can call it that. Not that Rajas would. Does it qualify for heartbreak if the relationship was never official? If a tree falls in a forest and no one updates its status on Facebook, does it make a sound? Deep, dire thoughts, these. Post-apocalyptic thoughts.

I pull The Clunker over to drop Martha off at Walmart. My eyes still don't want to stay open, despite the ridiculous amount of yerba maté I've consumed. I rub them to try to get the sleep out. Martha and I stayed up all night talking. Trying to ease the pain of Rajas's betrayal and his response to my ultimatum. Trying to get my heart on the same page as my stupid, shortsighted, stubborn pride. I can't fathom what it will be like to see him today. Added to Jacinda's silent treatment.

Martha touches my hair. "Maybe he's already come to his senses, my love."

Tears spill out of my eyes. "He would have called. Or texted. Or something."

She hugs me, dries my cheeks with her thumbs. "If he's stupid enough to choose anything over you, then screw him." Frowning, she adds, "Not literally."

"He had his reasons. Maybe I shouldn't have been so adamant."

She touches her forehead to mine. "Do not waiver, darling. You did the right thing. You can't let Rajas, or anyone, take you for granted."

I swallow.

She kisses me on the cheek. "Call if you need me. I'll be at your side in a heartbeat." She forces the door to let her out, singing James Taylor's "You've Got a Friend."

I manage a small wave and pull The Clunker away. Sipping my maté, driving slowly, I double-, triple-check the clock. Fifteen minutes until first bell: the Bane of my Existence, Global View. And three and a half hours after that, lunch—without Rajas.

The tears start again, plopping into my drink, turning it bitter and salty.

I park The Clunker and make my way into school. I keep my head down, hiding behind a long brown curtain of hair, hoping no one will notice I've been crying. But as I walk, students grow silent, eyes averted, only to burst into whispers after I pass. Down the hallway to my locker, a commotion. Like a replay of yesterday, a crowd has gathered, growing larger, snickering, muttering.

My stomach plummets.

The crowd is at my locker.

A murmur. Heads swivel to look at me. Silent, watchful eyes. Phones light up. People swing out to give me a wide berth. Just like yesterday, with Brookner.

Oh, no. No no no.

At my locker, I drop my bag. It tips over. My heart stops.

A student locker has been struck with lightning. My locker.

Deep red marker: EVENSONG SPARKLING MORNINGDEW is a HYPOCRITE! HYPOCRITE! HYPOCRITE!

Oh God.

What should I do? What should I do? Disappear? Say something? Scream? Run away?

I look around for an ally. Someone to help me. But I don't have anyone. There is no one to help or defend me.

I reach for my bag. My stuff has spilled out. Tampons, pens, papers, all over the cold floor.

—Is that really her name?

—It says hypocrite!

—I told you she was a homeschool freakazoid.

—Nicki told me that she heard that Jacinda said—

Just get me out of here! Where are my keys? Damn it! My hands are shaking. Martha. I need to call Martha. I fish around my bag. My phone! It drops from my hands and clatters across the floor. I kneel to get it—

Someone is here, handing me my things. Next to her, someone else is helping. Did Jacinda have a change of heart? I look up.

It's Marcie. She gives a sad smile, along with a girl I don't know.

Hands press gently on my back. Rajas? Please be Rajas! No, it's a woman's voice: "Come on, hon. Come with me. Marcie and Sarah will get those for you."

I stand. The arm encloses me and leads me away, behind the two girls carrying my stuff. "Everything will be okay," soothes Ms. Franklin. I watch the floor.

Quiet settles over the busy main office when we walk in. Along with some other teachers, Ms. Gliss looks up from her cubbyhole mailbox. Her eyes are cold but I think I detect a hint of pity.

Ms. Franklin deposits me in Dr. Folger's empty office. Marcie and the other girl—Sarah, Ms. Franklin said?—put my things in the other chair. They slip away without a word. Ms. Franklin says something to one of them. I stare at Dr. Folger's Slinkies. I can't even think.

Sarah comes back in. "Here. Hot chocolate." She sets a mug on the edge of Dr. Folger's desk. It's got a cartoon of a kid pushing on a door that says pull. Sarah tucks her hair behind her ear. "It might seem like it right now? But it's not the end of the world, trust me." She leaves.

For some reason I think of Hannah Bramble: her calm energy, her softly swishing tail. Hannah would agree this isn't the end of the world. But everything else—the Cornell diploma on the wall; the lightning on my locker; my heart, aching for Rajas; the echoes of laughter in the hallway—screams that this is Armageddon.

Tapping on the door. "Knock-knock, mind if I come in?" Dr. Folger dips his head. "Hello, Evie."

I put my head in my hands. "This just keeps getting worse."

"Indeed." He sits and lowers his voice. "Are you all right?"

"No. Yes."

"Mr. Heck is already working on your locker. I'm sorry this occurred. Do you know who did it?" He sounds like he already has a theory. "Someone who knows your full name?"

"Or who knows someone who does." Like Jacinda knows Brookner. The cold sweat on my forehead is making my hair stick to my face. I run a hand through it and sweep it over my shoulder. "Yes. I've got a pretty good idea."

He taps a miniature Slinky on his desk. Neither of us speaks.

Dr. Folger shifts and clears his throat. "The difficulty, of course, is the anonymous nature of the postings. The uncoupling, if you will, of the responsibility that should accompany freedom of expression."

I regard him a long moment. My involvement in PLUTOs is clearly an open secret between us, but if I want any hope of going to Cornell, I cannot confess. Especially now that things are devolving into such a tar pit hellhole. I take a deep breath and choose my words carefully. "Maybe...maybe the PLUTOs people thought anonymity would actually help. It can be hard for students to speak out against authority. It can be scary, especially when their future is at stake."

"I have no doubt that's what she—" he pauses meaningfully—"or he, or they, had in mind. As it happens—"

"It's like voting," I interrupt. I feel a little panicked, yet I want to make my point. "People don't have to sign their names on their ballots, because then they might be intimidated into not voting their conscience. Or maybe not voting at all."

"Ah. The flaw in your analogy is that, with a ballot,

speech is constrained. One must adhere to the choices."

"But you can write in whoever you want."

"One is still limited to a name. And ballots, by design, are not inherently hurtful. They cannot be directed *at* someone. I'm afraid this blog, and the lightning strikes—"

"Are hurting people." I study my hands.

"Yes."

I close my eyes. "But that doesn't change the fact that students have a hard time speaking up. This school is not a good democracy."

"Indeed, Evie. You've put your finger on it: this school is *not* a good democracy. And I'm not convinced that it should be."

"But it's— that's—"

"Heresy?" He holds up a finger. "What if a school, by necessity, cannot be a democratic institution? Does that necessarily negate the good we do here? Open your mind to the question. That's all I ask."

Ms. Franklin knocks on the doorframe. She hands me a pass. "Good luck, hon."

Dr. Folger tilts in his chair, a bow of dismissal. "Come back if you need respite, Evie."

"Thanks." I gather my things and get going.

When I arrive at my locker, Mr. Heck is scraping off the last bits of lightning. "Thank you so much," I tell him.

"Just doing my job." He closes his toolbox and collects

the curled scraps of cardboard. I wait for him to turn the corner before I dig a pen out of my bag and get to work on the hall pass Ms. Franklin wrote. Luckily, her writing is a lot like mine.

When I'm done, I take a deep breath and open Brookner's classroom door.

Textbooks are open on each desk. Stiv is reading aloud. Brookner's not here. In his place, at his desk, sits a young woman. Frowning, she places a pen on her book, as if to mark her place. Stiv stops reading.

There's a message on the board, but not in Brookner's writing. Elegant cursive loops announce, *My name is Ms. Bemis, and I will be filling in for Mr. Brookner while he is on administrative leave. I cannot comment further, so please don't ask me to do so.*

I hand Ms. Bemis my pass.

Jacinda is staring at her textbook like she expects it to come to life at any moment. Marcie gives me a tiny, pitying smile.

Ms. Bemis squints at the pass. "And they wish for you to return as well?"

I nod.

"Very well. Let me check you off. Evie..." She runs a finger over the roster in front of her.

"You mean Evensong!" says someone in the back of the room.

"Morningdew!"

Chortles from the last row of desks.

Jacinda and Marcie keep their eyes glued to their books.

Ms. Bemis does not respond to the comments. "Jacinda Harrod?"

Jacinda's head whips up.

"Your presence is requested in the main office."

The class goes dead silent. Jacinda peels her gaze off Ms. Bemis to lock eyes with me. She looks like she will kill me the moment we are alone in the hall. I set my jaw. This won't be pretty.

You are a child of the universe, no less than the trees and stars; you have a right to be here. And whether or not it is clear to you, no doubt the universe is unfolding as it should.

—Max Ehrmann, lawyer and writer, 1872–1945

22

"Rat out your friends much?" sneers Jacinda as soon as I shut Brookner's classroom door. She checks the hallway to be sure we're alone. "Dr. Folger already gave me the third degree yesterday. I don't know why I didn't just tell him it was you."

"Because then you would have been admitting your own guilt." I grind my teeth and keep walking.

"Um, hello? The main office is that way."

"The Clunker is this way."

"So? I thought—"

I whirl around and point a finger at her. "Listen. I did not rat you out. And I didn't strike Brookner's lightning, got it? We need to talk."

"I'm not getting in your smelly car."

"Fine." I spot an empty classroom. It's unlocked. "We'll talk in here. Keep your voice down."

Confusion seems to muddle her anger as she follows me into the classroom. "Where's Dr. Folger?"

"He's not coming. I doctored the pass Ms. Franklin gave me. I made it look like they were requesting you. But really, it's just you and me."

She glares at me. "What, no Raj? I'm surprised you have the courage to—"

"We broke up." There. I said it.

"You did?" Seeing the look of shock on her face is like taking a bullet to the chest.

Unable to speak, I nod.

"Why?" She seems so surprised that she's forgotten her rage.

"We had a fight." I swallow down the lump in my throat. "About the Brookner lightning."

At the mention of his name, Jacinda's rage resurfaces. Her cheeks flush a dark crimson. "John didn't do anything wrong. We were in love! And now they are investigating him! He's an innocent man. And he..." She convulses into sobs, hugging herself. "H-he said we had to end it! He said it's over."

"Because of the lightning?"

She doesn't answer. She doubles over, crying. I put my hand on her shoulder. Well, thank God. Brookner broke things off. Still, I hate to see Jacinda so upset.

Jerking away from my touch, she dabs at her eyes and looks up, angrier than ever. "You! You got what you deserved."

"I didn't post the lightning, Jacinda. I wanted to." I press my hands to my heart. "I thought about it, but it wasn't me. I swear."

"Oh really." She narrows her eyes. "Then who was it?"

"Does it matter?" A question Rajas asked me yesterday. At that time it did. But now...what would be the point in tearing Rajas and Jacinda further apart?

"Ohmigod!" Flustered, angry. "Yes! It matters!" She flops onto a chair.

I sit next to her. "I wanted to talk to you about..." I study the pocks marring the smooth surface of the desk in front of me. "Maybe we should think about shutting down the blog."

She snorts. "Now that it says something about *you*, you want to shut it down? No. I don't think so."

Crap. The lightning was bad; what if the blog is worse? "I haven't seen it," I say.

"Well, there's nothing on it that isn't true. It says that you are a hypocrite, because you promised not to do stuff without telling your friends first, but you did anyway. And it says that you think you're smarter than everyone at this school. You think you're above it all."

I put my head down on the desk. "How do you know what it says? Brookner wasn't here to show—"

"I just know!" she snaps.

But it's too late. Her phone isn't in sight, so she can't say she checked the InterWeb. We both know she wrote it.

I roll my head from side to side on the desk, just wanting everything to go away. "I think we should shut down the blog. But, despite what you think about me, I'm not a hypocrite. I won't change my promise. I won't shut it down unless you agree."

"Well, I do not agree."

Head still on the desk, I massage my scalp. My brain hurts. So does my heart. "Just think about it. That's all I ask."

She doesn't respond. The quiet lasts so long that, after a while, I look up to check whether she's still here.

She's staring at me, arms crossed, foot waggling. "I hope you know that it won't take Raj long to move on."

Oh man, she's going for the jugular.

"I mean, no one even knew you guys were together. Raj, like, didn't want people to know. Did you ever wonder why he always took you to the shop room?"

"Fine, Jacinda. You've made your point." Tears leak out of my eyes. I think I liked it better when she wasn't talking to me.

"You seriously had me fooled. I thought you were different. But you're not. You're the same as everyone else. You're just as mean and backbiting, and you—"

"Jacinda."

"What."

"How would I have gotten in? To post the lightning? I don't have a key. Have you thought about that?"

She blinks rapidly. Her lips purse. "I—um—"

"Maybe you should give me a little more credit."

"I think that you already give yourself more than enough credit," she mutters. She's lost some steam.

I stand to leave. I've said everything I can.

"And to think I was sticking up for you." Her voice is quieter but still thick with anger. "I, like, defended you to everyone. Everyone thought you were a know-it-all and a total weirdo. Raj and I? We vouched for you. We said you were cool. Well, not anymore. Now you're on your own."

"That's okay. I'm used to it." I grab the doorknob.

"Everyone hates you for making Brookner leave."

"I'm sure." I open the door.

"And Ms. Gliss knows it was you who did her lightning. She told me. She said—"

That's it. That is *it*. I close the door and turn back to Jacinda. "I take it you didn't bother to tell her *you* were involved with that one? God, Jacinda! We were a freaking *team* when we started PLUTOs! You knew Ms. Gliss was out of line. You wanted to do something good for the school! You went on and on about the sexism and sizeism Cheer Squad has to put up with. And what?

Now you're back to Ms. Gliss, kissing your coach's ass like a good little cheerleader?" My hands are fists. "You don't think I'm different? Fine. But you should do some soul-searching if *you're* posting lightning calling *me* a hypocrite."

Without waiting for her response, I open the door, wishing that, instead of the school's main corridor, this doorway led to another world—a peaceful homeschool world, a sustainable community of my own design. Far, far away from here.

In the banking concept of education, knowledge is a gift bestowed by those who consider themselves knowledgeable upon those whom they consider to know nothing... The teacher presents himself to his students as their necessary opposite; by considering their ignorance absolute, he justifies his own existence.

— Paulo Freire, educator and theorist, 1921–1997

The next morning, I poke at breakfast while Martha braids my hair. We get ready in silence. Even Hannah Bramble can't make me feel better. I'm stuck. I pitched my tent on skunk scat, as Rich would say, and now I must sleep in it. If I drop out of school or start cutting classes, Cornell will find out.

Climbing into The Clunker for school takes every ounce of my fortitude. At least it's Friday. Eight hours until blessed freedom.

When I drop Martha off at the Mart of Wal, she cups my face in her hands. "Be strong." She kisses my cheek. "I adore you, darling."

School is buzzing when I get there. The hall is clogged with clumps—larger than usual—of waving arms and kids talking over each other, wielding phones. Their eyes follow me as I push through the crowd, but it doesn't quiet, doesn't pull me into its focus the way it did yesterday.

And then I spot it. Holy crap. A student locker struck with lightning. Brown cardboard with painted letters, a girl crying as she tries to rip it down. DAVINA IS A SLUT!

Oh God. Please tell me this is just a dream—albeit a freaking nightmare.

I double back to the library. I need to check the PLUTOs blog.

Along the way, another crowd, another locker: MATT JOHNSON CHEATS ON HIS GIRLFRIENDS!

I speed up into a jog.

In the library, a bubbling herd of kids—the downtrodden proletariat who can't afford iPhones—surrounds the computers, trying to get a look at the PLUTOs website. The librarian is trying to shoo people away. "Students, these computers are for academic purposes only! Class research! Not rumor-mongering—"

No one listens. I recognize Matt Johnson, jostling for a view of the screens. Then, a loud collective groan. Through the crowd, I catch a glimpse. All four screens have gone inky black. The librarian pops up, victoriously waving a three-prong plug. "The computers will remain off, and the internet unavailable, until further notice. Chop, chop. To your classes. Now. Skedaddle!"

Grumbling students take to the hall. Matt and a couple of others mutter at me, almost too quiet to make out their brutal words. *Homeschool freak. Go back to where you came from.* I blow out a deep breath. Fine. I get it. I come in and shake things up a little, and things are getting feral. Maybe they believe the lightning Jacinda posted. Maybe they think I'm a hypocrite. Or worse.

But I had nothing to do with these recent strikes! How can I tell them?

Surely Dr. Folger knows these weren't my doing. Please, let him know it wasn't me.

I'll tell him myself.

The main office is busier than usual. Dr. Folger's office door is closed.

"Hi, hon," Ms. Franklin says. "Rough day yesterday, huh?"

"Today too," I say. "Is Dr. Folger here? May I see him?"

She frowns. "He's in a meeting at the moment."

"Can I wait?"

Ms. Franklin leans forward and motions me closer. She lowers her voice. "He doesn't think you were involved with what happened today, hon. He's meeting with Dr. Jones right now. They are looking into whether they can shut down the PLUTOs website. They're trying to verify their authority and persuade the blog administrators to delete it. Now, if the person who started it would just shut it down," she pauses, "life would certainly be simpler—"

The three-minute warning bell makes us both jump.

Ms. Franklin sips her Diet Coke. "He'll send for you if he needs to. Best for you to get to class now. And take what I said into consideration."

My feet are made of cement. I look again at Dr. Folger's office door.

"Go on, hon."

"Okay." I don't want to leave, but I try to trust Ms. Franklin's advice. The woman has her finger on the pulse of the school.

In Brookner's classroom, Ms. Bemis is attempting to instill order over chaos. Jacinda stares at me while I take my seat. Her skin, usually so luminous, is dull and sallow. Her hair is flat instead of spiky. Her foot is wiggling.

Ms. Bemis starts taking attendance, but no one stops talking. Static on the PA interrupts Ms. Bemis and manages to hush the class.

"Students, teachers, if you'll excuse the interruption." Dr. Folger pauses. "I will again remind you that bullying, whether online or in print, is a crime, as is defacement of school property. It will *not* be tolerated. A forensics team is gathering evidence as I speak." Around me, people exchange looks. Is he serious? "Students who are involved are encouraged to come forward of their own accord. That is all. Good day."

I'm scribbling a note to Jacinda: *It has to be shut down.* I flip it toward her when Ms. Bemis isn't looking.

Jacinda picks the note up and taps it on her desk.

I hold my breath. Will she agree?

She opens the note, smoothes it out. Clicks her pen.

"Please open your books to page 183." Ms. Bemis's tone sounds more like begging than instruction.

Jacinda, writing with one hand, lifts the other one skyward. "Um, Ms. Bemis?"

Oh no. She's going to show the note? I was so careless. Is it enough to incriminate me?

Jacinda clicks her pen closed and folds the note while she talks. "May I use the restroom?"

Ms. Bemis looks around, like she's worried an early bathroom excusal will set a bad precedent. "Class just started, I don't think that's such a good—"

Stiv pipes up, "Mr. Brookner always let us."

Jacinda smiles at Stiv. Satisfied that this is permission enough, she stands, scooting her chair with the back of her knees. "I'll be right back." She drops the folded page on my desk as she goes to the door.

"I really don't think—" Ms. Bemis swallows, folds her arms across her chest and reverses tack. "Okay. Yes. Go ahead." Which is smart, since Jacinda's already at the door.

I slide the note onto my lap and open it. Underneath my imploring scribbles, Jacinda wrote, *Do what you want. I'm done with this.*

Jacinda looks back before leaving. She seems angry. And sad.

When I pick her up after school, Martha is holding a bag of Oreos. She shakes it as she climbs into The Clunker. "I come bearing gifts." She rips open the package and hands it to me.

"Thanks." I nibble a cookie. My appetite's been terrible lately. "You realize this is actual processed food. High fructose corn syrup, artificial flavor, the whole nine yards."

"Darling, after the week you've had, I figure you can handle the hard stuff. I was relabeling the cookie section when you called..." She twirls her hand and trails off. Neither of us needs to replay the tearful call from my lunch hideout—my self-imposed solitary confinement in The Clunker.

I take a bigger bite. "Sweet Baby James, that's good."

"Give me one of those." She snatches a cookie from the bag, pokes it into her mouth, almost swallows it whole. "Now. You're sure, my love? That you want to delete the blog? You know, the Black Panthers didn't turn tail when the going got tough. Turn tail. Ha!" She chuckles. "Got to remember that one."

"PLUTOs isn't the Panthers, Martha." I straighten my shoulders and remind myself—or maybe convince myself—that I'm strong, that I know what I have to do.

"It's been derailed into something awful. Just... wretched. PLUTOs was supposed to empower people. Not hurt them."

"Hmm. 'Let us not become the evil that we deplore.'"

"Right." I frown. "Who was that? Wait, don't tell me. It was after the September eleventh bombings. A congresswoman from California...Barbara...It can't be Barbara Boxer."

"No, Barbara Lee. From Oakland. Birthplace of the Black Panther Party, not for nothing." She takes another cookie. "Sounds like Jacinda more or less gave you permission to take it off-line."

"Pretty much." I brush Oreo crumbs off my sweatshirt.

"It was probably the best she could do, poor thing."

In shock, I jerk the steering wheel. "You're on her side?"

"Hell no, my love! Hell no. I'm just saying she's probably confused, being new to the insurrection and revolution business."

"Before you start feeling too sorry for her, keep in mind that she was totally into it when we started PLUTOs."

"Noted."

"And she surely doesn't have the market cornered on confusion."

"Got it."

"And I'm not Angela Davis or Huey Newton. I'm pretty new at this too."

"Right."

"Don't patronize me, Martha. I'm serious."

"Patronize you? I would never. Perish the thought, my love!" She grins, but I'm in no mood for her humor. She pinches me on the thigh and starts humming a Feist song.

"Martha?"

She reaches for my hair. "Yes, darling?"

"My boyfriend dumped me. My best friend won't talk to me. My future is in a garbage can. Everything has turned to crap. Can you please just let me be a sullen teenager, just this once?"

She tugs my hair. So much for trying.

When we get home, I boot up the computer. I sign in to the PLUTOs account.

OPTIONS. DELETE BLOG.

"DELETING CAN NOT BE UNDONE. ARE YOU SURE YOU WANT TO DELETE?"

I click YES.

Martha watches over my shoulder. We both stare at the screen, looking more through it than at it, until a box comes up.

BLOG DELETED.

"There. It's done. The revolution is dead." I put my head on the table. "This one, anyway."

She rubs my back. "I'm sorry it didn't work out, my love. But you must keep the faith, keep fighting—"

I moan. "No more pep talks."

"You kick-started some dialogue at The Institution of School. You learned for yourself the evils of Freire's notion of banking education. You spread the idea of transparency, and that is just what the world needs."

I hold up a hand to stop her. "I'm going to bed."

Martha nods, finally taking the hint. "I'll bring you some tea."

"Don't you have a shift at the co-op, or HSP coffee pals, or something? You should go."

She wrinkles her nose. "I'm not going. I may have worn out my welcome."

I screw up my face into a question.

"Darling, your enthusiasm is overwhelming. Go to bed."

Too tired to argue, I climb to my loft and flop down on the futon. At least it's over. I turn onto my side and pick at my bedspread, trying not to think about Rajas, and Jacinda, and Cornell. I breathe deep. The worst is over. The worst is over. Isn't it?

24

The trouble ain't that there is too many fools, but that the lightning ain't distributed right.

—Mark Twain, author and humorist, 1835–1910

Did you see it?

Which one?

Before first bell on Monday, a jabbering horde of students assemble around a locker. A locker with a lightning strike. Red poster board, black marker. DON'T TRUST JASON DRELLER! HE IS A LIAR!

But I shut the blog down! What is happening?

Another student's locker: S. J. IS A TEASE!

Further down, my geometry classroom. Paper lightning plastered to the door. MS. THEODORE IS RACIST.

This is turning into a nightmare. The Tenth Circle of Hell.

I turn the corner. Another crowd.

My locker. Again. Lightning. EVIE MORNINGDEW RUINED OUR SCHOOL!

I elbow through the crowd and pull at the lightning bolt, try to rip it off. It's stuck tight.

Behind me, kids are murmuring: *That is so true!* and *She deserves it!* and *School sucked before, but now it's worse.*

Kicking now, I dent the dull metal of my locker. I scratch at the cardboard. A fingernail bends back and rips away from my skin, but the lightning doesn't budge. I kick again, and again. It's useless. I slump to the floor.

"Show's over!" I yell. A few people detach from the crowd and float away. The remaining onlookers mutter, blink, stare.

"Please! Go!" I cry, batting at my tears. Bitter tears, frustrated and impotent. I pull up my hood to hide.

"Guys, you've seen what there is to see." It's Stiv. "Dr. Folger will be here soon, and he's going to be pissed at anyone hanging around."

People must believe him, because I hear feet shuffle away. But Stiv is still standing here. And I'm still sitting here.

"Thanks," I say to his legs.

He blows out a breath. "Yeah," is all he says before he walks toward Global View. And is stopped in his tracks by another kid.

"You're on *her* side, now?" The guy blocking Stiv looks at me like I'm dog crap. "Why? You nailing her? You hitting that?"

Stiv glares. "Drop it, Brian."

Brian shoves Stiv.

Stiv throws down his books. "You don't want to start something. You really don't."

The crowd rematerializes, all jeans and shoes from this angle.

Brian shoves Stiv again. "Oh really?"

"I'll give you one more chance to walk away," Stiv warns. "You mess with me, you mess with the whole soccer team."

"Yeah, you do!" A boy pushes his way through the mob to stand at Stiv's side.

"Hells yeah!" Another soccer player shows up next to Stiv. They fold their arms over their chests, forming a wall.

Brian's eyes dart from Stiv to the other guys; he looks like he's debating whether protecting his pride is worth getting pummeled by three soccer players.

"What is the meaning of this?" Dr. Folger booms. Kids scamper.

Dr. Folger draws himself up, his suit coat straining at the shoulders. "Mr. Wagner? Mr. Beers? Mr. Buxford and Mr. Cobb. Shall we meet in my office?"

Brian shakes his head. "No."

"Indeed, that was a rhetorical question. Come with me."

The four boys start walking. As they pass, they cast their eyes down at me. They are seething. A couple of them look like they will kick my ass as soon as Dr. Folger is done with them, and as soon as they've finished their own war.

Dr. Folger pushes his hands into his pockets. "Evie. Mr. Heck is quite busy, but he will attend to your locker posthaste." I search his face for the customary warmth. It is not there. "Please stand and get to class." He catches up to the four boys.

I thud the back of my head against my locker to unstick my brain. Think. Stop crying. Things have snowballed out of control: it's an avalanche, a growing snowslide careening down a mountain. I knock my head against the metal again. The avalanche already smothered me last week. What's another foot or two, if I'm already buried alive? At least today's lightning strike is true. I *have* ruined the school. But what about the other kids' lightnings? Were they deserved?

A snowball, an avalanche. Dr. Folger and the superintendent haven't been able to stop it. So much for their top-down approach. And the bottom-up, grassroots approach is what started this mess in the first place. My stomach contorts. This is overwhelming. How can you stop an avalanche?

And there is another, more basic question: how are people getting in after school hours to post lightning? The place is supposed to be locked tight.

In Global View, Stiv doesn't make an appearance, nor does Matt. Marcie won't meet my eyes. And Jacinda? I don't even bother trying to talk to her or write a note. What's the point? The blog is down. She wanted to wash her hands of it, of me. But this huge wall between us is killing my heart. The heartbreak of a broken friendship—why don't they show that in the movies? It's every bit as bad as the hurt from Rajas.

Rajas.

I need to talk to him. Which will be as much fun as jumping into a meat grinder.

At lunchtime, the cafeteria thrums as if the entire student body is on the verge of anarchy. It feels like an unseen force is thrusting people into constant motion. Everyone is pacing around, orbiting tables, circling prey. Fights break out. Teachers—there are more here than usual—spring into motion, knocking over chairs to push sparring kids apart.

At tables, people aren't talking, they're shouting.

Except Rajas's table, which lapses into dead silence when I show up. Jacinda's not here. She must be at Cheer Squad? No, that can't be it, because Marcie's here.

"Can I talk to you?" I ask Rajas over the din of the surrounding tables.

He looks impassive, except for the blotches rapidly staining his skin. Please tell me it's because he misses me. The audacity of hope. More likely it's embarrassment that I'm addressing him in public. Or pity over the lightning strikes against me? A surge of anger makes my hands pulse. I don't need his pity, I don't want it. This girl is different.

I say it again. "Can we talk?"

Rajas scratches his nose. "Yeah, okay."

"I assume you'd prefer to go somewhere private?"

"Sure." If he caught my irony, he doesn't let on. He grabs his tray and empties it in the garbage as we go out the door.

We walk in silence until we're passing the gym.

"Stop," I tell him. Because he's leading us to the shop room, and I can't bear the thought of it. As much as I've tried to shut them out, Jacinda's words still echo in my mind: *Did you ever wonder why he always took you to the shop room? No one even knew you guys were together. Rajas didn't want people to know.*

I thought it was so we could have each other all to ourselves. To talk and kiss and kiss some more.

Was I really that naive? Humiliating. Time to change. Nobody puts baby in a corner.

Rajas leans on the gym doors. "What do you want to talk about?" His voice is neutral.

I want to talk about the way we broke up! I want to talk

about you choosing Jacinda over me! I want to talk about you telling me you love me! I want to know if your heart is as wrecked as mine! But I don't say those things. Instead, I clear the lump blocking my throat and say, "I want to talk about how people are getting into school. At night. To post the lightning."

He jerks his head around to make sure no one is listening. "How would I know?"

"Please, spare me the innocent act. I just want the truth."

He runs his hand through his hair. "Don't know. That is the truth."

"Does Jacinda? Does she know?"

"She's not talking to me."

"Really? Why? Did you come clean and admit it was you who—"

"Eve." He holds up a hand to indicate he doesn't want to talk about it, just as a group of girls walks by.

"Hi, Rajas," says one of the girls, smiling broadly and waving with her fingers.

"Hey, Rosemary."

"See you after school?" she asks.

"Yeah." He smiles his crooked smile. "Of course."

"Good!" The girl bounces a little. When they continue on, she and her friends burst into giggles. They look back at Rajas before disappearing around the corner.

See you after school. And now my heart is beyond broken. It has circled back from being numb, and is crumpling into itself. It's a black hole in my chest from which nothing, not even light, can escape.

"Eve, I—"

"Okay. Thanks for the information." I take off.

I manage to hold back my tears until I'm in The Clunker.

In the driver's seat, I crank the ignition. Her name was Rosemary. I've seen her around. First year student, I think. Always giggling and looking a little boy crazy. Have she and Rajas been seeing each other all along? Wouldn't Jacinda have told me? Or maybe Rosemary had her eye on Rajas and she was just waiting for us to break up. Except that she wouldn't have had to wait, because no one—other than Jacinda—knew we were together.

I stomp the clutch and pry The Clunker's gearshift into reverse, then jam it back into park. There's still half a day of school left. I hit the steering wheel, shut the engine off. My fingers hurt from trying to rip the lightning from my locker. And the tears keep coming.

25

If we don't fight hard enough for the things we stand for, at some point we have to recognize that we don't really stand for them.

—Paul Wellstone, U.S. Senator, 1944–2002

On Tuesday, a police car is parked in the student parking lot. A cop stands beside it, looking menacing, trying to dissuade students from breaking into fights.

Locker. ABRAM PAUL IS AN ASSHOLE!

Classroom door. MR. WOLMAN SUCKS UP TO RICH KIDS.

I have to talk to Dr. Folger. Just to...I don't even know. Express my condolences at the accelerating decline of The Institution of School? Bear witness to the whirling vortex of a toilet flush that is his school? And my role in creating that cosmic sewage? Should I confess? Should I have known this was going to happen? Should I have seen it coming?

When I open the door to the main office, Ms. Franklin

waves me in. "He's expecting you, hon."

I take a deep, cleansing breath and knock on Dr. Folger's office door, which is slightly ajar. Sitting at his desk, Dr. Folger looks contemplative. He's holding a Slinky over the floor, springing it up and down. "Evie. Come in."

I sit. My throat is dry. What should I say? I put my hands on my lap and try not to think about his Cornell diploma. "Dr. Folger, I—"

"Please, Evie. For your own sake, let me do the talking." He sets down the Slinky. "Let us start at the beginning.

"I strongly suspect that you, and quite possibly an accomplice or two, began the PLUTOs website. I believe that you were behind the lightning strike against Ms. Gliss."

"But I—"

"Enough." It's the harshest tone he's ever taken with me, and it makes me want to crawl under the chair. Dr. Folger steeples his hands and taps index finger to chin. "You should count yourself very fortunate indeed that I lack the evidence to prove my suspicion."

Guilt singes the tips of my ears. And relief washes through me. He wasn't able to connect us to the blog. And obviously neither Jacinda nor Rajas has been persuaded to confess. They don't hate me quite enough to self-destruct. Thank God for small favors.

"Assuming my suspicions are correct, I have no doubt that your intentions were honorable, if grossly—and I do mean grossly—misguided. Alas, we have covered this ground before." His chair pivots as he leans back. "The blog has gone off-line, and that is good. But we are approaching a crisis point here. I've put the school on veritable lockdown and posted security guards at the main entrances. We are petitioning the school board to fund an alarm system. But as you can see, students are still finding their way into the building after hours."

I keep my face neutral. Rajas says he's not using his key, and I believe him. But kids are trickling in somehow. Where is the leak?

"This is disturbing, to say the least. And momentum has not shifted," Dr. Folger continues. "Indeed, the lightning strikes are occurring with even greater frequency. This is becoming, to use an expression from my younger days, a shitstorm."

I smile at his term, but his eyes don't concede one iota of levity.

"I've said it before: I like you, Evie. But I am not happy, not by any stretch of the imagination, about this situation." His gaze fills me with so much remorse that I need to look away.

"Evie, you may fashion yourself something of an advocate for democracy—"

"But can I just—"

"No." He lifts a finger in warning. "No. I am not finished."

Chastened, I nod and sit on my hands to keep quiet.

"Now. If you want to be taken seriously, if you are truly the advocate for justice you think you are, you must accept responsibility for the consequences of your actions. *All* of the consequences, intended or not.

"If you are the person I think and hope you are, you will put your strong ideas to work. You will do everything in your power to rectify this situation." He dips his head. "That is all. You are excused, Evie."

Dismissed and then some, I leave. Dr. Folger's disappointment is an acid eroding the scant remains of my heart. I can't even look at Ms. Franklin, because if she gives me a sympathetic smile, I'll dissolve into tiny pieces. Dr. Folger wants me to do something. But I'm so empty. What's left to do something with?

Learning carries within itself certain dangers because out of necessity one has to learn from one's enemies.

—Leon Trotsky, Marxist theorist and Bolshevik revolutionary, 1879–1940

Wednesday morning, one police officer monitors the bus circle. Another leans on his cruiser in the parking lot.

Inside, a locker: JAMIE CLEARY HAD A NOSE JOB!

A classroom door: MR. CAMPOTO GIVES FOOTBALL PLAYERS GRADES THEY DON'T DESERVE!

Another locker: SCOTTIE FOREST IS A TOTAL FAG. Sobbing, a kid is pulling at the lightning. He looks desperate. I run over and help him pull it down. This one comes off, thank God. "Thank you," he whispers, but his face changes when he sees who I am. "You," he snarls. "You started this. Get away from me."

I leave, taking the lightning with me. Scottie's got enough to deal with, without being associated with the loathsome Evensong Morningdew. Anger pulses against my tired, empty skull. I rumple the cardboard lightning and stuff it in the garbage. This homophobic slur is by far the worst. It's antithetical to why we started PLUTOs. The diametric opposite. We wanted a flashy way to confront abuse and oppression. Instead we turned the fight for justice into plain old bullying. Anonymous bullying, no less. The most cowardly kind.

PLUTOs striking Ms. Gliss was warranted. I stand by that. And Brookner got what he deserved. As for the other strikes against teachers…are they true? Were they justified? I don't know. I'm not a big fan of Ms. Theodore, but is she racist? It's not impossible.

Then there are the strikes against kids. Maybe some people are assholes, and do cheat on their girlfriends or their tests. Or someone got a nose job. Who cares? It's personal. They're not oppressing others. Striking lightning for that stuff is just plain petty.

And calling someone a fag? That's worse than petty: it's hateful. Inexcusable. It's taking the lightning and turning it into a tool of oppression.

Dr. Folger is right. I have to act. But how? If Rajas and Jacinda were with me, maybe we could do something. Maybe, although I don't know what. But they aren't with me. I'm alone. I'm the school pariah. Struck twice by lightning, blamed for ruining the school. At this point, I have as about as much influence as a leper in a cave.

In Global View, Jacinda looks sullen and pallid. She rests her head on her desk most of the period, but at least she's here. Some days she doesn't come to class at all.

At lunchtime, I hide out in my Fortress of Solitude, The Clunker. I choke down a few bites of apple. I Zen out and try to take deep yoga breaths. Think. A solution. I stare at the familiar cracks on the dashboard. I roll my head on the steering wheel. The only thoughts I can muster are questions: How are people getting into school to post the lightning? How did things go so wrong? How can I make it all just go away?

I can't think. I have to get out of here. At least for now. If I make it back before geometry I won't get detention. I drive in a daze and I end up in the Walmart parking lot. Out of habit, I suppose; I didn't make a conscious decision. Since I'm here, should I call Martha? She'd come flying out in a heartbeat. But she's been missing shifts as it is, thanks to me. What if she got fired? I don't want to add her to the list of people getting hurt.

Ugh.

A revolution, taking a moral stand, is one thing. Hurting people is another. Being hurt.

Betrayal. Heartbreak. Jacinda. Rajas. Cornell.

I groan and crawl into the back of The Clunker and lie down. I've got to think of something. I have to.

Think of Scottie Forest and Matt Johnson and Jamie Cleary and Davina Whoever and the others. And Stiv and the kids who are fighting each other, set off by the divisive lightning. The whole school is imploding.

Focus.

But my mind won't center on anything other than all the hating, the pain.

I rub my temples. Time to try to stoke up some positive energy.

Bam bam bam!

Holy crap! I'm startled nearly out of my skin because someone's knocking so hard The Clunker shimmies.

Bam bam bam!

What now? Walmart security guards? But you're allowed to camp in Walmart parking lots! It's the only good thing about them! I grab the latch and slide the door open to tell whoever it is to—

Brookner. Brookner is standing in front of me.

He rocks onto his heels. "Evie."

My stomach clenches, churning resentment and disgust. "How did you find me?"

"I have my ways."

"What are you doing? Are you stalking me? This is all your fault! Everything went to hell because of you!"

"Now now. Don't be snippy. May I come in?" Brookner asks.

I glare at him. "Are you kidding me? You really think

that's a good idea? To be alone in a van with a female student?"

"Hmm. You might be right. I'll stay out here." He wags his head in the direction of his car. "Booker's in there. Better that he can see me. More reassuring."

I peer past Brookner and give a small wave to Booker. He sags in the passenger seat, looking miserable. He looks down at something.

Brookner follows my gaze. "He takes that snake with him everywhere now."

"Just make sure he keeps Javier well fed. I'd hate for him to—" Wait. Enough distraction! "What do you want?" I demand of Brookner. "Go on in and do your shopping."

"I'm not here to shop. I'm here to talk to you."

"So you *are* stalking me?"

Instead of responding, he adjusts his glasses. For the first time, he seems to notice my eyes, red, chiseled out from dark circles caused by tears and lack of sleep. "Evie, have you been crying?"

"No!"

He raises an eyebrow.

We're both quiet, as if daring the other person to talk first. Brookner leans on The Clunker. "Well. You know that I've been put on leave? That I'm being investigated?"

"I would feel sorry for you, except that you completely deserve it."

"Yes, well. Kind of nice, the quiet. We're making the best of it. It gives me a lot of time to think. Maybe I'll homeschool Booker. He's been keeping me company, helping me dig up some new quotes." He smiles. "I've got a good one. It's contextual. 'Great spirits have always encountered violent opposition from mediocre minds.'"

My breath catches. "Einstein." It's one of my favorite lines of all time.

He nods.

I straighten my spine, recover my anger. "I take that to mean you consider yourself a great spirit?"

"You don't?"

"Consider *you* a great spirit? No."

He laughs. "We're a lot alike, you and I."

I cross my arms. "No we're not." I sound every bit the petulant teenager, but I don't have the energy for anything else.

"We certainly are. We both fancy ourselves mavericks. Idealists. We question the arbitrary boundaries society places upon us."

"I don't do sketchy things. I don't hurt people."

"Oh no? Well. I wonder...how do you suppose Ms. Gliss felt after the first lightning strike?"

"She deserved it. Besides, why would you assume that was me?"

"Please." He waves a hand, like he's not interested in

that argument. "Posting anonymously on the internet. Not giving someone a chance to redeem herself, or at the very least, respond to the charges. How sketchy—to use your term—is that?"

"She could have posted a response," I mutter.

"And how effective could that have possibly been?"

I don't answer, because he's right. About *one* thing. It wouldn't have done any good for Ms. Gliss to respond.

There's a spark in his eye. "Perhaps I shouldn't speak in the past tense about Ms. Gliss's response."

"What's that supposed to mean?"

"Perhaps she's leaving the door open, as it were, to the possibilities of diluting the accusations against her, hmm?"

I blink.

He chuckles. "You're not the only person with a strong mind and ideas in her head, Evie. You should give people some credit." Pressing his elbow against the door frame, he shifts his weight, turns, and leaves.

But I do. I do give people credit. Don't I?

Jacinda says I give myself too much credit. "You're the one who should give her some credit!" I shout at Brookner.

He swivels around to face me. "And what, pray tell, is that supposed to mean? Enlighten me."

"You manipulated Jacinda. You made her think it was okay to be dating you."

Scanning the parking lot for anyone who might have heard me, he walks back toward The Clunker. "On the contrary. I simply treated her like a human being, with whom I enjoyed talking. I made it very clear that we must wait until she graduated, until she was no longer a student, for our relationship to progress."

"Then answer me this: if you're so sure that you didn't do anything wrong, why did you break it off with her?"

"Besides the lightning strike and the ensuing investigation?" He takes off his glasses and rubs them on his shirt. "Let's just say that a mutual acquaintance paid me a visit."

I lean back, realizing. "Dr. Folger."

He puts his glasses back on. "You know, Evie, for someone who prides herself on her precocity, you really can be quite dense." He jogs to his car, jerks the door open. He says something to Booker and ducks in.

Seething, I watch him drive away.

He's abhorrent. But he's done me a favor. He's given me some clues, some pieces of the puzzle.

I know how people are getting into school after hours.

27

A strong woman is a woman who is straining.

—Marge Piercy, poet and novelist, b. 1936

Long after the dismissal bell, the school feels like an industrial wasteland. Even more than usual. Hollow creaks ease into silence, and echoes skitter off the walls and lockers. Sports and activities have wrapped up, but a smattering of stragglers remains, so if I bump into one of the new security guards, my presence here is not entirely suspect.

Now. If a door is being left unlocked at night for people to sneak in and out, it would have to be somewhere kids know about, but obscure enough for Dr. Folger and the security guards to overlook. And if it has something to do with Ms. Gliss...I'll start with the gym.

Lights off and empty, the gym seems cavernous. Paper murals slouch from masking-tape points, covering walls and windows. *Go Purple Tornado! Show your spirit!* The Cheer Squad's preparation for the homecoming pep rally tomorrow, the one Rajas mentioned. Rajas. My heart sags, tired and achy, thinking about him.

I give myself a mental kick; no time for heartache. I'm on a mission.

Checking again to be sure no one is around, I jog to the emergency exits. Both sets are locked. I make my way into the girls' locker room. A few of the lockers are still open, and someone has left her shoes on the floor, but it's deserted, lit only by the flickering Exit sign over the door to the fields. This would be the perfect door for Ms. Gliss to leave open. It would make so much sense. I check the latch.

It's locked.

Crap. Maybe Brookner threw me a red herring? Maybe it's not Ms. Gliss.

Sighing, I turn to go. Wait. A creaking sound—a locker door? No, it's my imagination. I'm alone.

I head back out in the gym—and there's a *click* and movement: the door to the boys' locker room slipping shut. This time I'm sure it's real. I tiptoe-jog across the gym and go in. The smell hits me first: sweaty jockstraps, musty cleats, body odor. The layout is a reversed version of the girls' locker room. Mr. D's office door is closed. I tiptoe to the door that exits to the fields.

And there she is. Ms. Gliss. She's biting a piece of duct tape, using her teeth to rip it from the roll. She props the door open with her foot. Holding the latch down, she stretches a strip of tape over it. With a turn of her head, she bites off another piece, uses it to cover the strike plate. She runs her fingers over the tape, as if making sure it will hold.

Brookner was right: Ms. Gliss is leaving the door unlocked. She *wants* people to post lightning. It makes sense. The more teachers who get struck by lightning, the less bad she'll look. Mr. Brookner, Mr. Wolman, Mr. Campoto, Ms. Theodore…who's next? Step on up, faculty. Misery loves company.

Ms. Gliss eases the door into the frame. I duck behind the lockers before she turns around.

"I know you're there." Her voice is shrill. "Evie. Would you like to tell me what you're doing in the boys' locker room after school hours?"

Damn! Think. Do I want a confrontation? If I bolt, I could probably make it to The Clunker. But I'd have to come back to undo the tape and lock the door. Tonight, and every night after that. And what if Ms. Gliss started changing doors? I'd have to search for the right door every night. When would it end?

If I stay, maybe I can convince her to stop.

Stay or run? Fight or flight?

I step out from the lockers. If I'm honest, I made my decision long ago: Stay. Fight.

"I saw you taping the lock," I say.

She starts walking, passing me on the way to the gym.

"Hey!" I hurry to follow her. "Wait."

In the gym, she twirls around. "What do you want?"

"I *saw* you taping the lock."

"Really? Let me tell you what I saw: I saw a female student in the boys' locker room. A student who is in school, after hours, without a reason." She pushes her hand through the roll of duct tape and wears it like a huge bracelet. "I'm afraid I have no choice but to report you to the authorities, since I can only assume you are here to post a lightning, something damning against a student. Or, more likely, a teacher."

My stomach starts to fold in on itself. "But I wasn't—you can't—"

"No? I'm really sorry, but it's just my obligation, m'kay? I've been targeted myself, you see." She lifts her hand to her hair, the duct tape falling to her elbow. The corners of her mouth turn down. There is a hint of sadness in her face. Is she human after all?

She sucks her teeth. "I'm afraid that, at this point, with all the damage that's been done, Dr. Folger will probably have no choice but to suspend you. Or possibly expel you."

My mouth goes dry. Expelled? She wouldn't turn me in to be expelled, would she?

Yes. Of course she would. And I don't know why I

didn't see it before, but it's not just because she's angry. It's because she's hurt.

"Wait. No." I dig down for my resolve. "You are the one rigging the door."

Ms. Gliss curls her lips. "How about we both go to Dr. Folger and offer him our different points of view? Who do you think he'll believe? Me, a tenured faculty member who's been teaching and coaching for eleven years? Lightning strike notwithstanding," she frowns. "Or you. A student with no history, who's been here for...how long is it? Oh yes, I remember! Didn't you show up *just exactly* when all this trouble started? Wow, what a coinky dink." She taps her chin, as if mulling it over. "Yes, let's do that. Let's go to Dr. Folger together. I like my chances."

Dr. Folger has all but given up on me. What if he believes Ms. Gliss? Even if he didn't, he'd be obligated to investigate. The superintendent might step in. Dr. Folger's hands would be tied. No more leniency.

"But we both know the truth," I say.

"Do we? The truth where you slandered me for being human and having a bad day, and now I'm being reviewed by the school board? Or the truth that you came to this school and all hell broke loose, and you should be expelled?" She fiddles with her duct tape bracelet. "I was going to apologize to Marcie, you know. I brought in frozen yogurt for the whole squad, because I felt bad. That was the morning I found your pleasant surprise on my door. Well, Evie. I'm a bigger person than you might think. Tell you what. How about I do you a huge favor and let you off the hook this one time?"

I can't meet her eyes. I'm so confused—she was going to apologize to Marcie? "Okay," I mumble.

"Well then. You may go."

"Thanks." Wait a second. *Thanks?* Why am I thanking her for letting me go after I witnessed *her* doing something wrong? Ms. Gliss should be held accountable—for what she said to Marcie and for what she's doing now.

Talk about irony. Accountability is why we started PLUTOs in the first place. We wanted Ms. Gliss to have a reckoning.

I curl my hands into fists.

I don't want irony. I don't even want revenge.

I want justice.

The most common way people give up their power is by thinking they don't have any.

—Alice Walker, author and activist, b. 1944

I walk through the nearly empty parking lot, climb into The Clunker, and rest my head on the steering wheel. Dusk is beginning to settle; the days are getting shorter. My shoulders hump in an involuntary shudder of humiliation and rage. And impotence.

No. I refuse to give in to these feelings. Ms. Gliss will not stop me. I will think of something. Gritting my teeth, I crank The Clunker to a start.

I fight the gearshift into first and swerve to avoid two cheerleaders emerging from school, pom-poms in hand. Which is weird because I was sure the place was empty. They must have been doing last-minute pep rally preparations.

Wait. The pep rally!

I stomp on the brakes, turn the engine off. Hop out

of The Clunker and run back into the school. The main office is locked; Ms. Franklin has already left for the day. I pound on the door.

Dr. Folger looks up from the teachers' mail cubbies. His eyebrows rise as he opens the door. "Evie."

"A speak-out! An open mic for students to talk!" I'm breathing hard, from running and from excitement. "That's what we have to do!"

He straightens the stack of papers he's holding, sets them down on Ms. Franklin's desk.

"You said I should come up with a solution to make things right. This is it. It's perfect! There's a pep rally, so the whole school will already be together."

He regards me for a long moment. "Let us sit down, shall we?"

I explain as I follow him. "PLUTOs started for a reason: to empower students to speak up against injustice, and to hold teachers accountable so they can't abuse their authority. I mean, just for the sake of argument. That's why I assume PLUTOs started…" I trail off.

In his office, I plop down onto my customary chair. Dr. Folger takes a seat behind his desk, adjusts his suit jacket.

"Students need a form of expression. We need a way to talk to each other and reopen the lines of communication. More of a give-and-take, instead of the lightnings, right?" I don't wait for his answer. "Yes. Freedom of speech. I'll always believe in it. But, if the problem with PLUTOs and the lightning is that it's anonymous, then a speak-out—"

Dr. Folger holds up a hand. "Please excuse the interruption, Evie. But I have a question."

"Okay."

"A pep rally is designed to invigorate students, rile them up, if you will. Do you think it wise to invite dialogue at such a heated time?"

Good point. I deflate a little.

His smile shows a twinkle of camaraderie. "On the other hand, administrators and faculty, as a rule, are not keen to cancel classes. In that regard, a pep rally presents a rare opportunity for the entire school to convene. As you have pointed out." Dr. Folger leans back. I'm expecting him to reach for a Slinky, but he doesn't. Instead, he says, "As it happens, I've considered the idea."

"Really?" My eyes go wide. "Wow."

"Don't sound so surprised. I have some practice with free-speech rallies." He grimaces. "Alas. I digress."

In my mind, Martha winks and chides me: *The trick is to make it seem like his own idea. Sunlight.*

"I've discussed the idea with Dr. Jones," Dr. Folger continues. "Something must be done to contain the chaos. As we see it, we are coming down to two choices.

Either I clamp down harder and create a no-tolerance state of—"

"Fascist dictatorship?"

He chuckles. "Not quite the term I would use, but…that's the general idea. Or, the other option is to create a valve to relieve some pressure. At its best, a speak-out would function as a safe yet effective means for students to discharge steam."

"Since clearly, from all the lightning, people have a lot to say."

"Be that as it may, I'm not convinced that what has been said has been worth saying. Much of it was neither warranted nor helpful."

"Right." I take a deep breath. *Evensong is a hypocrite! Evensong ruined the school!* Warranted, maybe, but not helpful. But as bad as they were, those don't compare to the horrendous injustice of being called a fag.

"A speak-out adheres responsibility to freedom of expression. When one speaks in front of a crowd, one is accountable for his or her statements."

I nod. "No vicious, anonymous accusations."

"They certainly would not be anonymous. Whether or not they would be vicious would remain to be seen." He taps his desk. "The bottom line is, Evie, I simply cannot take the risk."

"Wait. I thought you were into it."

"As an *administrator,*" he annunciates slowly, "I simply cannot take the risk."

"As an administrator."

"Indeed." He folds his hands on his desk blotter. "In any event, a successful speak-out would have to be student-led, don't you agree?"

I pick up the rainbow Slinky, fiddling with it while I think. "Definitely. Yes. Because if the idea came from you, or a teacher—if it was top-down, it'd be just another tool of The Man. Kids would reject it."

"So we are in agreement."

I wrinkle my forehead. "I'm confused. You said you couldn't condone a speak-out."

"That's correct."

"So how do we agree?"

He doesn't answer. He swivels to stare at the wall, his diplomas. Cornell. "I am reminded of one of our initial conversations about creating democracy and social justice." Turning back to me, he clears his throat. Lines etch his face. "Why are you here, Evie?" The impatience in his voice stings.

"To tell you my idea about the speak-out."

"You want my permission. My blessing."

"I guess so—"

"You don't have it."

I swallow.

"But that wasn't my question. I meant, why are you

here, at this school? To what end did you enroll?"

"I—I wanted to see what high school was like."

"That, as we used to say in the movement, is a cop-out."

Ouch.

"Let us be honest with each other. You are no passive wallflower, Evie. You did not come here to observe. If you had, none of this would have occurred. As you know, this school has undergone a tremendous shift, due largely to your actions."

"I thought you liked—"

He holds his hand out for the Slinky I'm playing with. I set it in his palm.

"I will say this," he says, "and then I will ask you to go home and reflect on it. The notion is as simple as it is important, if you are to embrace your calling as an agitator for fairness and justice: you simply cannot, and must not, expect the blessing of the very authority you are working to undermine."

I try to absorb what he's saying.

"I think you understand me."

"You're saying I shouldn't expect a stamp of approval from The Man."

A terse smile. "Indeed."

"You're saying I'm on my own."

Without a word, he stands.

Hint taken.

Social Justice 101: What happens when the revolution you started turns around to bite you in the butt. Social Justice 102: why you shouldn't expect help—from friends or from The Man.

These classes should come with a warning: Enroll at your own peril. Courses guaranteed to induce fear and loneliness. And make you take risks you never dreamed you would.

Women are never stronger than when they arm themselves with their weaknesses.

—Marie Anne de Vichy-Chamrond, Marquise du Deffand, patron of the arts, 1697–1780

Looking at the stars visible through its translucent roof, I try to find some solace in the beauty of the Dome Home. Martha pulls my hair out of its elastic and runs her fingers through it. We are sitting cross-legged on her bed. "I'm sure you can make Jacinda see the light, darling."

"Not without a thousand-kilowatt bulb and some major retinal damage."

"She'll come around. Push a little, then back off and give her more time."

"There's no more time to give. The pep rally's tomorrow." I rub my face in misery. "I can't do this, Martha. I thought I could, but I can't."

"Of course you can. You're strong, my love."

"I don't feel strong." I close my eyes. "It's going to be brutal, like the massacre at Wounded Knee. Except minus the ethnic cleansing." I sigh. "I just wish I had someone on my side."

"Well, you should've known not to count on The Man for support." She *tsks*. "Too bad. That one almost had me fooled."

"Dr. Folger won't help me, but he won't stop me, either. That's what he was trying to say."

She snorts. "That's quite an endorsement."

I blow out a big breath. "Man, Jacinda would be perfect. Everyone would listen to her."

"I'll come with you, darling. I can be your cheerleader."

"Showing up with my mom in spanky pants won't help the cause. I'm already universally despised."

"Surely you exaggerate." She begins to braid my hair.

"Surely I do not exaggerate. When will you comprehend I'm the school untouchable? Everyone, and I mean everyone, teachers included"—I shiver at the thought of Ms. Gliss and her duct tape—"hates me. We're not talking mild disapproval here. It's elemental, vampire-versus-slayer hate." I take a deep breath and feel Martha do the same. The tugging while she braids feels good.

"Yowza, you're tense."

"Comes with the territory. Of being hated with a fiery passion—"

"Of a million burning suns? Of a thousand-kilowatt bulb? Of vampires? And Colonel Forsyth?"

"Finally, you're appreciating the magnitude of the situation."

She drops my braid over my shoulder. "Lean forward, I'll rub your back."

We are quiet awhile, thinking.

"It's the hard thing to do," Martha says eventually, "but it's the right thing to do."

"I know." I set out to create justice, not ruin the school. "I just hope it works. We have to bring some sunlight back." I swallow hard. *Sunlight.* There's something else that needs to be brought into sunlight: a final piece of the puzzle. My heart squeezes at what I need to ask Martha. I'm not sure I want to hear the answer.

"Martha, why aren't you going to HSP anymore? Or meeting them for coffee?"

She sniffs. "I'm through with the Horny Singletons, my love."

"You wore out your welcome, you said?"

"*C'est vrai.*" Kneading my shoulders, she starts humming an Ani DiFranco song, the one about goldfish having no memory.

I take the plunge. "Why don't you just tell me the truth?"

Her hands freeze for a moment. "What do you mean?"

She runs her thumbs down the grooves along my spine.

"I figured it out. It was you, not Dr. Folger."

Another pause. "I'm still not following."

"I'm shining light on the fact that you haven't been forthcoming with me."

"Darling—"

"Know how I put it together? Brookner said something about why he broke it off with Jacinda. He said, 'a mutual friend paid me a visit.' I figured he meant Dr. Folger. And then it hit me: you recognized Jacinda's name, way back when I sprained my ankle and she and Rajas brought me home." Saying Rajas's name feels like needles jabbing my throat. "Jacinda had put up a flyer for baby-sitting. A flyer you saw at HSP."

Silence.

"Jacinda knew Brookner before she had class with him. From baby-sitting. Brookner found her the same way you did: the flyer at HSP. He's one of the Horny Singletons."

"Darling."

I turn around to face her. "Why all the secrecy?"

"We don't do much with last names at Horny Singletons—at HSP. It's not the kind of place where you give out business cards. And there's a lot of Johns in the world."

"You must have known he was a teacher."

Her hands drop to her lap. She doesn't answer.

"So...that night when Jacinda was baby-sitting and Javier the snake got loose, you ended up coming home early. Were you out with him? With Brookner?" I start to unwind the braid Martha started. "You know what? Don't answer that. I don't even want to know."

"Evensong Sparkling Morningdew. You know I would never, ever, in a million years, knowingly do anything that might hurt you. But you are always encouraging me to have a social life."

"But Brookner is crap nasty!" I make a face. "Okay. I'll admit, at first he sucks you in with his smarts and his stupid meta-ironic nerd glasses. But the man is a toad."

"Preach it, sister."

"Why did you keep it a secret? It's just plain weird of you not to—"

"You've been so amazing, darling. Creating PLUTOs, making new friends, sticking up for yourself, taking a stand. I've just been in awe." Unaccustomed to tears, Martha's eyes become a roadmap of veins. "When I put it together that John Horny Singleton was John Brookner, when I found out what he was up to—"

"You went to him yourself. You told him to stop with Jacinda, or else."

"Yes, darling," she murmurs, smoothing a finger under her eye. "I did."

"Why not just tell me everything? We always tell each other everything."

"I didn't want to interfere! I was—I am—spitting mad at him. I couldn't let that jackass continue to be a predator!" She stops mid-rant, shaking her head. "I wanted to do it quietly, without focusing attention. This isn't about me, darling. This is your fight. I didn't want to steal your thunder."

"Funny. This whole thing started out with lightning, not thunder." I slide off the bed.

"Evensong—"

I hold up a hand. "I'll be okay. I get it. I forgive you. I just need some air."

Outside, I lie down on my favorite little hillock.

The cold air is dappled with wispy stratus clouds, haloing the thin sliver of moon. A barred owl's plaintive hoot—*Whoooo, whoooo, who cooks for you all?*—reminds me to breathe. Hannah Bramble's bell clunks faintly as she lows in the barn. I hug myself to keep off the chill. Above me, Vega shines huge and powerful, the earth speeding toward her at twelve miles a second. How is that possible? How do we not get blown off the planet by the sheer force of the universe?

I breathe and breathe. What if the earth could stop moving? Would time stop? I long for it to let me go back. Let me stay homeschooled, let me get into Cornell. Let me trust Martha to tell me everything. Let me meet Jacinda, let me fall in love with Rajas without all this. Let me not be alone and shunned.

I tremble from cold, from tears I'm sick of crying.

I've come this far. I'm a part of this world, as much as the owl and the moon and Hannah Bramble. And I'm not going down without a fight.

30

Real courage is when you know you're licked before you begin, but you begin anyway and see it through no matter what.

—Harper Lee, author, b. 1926

You know, this would be a whole a lot easier if Jacinda didn't hate me so much. With her help, a speak-out would be manageable. Maybe even successful.

I'll give her one more try. I have to.

In Global View, Ms. Bemis might as well be a kitten stuck up a tree, she seems so ineffectual. The whiteboard, once a site for controversy and provocation, now bears the forlorn suggestion, *Silent study, please review chapters 20-21*. Half of the class has vanished. Did they change their schedules, or are they permanently skipping? Who knows? The remaining students rearranged the seating chart. Now I sit alone.

Without allowing hope to creep into my heart, I trek over to Jacinda. Marcie and another member of Cheer

Squad sit to her left and front. They are in uniform for the pep rally. They chant softly, practicing cheers, inspecting the hems of their skirts. Jacinda is touching up her nail polish. It's a scene from a movie—cheerleaders being shallow and cliquey. Before I came here, I thought that's all there was to them. Jacinda taught me there's more. But right now, that's pretty hard to see.

As I take a seat, my book slams onto the desk, a nervous accident. Heads lift like startled deer interrupted from grazing. Ms. Bemis frowns and marks something in her roster.

"Jacinda, can we talk?"

Jacinda dips her nail polish brush into the pot, twists the top shut. She blows on her fingernails and nods at something Marcie is whispering.

It's a united front. How good must it feel for so many people to have your back? My heart bristles with envy.

I try again. "Can we talk...alone?"

Jacinda looks at me, her dark eyes wary. "Anything you want to say to me should be something you can say to the whole squad." Hmm. A clever way for her to curtail any talk of Brookner? Or is she feeling so vulnerable she needs her team?

"It's private."

I search Jacinda for the girl I used to know. What happened to all the love and goodwill that used to tumble out of her? Where's the slow burn of her generous wit? I long for the friend who came to my rescue/non-rescue at the creek, who giggled with me about Rajas, who helped start PLUTOs. But that Jacinda is gone.

I lower my voice. "I'm planning a speak-out, for after the pep rally. I think it could help bring the school back together, and still give students their free speech rights. But without hurting people, you know?" I swallow. "I really need your help."

Jacinda's toe starts tapping. "I have to—" Her eyes pop wide, looking past me.

I turn to look. Ms. Bemis is crossing the room to open the door for Ms. Gliss. Ms. Gliss, who smiles at her Cheer Squad. Then, catching sight of me, her smile degenerates into a scowl. Frost lines my stomach.

Ms. Bemis looks glad of the interruption. "How can I help you?"

Ms. Gliss recovers her smile. "I need my Cheer Squad. Dr. Folger excused them so we can finish preparations for the pep rally."

"Oh." Ms. Bemis turns to the cheerleaders. "Okay girls? Go ahead."

"Please!" I whisper. "I really need you."

Jacinda flicks a glance at Ms. Gliss. As she tucks her things into her purse, she says, "I just…can't." Then, louder, "We're not buying what you're selling." She lifts a shoulder and turns. "Come on, girls. Let's go."

The door clicks shut behind them.

So that's it. It's official. I'm on my own.

Maybe I depleted my tear allotment for the week, or maybe I'm too tired for sadness, because all I feel is nothing. I open my textbook and stare at it, but the words won't arrange themselves into any meaning.

The bell rings.

In the hallway, eyes down, heading to my locker, I bump into someone.

"Sorry," I mutter, but I don't bother looking up. I know who it is. I know the feel of the chest, I know the warm, spicy smell.

Rajas brushes a finger down my arm. "Eve. Are you okay? Talk to me."

"You made your choice." What else is there to say? I push past him.

How much worse can this day get?

I have a feeling I'm about to find out.

The idealists and visionaries, foolish enough to throw caution to the winds and express their ardor and faith in some supreme deed, have advanced mankind and have enriched the world.

—Emma Goldman, writer and anarchist, 1869–1940

The pep rally is period seven and eight combined, so it can go on interminably, until the end of school. Or perhaps till the end of time. I crack the gym door and peer in. Everyone's here. The place is teeming, the walls seem bowed outward like they will burst. In full spanky pants regalia, the Cheer Squad has whipped the entire school into frothing paroxysms of pep. All the athletes have their purple jerseys on. The student jazz band is playing. The collapsible wooden bleachers, expanded down to the court lines, vibrate with all the cheering and yelling. They look on the verge of collapse under the stomping feet.

Dread slams into me, hard. This was not a good idea. It isn't going to work.

With trembling fingers, I pocket my keys and put

down the posters I've brought in from The Clunker, the ones Martha helped me make.

Students speak out!

Speak truth to power!

Freedom isn't free!

They seem flimsy and pathetic now.

The Cheer Squad has its own signs, stiff and perfect-looking, which are propped against the gym wall. One has tipped over; I can make out a few of the stenciled words.

Oh God. Unbelievable.

Jacinda didn't want to help me, isn't ready to be friends again. Fine, I get it. But this?

The tipped-over poster has my name on it! *Evensong, you—* I can't see the other words. A replay of the lightning struck against me, no doubt. Which one? Hypocrite? School-wrecker? Or worse.

Backing into the hall, I close the door and sink to the floor. My puny signs slump down next to me. I can't bear to go in.

Deep breath.

I'll just wait out here. For now. The hall clock says 2:13. I'll go in at 2:15. Two more minutes. Two minutes before I confront the entire student body. And faculty, including Dr. Folger. Two minutes until I lead myself to my own slaughter.

One minute thirty seconds.

Breathe.

The big hand ticks to 2:14. One more minute.

The doors rattle from the noise of the crowd, the brewing storm.

I'll go straight to the microphone in the middle of the gym. I'll say what I have to say. I'll start a speak-out.

Applause erupts, echoing into the empty hall. Rhythmic shouting from the Cheer Squad, a stampede of foot stomping in the bleachers. I put my head in my hands. Dr. Folger was right. I must have been crazy to think that a pep rally was good timing. They're going to chew me up and spit me out.

No. I won't be cowed. It's the hard thing to do, but it's the right thing to do. I will be strong.

This girl is different.

Breathe.

Twenty-five seconds.

The storm swells.

2:15.

It's now or never.

I gather up my signs but they slide out of my hands like they're scared of their fate. I shuffle them together and bump them along into the gym.

The screaming batters my eardrums. In the bleachers, students are shouting, standing, leaning into each other, pumping fists. Teachers and staff are seated in the first rows, clapping along with the Cheer Squad and jazz band. Ms. Gliss is standing in a far corner. Near her, a man in a suit is scowling importantly. Is he an observer from the school board? Ms. Gliss tucks her hair behind her ear and follows the cheerleaders with her eyes. She looks pleased. Jacinda and the rest of the Cheer Squad sweep down the sidelines, wiggling their fingers and yelling at the crowd to *Show your spirit!*

My pulse pounds. Sweat stipples my forehead. Forget yoga breathing; the best I can manage at this point is to pull in enough air to stay alive. I put my signs aside—I can barely walk as it is.

As I make my way to the middle of the gym, people start to notice. Little by little, decibel by decibel, the noise dwindles.

A cord snakes to the microphone at center court, set up for the girl who warbled *The Star-Spangled Banner*.

I walk. The crowd quiets. I'm at the half-court line.

Is the microphone on? I give it a tap; it lets off a piercing shriek. Students clamp their hands to their ears. A groan ripples through the bleachers.

I clear my throat. "Let's—let's thank the Cheer Squad for such a fantastic pep rally!"

A moment of absolute silence, followed by a faint smattering of applause.

So furious you can almost see steam coming out of her ears, Ms. Gliss is stomping toward me. Until someone catches her by the elbow. It's Dr. Folger, standing near the man I assume is from the school board. Dr. Folger whispers something to her, and her eyes go wide. She steps back.

A screeching wolf whistle emanates from high in the bleachers. Jacinda grimaces. Sexism against Cheer Squad, like she'd said. In a nanosecond, she regains her composure with a smile and a high kick. She keeps looking at me, but her glare doesn't seem as hateful as it was in Global View. Wishful thinking? Stress-induced hallucinations?

Where is Rajas? I don't see him. Maybe he ditched the rally. He's not the pep type. My heart contracts.

Deep breath. "You're probably wondering why I'm out here. There's been a lot of—"

—Shut the hell up!

—Get off the mic!

"I just want to—" The microphone squawks feedback again.

Jacinda turns to her squad. Index fingers pointed at the ceiling, she cocks her thumbs like pistols. A signal. The cheerleaders run to fetch their signs, marching back single file. Marcie is behind Jacinda. They hold their posters close to their bodies, words facing in.

So. It's sabotage. She knows my plan because I asked her for help. Rookie mistake on my part. She's about to stone me in front of hundreds of people.

I lean into the microphone again. Not looking at Jacinda, not looking at Dr. Folger, not looking for Rajas. I close my eyes and speak. "They say that sunlight is—"

—Go back home, homeschooler!

"I wish I could." I laugh, a frail cackle that the mic broadcasts. The sound of public humiliation.

Yoga breath. Be strong. "I thought if I—"

—Freak!

Squaring my shoulders, I say, "James Garfield said, 'The truth will set you free, but first it will make you miserable.'"

The Cheer Squad lines up behind me. When will they show their posters? As soon as everyone sees the *Evensong* one—whatever it says—my public stoning will commence.

I talk fast. "I just…I think it's important to speak out. We should all do it. But we have to be responsible. I made some mistakes, and I apologize to anyone I might have hurt—"

Jacinda gives four sharp claps. "Cheer Squad! Ready? Okay!"

"Truth is important," I press on. "But I'm starting to think that what's even more important is kindness."

Jacinda hollers, "Five, six, seven, eight!"

I have to hurry. "And I think we should have an open mic, for a speak-out!"

"Go!" The Cheer Squad flips the posters and lifts them high.

The crowd surges.

I'm toast.

To suppress free speech is a double wrong. It violates the rights of the hearer as well as those of the speaker.

—Frederick Douglass, abolitionist and author, 1818–1895

I step back from the microphone. I have to get out of here. I'm done. I tried.

They won. I got creamed.

I start walking.

To the side, someone hops down from the bleachers. Running his hand through his coal black hair, he jogs toward me. Rajas.

More public humiliation? No thanks. I walk faster.

"Evie! Wait!" Jacinda's voice. It's too loud. Amplified. She's talking into the mic.

Rajas catches up to me and grabs my wrist.

I snap it away. "Back off!"

Jacinda's voice: "A speak-out is such a great idea."

The bleachers start to quiet. But it's a warmer quiet for Jacinda, without the steely edge of hate.

"I have a quote to share too?" Jacinda says. "It's from this guy Felix Frankfurter. Talk about a seriously tragic name!"

Eager to complete my stoning, and enamored with Jacinda, the whole school laughs.

I get to the doors. Rajas is right behind me.

Jacinda continues, "Frankfurter said, 'Wisdom too often never comes, and so one ought not to reject it merely because it comes late.'" A pause. "Evie! Come back."

I turn around; I can't help it. Jacinda's hands become pistols again. As one, the Cheer Squad turns to face me, holding their posters overhead.

There is a low murmur, and a bit of applause.

The posters, they are…not what I thought.

Free speech for all!

Speak out!

Speak truth to power!

Jacinda is running toward us, holding the poster with my name: *Evensong—you are fearless!*

Confused, not daring to hope, I look at Rajas.

He smiles his crooked grin. "If you'd stop and listen for a second, I've been trying to tell you."

Jacinda says, "I'm so sorry, Evie!"

My whole body liquefies with relief, with cautious hope.

"I couldn't say anything to you when Ms. Gliss showed up. But my squad and I talked about it. Because I knew...we could see that you were right, a speak-out was a super good idea." She fingers her spiky bangs. "I'm still kind of a mess about the whole thing with, you know—" Jacinda's shoulders twitch, as if it's an enormous effort not to sink into Brookner quicksand. "Anyways, guess what! I saw you and Ms. Gliss yesterday coming out of the boy's locker room! I, like, totally overheard everything! I cannot believe that she's the one who's been leaving the fricking door unlocked!"

"You—you were there?" There was a witness. Justice prevails!

She's nodding. "Yes! And I went to Dr. Folger and told him what she did!"

Which explains the look on Ms. Gliss's face when Dr. Folger spoke to her just now.

"I'm sorry, Evie. I'm a serious mish-mosh about the relationship and," Jacinda winces, shakes her head, "I can't believe I posted lightning against you. I'm so, so sorry. I don't expect you to forgive me, but—"

"You're already forgiven," I say. "I've made a ton of mistakes too. And I miss you so much."

Her eyes go wide, all dark eyelashes and shimmery makeup. "Really?"

"Really."

She hugs me. Everyone is watching us. "You need to get back." I twirl Jacinda around to face the noisy throngs. "Your public awaits."

"Do you forgive Raj too?" She turns back to Rajas and me. "Raj told me he did the—you know. The Brookner lightning. And I mean, I'm mad? But also I'm just trying to deal with it all..."

Maybe I was too harsh with Rajas. Then again, maybe I wasn't. He went behind my back, fed me to Jacinda, hid me from view, is already seeing someone else, and hasn't even tried to apologize for any of it. And yet. I thirst for him. "I don't know."

Rajas walks away.

So that settles it. "See?" I tell Jacinda. "He won't even fight for me."

"He misses you." Tilting her head, "Don't you want him back?"

I want to scream *YES! I feel like my heart's been ripped out!* But he is putting more distance between us, walking away, taking his crooked smile with him, his warm lips, his mind, his love. I squash my feelings down. "Like you said," I tell Jacinda, "if he truly loved me, he wouldn't have kept me hidden in the shop room."

Jacinda cringes. "That was so evil of me."

"Yeah. It was. But it's true. I mean, he has to be willing to take a stand about being together. Or anything else, for that matter."

A hush comes over the crowd.

Rajas is changing direction.

He's heading to the microphone.

Keeping his eyes on me, he stoops to speak into the mic. "I don't have a quote."

Go, Rajas! A girl's voice. Followed by a hoot of approval from someone else.

"Yeah. Thanks." His face is getting blotchy. "Just want to say, I think it's a good thing, to speak out. Speak your mind, even if the truth turns around to bite you in the butt." He pauses to accommodate laughter. "It takes courage. My girlfriend, Eve"—he points to me—"taught me that."

Oh my God.

Did he just do that? Anti-label Rajas publicly stated he has a girlfriend?

And that it's *me*?

"At least, she used to be my girlfriend," he says. "But I was an idiot and messed things up. And I never apologized. So, here goes." He gives a nervous smile. "I'm sorry, Eve. I was an ass."

"Ohmigod!" Jacinda pushes me toward the mic. "What are you waiting for! Go get him!"

People start clapping, and it goes rhythmic, a cadence building into a crescendo. They are waiting for me to do something.

"But I thought—isn't he seeing that girl Rosemary?"

"What? Rosemary?" Jacinda makes a face. "No!"

"But she was talking to him. They were planning to meet after school."

"Duh! Probably because of Raj's apprenticeship thingy. Her dad will be his boss next year."

"But…that's it?" I light up inside. I'm electric, radioactive.

"You aren't going to leave the poor guy standing there all alone!" Jacinda is still pushing me.

Until she doesn't have to push me anymore. Rajas is waiting for me with his beautiful crooked smile.

The crowd starts whooping, laughing, cheering.

Jacinda screams, claps, and runs up and down the gym. The rest of the Cheer Squad joins her.

My heart is like a magnet, my feet are on autopilot, until I'm here at center court and Rajas's eyes are dark as a new moon midnight and they're getting closer and now we're kissing. The crowd thunders, roars, but all I can think about is lightning—the real kind—and all I can hear is the echo of Rajas's words: *My girlfriend, Eve, taught me that.*

Whatever you do may seem insignificant but it is most important that you do it.

—Mahatma Gandhi, spiritual and political leader, 1869–1948

SUGGESTIONS MADE AT THE IMPROMPTU STUDENT SPEAK-OUT AT THE HOMECOMING PEP RALLY

Notes taken to edit...some we can put in a new weekly newspaper column, "Students Speak." It will highlight and look into the good ideas that come from students at monthly lunch speak-outs. The speak-outs will be co-facilitated by Dr. Folger, Kelly Lupito (student council president), and Evie Morningdew. The "Students Speak" column will be co-authored by Stiv Wagner (myself, Editor in Chief of the Purple Tornado News) and Evie Morningdew.

(Note: I started taking notes a few minutes into the speak-out, so I missed some of the first suggestions.)

* Teachers buy students lunch every Friday.

* Coke machines in the cafeteria.

* Boys should be cheerleaders for girls' sports.

* Open the unused courtyard (between the library and Home and Career Skills classrooms) for students to use in free periods.

* Once a month students teach the classes.

* Get exercise equipment like treadmills and elliptical trainers in the gym so we can use those instead of being gym class heroes. Because it's still physical fitness.

* Math club should get as much funding as the football team.

* Upgrade the bathrooms and keep them clean.

* Give Mr. Heck a raise because he does the most work in the school.

* Teachers favor athletes and cheerleaders and that's not fair.

* Make a school flower and vegetable garden, especially a rooftop garden.

* Make the school carbon neutral.

* Certain teachers cross the line with their girl students and those teachers should not just be placed on administrative leave, they should be fired.

* [Name of student] is an a**hole.

* [Name of teacher] is a b*tch.

[Note: At this point Dr. Folger stepped in and asked students not to name names but to keep their comments limited to ideas for improving the school or he would turn the mic off.]

* Kids should be allowed to bring water bottles to class and eat snacks throughout the day.

* There should be school hoodies you can buy even if you're not an athlete.

* Make the school buses run on natural gas or hybrid.

* People who take dance classes should get credit as a sport and you should be able to get gym class exemptions if you do sports.

* Paint murals on the lockers.

* Change the school colors and mascot because they're stupid.

* Start an Ultimate Frisbee team.

* Vote for favorite teachers and they get a raise.

* The school should lend out iPads.

* More parking for students.

* We should be able to go off campus for lunch—especially upperclassmen.

* Lunch is disgusting. We need better options.

* Homecoming and dances are lame. We need better stuff.

* We should be able to bring our pets to school.

* School shouldn't take attendance anymore.

* Start a worm-farm compost in the cafeteria for lunch scraps.

* We should get smartboards for the classrooms.

* Let us do internships as a school credit elective.

* There should be a student representative on the school board.

* Stop looking down on kids who aren't planning on going straight to college.

* Let us choose one class a year that we can pass/fail instead of letter grades.

* Kids who love to cook and menu-plan should have a shot at working in the cafeteria.

* We should fly the flag of the whole earth, along with the U.S. flag, on the school flagpole.

There is no reason to think a small group of thoughtful, committed citizens cannot change the world; indeed, that's the only thing that ever has.

—Margaret Mead, cultural anthropologist, 1901–1978

Finally, slowly, the last students trickle out of the gym. The whole space seems to breathe a sigh of relief.

When the dismissal bell rang, Dr. Folger had to interrupt the student at the mic—a popular junior named Jeremy—to insist that everyone leave so they didn't miss their buses. The speak-out was still going strong, ideas flying, all sorts of students with all kinds of amazing ideas, along with the occasional turd in the punch bowl, as Rich would say. At the end, Dr. Folger vowed that, from now on, students could hold monthly speak-outs during lunch.

The promise was greeted with stomping feet and a roar of approval.

Now, twenty minutes after dismissal, only the Cheer Squad remains. Their sneakers squeak as they reattach streamers and decorations for the homecoming festivities later this weekend.

I called Martha. She's taxiing from Walmart, and she's bringing provisions. Hopefully not stolen ones.

Rajas and Jacinda and I sit, leaning back against the full-length windows. "You should have seen your face!" Jacinda laughs. "You really thought we were holding evil signs?"

"Yes! I was steeling myself for the apocalypse."

"I felt bad. But I was confused, you know? I missed you so much, and then you told me your idea for a speak-out...but when Ms. Gliss walked in, I needed to, like, play it cool. You totally freaked her out yesterday, by the way. You were so brave, confronting her like that!"

"You were brave to go to Dr. Folger and tell him about her."

"Not as brave as you." She looks over at Rajas. "Or you, Mr. Romantic! Ohmigod, Evie, could you just die? I cannot imagine someone doing that for me!" A sadness descends on Jacinda; she must be thinking about Brookner, but she soon smiles again. "That was, like, so fricking sweet! You rock on with your bad self, Raj!"

Rajas shrugs. "Wasn't that big of a deal."

"Yes it was!" Jacinda says.

"Yes, it was," I agree.

"But I should have apologized to you a long time ago." He's frowning.

"Yes, you should have." I bump him with my shoulder. "You're not completely off the hook, you know. We still need to talk."

"Great. Every guy's favorite words."

"Oh, pish-posh!" Jacinda waves a hand. "Just forgive him already! He was only trying to protect me. As misguided as that was!" Another shadow crosses her face. Again, she shakes it off. "It's just a matter of time before you two are back together, and until you're, like, fully engaged in nauseating PDAs."

I can't help but smile. I turn to Rajas. "What happened to 'I don't like labels'?"

He scratches his nose. "Guess I managed to see the light. When it comes to that particular label."

Jacinda looks past us to someone entering the gym. She whispers, "Here comes The Man."

"Yes, yes, here comes The Man." Dr. Folger gives me a wink. "Didn't think I could hear you, Ms. Harrod?"

Jacinda looks horrified. "I'm so, so sorry Dr. Folger! I—"

"Jay, you didn't know?" Rajas becomes serious. "Dr. Folger has spyware in his suit pocket. It uploads directly to—"

"The InterWeb," I finish.

Her eyes grow wide. "Are you serious!"

Dr. Folger smiles. "Indeed they are not."

Jacinda juts out her pretty chin and swats Rajas's knee in fake anger.

"Well, Evie," says Dr. Folger. "I'd say the inaugural speak-out went quite well, all things considered. Would you agree?"

"Definitely. But we need to make sure all the students' suggestions are taken seriously. Stiv is game for starting a new column in the newspaper. But we have to create other ways to embrace change and implement—"

"Hold up, Eve," Rajas says. "How about enjoying the moment?"

"Right, I know. It's just that we've got momentum on our side now, and—"

"Evie!" giggles Jacinda. "Slow down! Take a breather!"

"Okay. I'll try." I smile. "Sorry."

"Don't be sorry," Rajas says. "That's why we love you."

My cheeks blaze, my heart flips at Rajas's words. *Love.* If it weren't for Dr. Folger's Cold Shower Effect, I might jump Rajas's bones right now, before I even decide whether I've forgiven him. Time for a change of subject.

"Do you want to join us?" I ask Dr. Folger. "Martha's bringing food."

His eyebrows rise. "It's unorthodox…but don't mind

if I do." Awkwardly, he sits on the floor, tugging at his ankle to cross his legs.

The door bangs open. "Revolutionaries! A feast! Organic corn chips! Salsa! String cheese! Courtesy of your local Walmart!" Martha plops the food down, along with a six-pack of juice spritzers. She sits. "Well, comrades. Sounds like the inaugural speak-out went quite well, all things considered!"

We exchange glances around the circle, stifling chuckles.

"And what's so damned funny?" Martha says.

Dr. Folger laughs. "I believe you are starting to sound like The Man. Watch out. In a few years time, you might have an office next to mine."

Martha throws up her hands. "Never! Perish the thought." She grabs the bag of chips and wrestles it open. We all dig in, eating like cave men around a fire pit.

I bite into a string cheese and reach for a chip. "So, Dr. Folger. How about that recommendation for Cornell? Jacinda wants to go there too, you know."

"Well isn't that interesting." His grin reveals a bit of salsa pepper stuck to his tooth. "As it happens, I have drafted a couple of letters. They're around here somewhere." He pulls two envelopes out of his jacket.

"Really? That's fantastic!" Jacinda beams like she's won a Nobel Prize. Or one of those MTV awards.

"Thank you! Thank you! Thank you!" I reach for the letters.

"Not so fast." He whisks the envelopes away. "Perhaps it would behoove me to hold onto these. After all, you've not yet been here a semester—"

"And witness the chaos that's ensued." Rajas gives a sly smile.

"Indeed," Dr. Folger nods. "How about we just file these safely away as a little...insurance policy, if you will."

"Seriously. You should!" Jacinda says. "Evie's such a bad influence. And I mean, look at everything that's coming up. Homecoming, of course, and winter formal—"

"Hey! You're all ganging up on me! Again!"

Jacinda's still reciting her list. "And prom, and spirit week, and graduation. Ohmigod!" She smacks my leg in excitement. "Are you thinking what I'm thinking?"

Dr. Folger and Martha exchange a look of exaggerated fear.

"Graduation speaker!" Jacinda chirps. "You'd be, like, so perfect!"

"Jay, that *is* perfect. Just imagine Eve's address," Rajas says. "'How to deal when a revolution turns around to bite you in the butt.'"

I shake my head. "No no no no."

"Why not, darling?" Martha looks distraught. "Don't tell me this experience has turned you off from social justice activism—"

Jacinda is trembling with excitement. "No, it's because she has something else in mind! I know! It's going to be, 'How I came here and made this school a better place,' isn't it? Isn't it!"

"Nope," I say. "Wrong again."

Jacinda pretends to pout. "What, then?"

Brookner's words are coming back to me, as imperfect as their messenger was. *For someone who prides herself on her precocity, you sure can be dense.*

But I'm finally beginning to get it.

It's not just about me anymore. It never really was.

This girl is different. Yes—but that's not the entire story.

The real story is much more interesting. I look around our circle, at the funny mix of friends sitting here, sharing this moment, crunching organic corn chips. I think about the kids who spoke out today, at the surprising and inspiring ideas some of them had.

I smile. "I'd definitely give the speech, if people elected me to." And it would be about how we're going to change the world. Together. Because this girl, this boy, these kids—all of us—are different.

ACKNOWLEDGMENTS

It turns out that being an author is a team sport. And boy do I have an amazing team.

Thanks foremost to Noah and Sam, for your sustained patience, silliness, and love. Thanks also to the rest of my family, especially Juanita and Earl Johnson, and Lisa Wichman—for your enthusiasm and careful readings—and to my Aussie family, the Everetts. (Hey Max—thanks for protecting Sam from all those fierce koalas so I could write. My shout, next time we're down under.)

Tremendous gratitude to my critique group: John Bemis, Jennifer Harrod, and Stephen Messer. E. B. White wrote, "It's not often that someone comes along who is a true friend and a good writer. Charlotte was both." You are my Charlottes, although non-arachnoid and hopefully much longer-lived.

Cheers to my agent, Ginger Knowlton, for constant kindness and for being in my corner. Thanks to my editor, Kathy Landwehr: smart, hilarious, and you make house calls? Doesn't get any better. Thanks also to Vicky Holifield and Jessica Alexander for insightful and gentle editorial touches, and to Mo Withee, Melanie McMahon Ives, and Loraine Joyner for a cover and design Evie would love. A raised glass to the entire crew at Peachtree Publishers for making this such a humane, delightful, collaborative process. Viva la Peachtree!

Finally, heartfelt thanks to the L-Hs for Ruby love; the angels; the TNS crew; and the rest of my dear friends—too many to name here, but if you're asking, "I wonder if that means me?" It does. It means you.